Mark B. Cohen

Mark B. Cohen was born and brought up in Glasgow. His mother was the author and journalist Evelyn Cowan, and his father, Paul, was a head maths teacher. After attending Calderwood Lodge Primary School and the High School of Glasgow, he graduated with an honours degree in Interpreting and Translating from Heriot-Watt University in Edinburgh. He then spent two years as a parliamentary research assistant before moving to the City, where he is now a director at a merchant bank. He lives in North West London and is currently working on his second novel.

If you would like to learn more about this book, or wish to get in touch with the author or receive details of his future novel, please visit the Brass Monkeys website at www.brassmonkeys.com.

'*Brass Monkeys* is a joyful, political romp. Like all outstanding satire, it darts in and out between comfortable truth and laughable unreality. The author learned much – perhaps too much – during his time working with me in the House of Commons!' Lord Janner of Braunstone

'An outrageously funny book, which stretches the truth into farce' Norma Major

'A sharp eye for the way things are, and a wild imagination for the way things might be, deliver a text that teeters merrily between fantasy and reality.' Matthew Parris, *The Times*

'Anyone with half an interest in politics will have huge fun with Mark Cohen's frenetically paced debut novel, which delves irreverently into the world of Westminster and the media.' *Yorkshire Evening Post*

'An anarchic, irreverent Tom Sharpe-style romp through the fields of politics and the media with murder, mayhem and extremely salacious shenanigans . . .a riot of laughs.' Cameron Simpson, *The Times*

'A highly risqué account of sleaze and skulduggery in Whitehall and Westminster' *Scotland*

'Will have you laughing out loud' *South Wales Argus*

BRASS MONKEYS

Mark B. Cohen

Hodder & Stoughton

First published in 1998 by Hodder and Stoughton
A division of Hodder Headline PLC

A CIP catalogue record for this title is available from the
British Library

ISBN 0 340 71297 X

Typeset by Palimpsest Book Production Limited,
Polmont, Stirlingshire
Printed and bound in Great Britain by
Mackays of Chatham PLC, Chatham, Kent

Hodder and Stoughton Ltd
A division of Hodder Headline PLC
338 Euston Road
London NW1 3BH

To my mother Evelyn and late father Paul
with love and gratitude

Acknowledgements

I'm enormously grateful to all my family and friends for their patience, support and many helpful suggestions during the writing of this book.

Brass Monkey Awards for a life-time's achievement in literary counselling go to: DHB, MSB, EC, ESC, PSG and LJL.

Very special nominations also to: LPA, CAB, WB, CLB, DJB, CC, JDC, MGD, JFE, SJF, KSG, VG, BJ, JNL, RBM and JGM.

(For reasons that may become apparent, initials have been used to protect the innocent.)

The Pop

Full TV Guide - Page 10
Bonking Bishop's sextuplets
kidnapped by Martians — *Page 13*
*Pop*Sport — *Pages 18-20*

Saturday January 1st 2000

VOX *POP* SAYS:

Europe's saddest hour

Yesterday's disaster at the Euro-Millennium Tower was one of the most tragic accidents ever to befall our continent.

Along with all of Britain, the *Pop* mourns those who perished.

Not just because they were Europe's most senior politicians, but as fellow human beings.

First and foremost, we commiserate with their nearest and dearest. Our hearts go out to all of them.

But, in the aftermath of the Brussels catastrophe, there are hard questions to be answered. And the *Pop* will be fearless in asking them:

- What were these 'structural weaknesses' that caused the 2.5 billion euro building to collapse so suddenly during its inauguration ceremony?

- Is there any truth in the story that it was all due to a linguistic cock-up on the pan-European Architects' Committee?

- If so, why have the Belgian police not yet arrested its chairman, Professeur Babelle?

- Most importantly, who was responsible for allowing the entire British Cabinet to attend this event - with such devastating consequences for our country?

The *Pop* demands to be told.

Meanwhile, we pay tribute to the late Prime Minister and all his colleagues. They will be sadly missed.

And we commend his party for moving so fast to elect a new leader and fill the terrible gap left behind. We wish Edward Burgins, our new Premier, well in these most difficult of circumstances.

He carries with him the goodwill of the entire British nation.

Good luck to you, Eddy!

New Premier to address the nation tonight

10 Downing Street today announced that the new Prime Minister, The Rt Ho Edward Burgins MP, wi broadcast to the nation 9pm tonight.

Earlier, Mr Burgins ha called for calm in the wak of the tragic events i Brussels.

Standing on the threshold o Number 10, he said that like the rest of the nation he was deeply distressed by events and saddened to be taking office in such circumstances. He would b in urgent discussion wit the remaining members o other EU governments t press for the most thoroug investigation.

But he maintained that th day-to-day business government would contin as normal, as his la predecessor would hav wished.

The seventy-two-year-o Premier looked sprigh but sombre as he fielde questions from jou

Continued on Page 2

"Everything to play for" in Olympic venue bid

Incoming Sports Minister Hugh Driftwood, today said he had every hope of securing the 2008 Olympics for Britain Speaking just as
(continued on Page 3)

Chapter 1

A reporter and cameraman from breakfast TV were camped outside the front door. They'd been there since first light, waiting for Hugh to appear. In the meantime, they were interviewing any of the neighbours they could lay their hands on. After all, if the rumours turned out to be true, any embarrassing details about his personal life would come in handy for the lunchtime news.

First in line was the eleven-year-old from next door, who was getting in his revenge for a complaint involving his skateboard and Hugh's car door. With evident relish and surprising eloquence, he laid into Hugh and the government he belonged to, before turning for good measure to every other politician whose name he could remember.

'Sod the lot of them,' he concluded triumphantly, dodging to stay on camera as the reporter hastily moved on. In Islington, the boy's parting glance implied, you messed with eleven-year-old skateboarders at your peril.

Meanwhile, oblivious to all the fuss, the object of his anger was asleep alone in an upstairs bedroom. In the final throes of one of those erotic dreams that had recently become an unwelcome feature of his early mornings, the last thing Hugh Driftwood expected was an audience of three million viewers outside his window. But that was what he was to get, and he was to find out about it the hard way.

At seven thirty, the television set on his bedside table clicked on automatically and a commentator began droning on about the Cabinet reshuffle. Through a sleep haze, Hugh listened with semi-detached interest. At least it wouldn't affect him this time. Or so he thought.

He was wrong. 'Speculation's growing at Westminster,' said the newscaster, 'about a surprise move for Hugh Driftwood, the young Sports Minister. In the short time since he took office in such tragic circumstances, the Prime Minister has been plagued by constant allegations of sleaze and corruption and is thought to be keen to inject fresh blood into his Cabinet. And after his recent triumph over the Olympic venue, Mr Driftwood is seen as a prime candidate for promotion.'

With a surge of panic, Hugh prised open his eyes and searched frantically for his glasses. He turned up the volume and regretted it. The football reception the night before had been in his honour, making early escape impossible. So he'd joined in all too enthusiastically and now there was a dull ache in his head, and his stomach felt as if it had finished its soak and was about to start its spin cycle.

There was worse to come. 'Our reporter, Posey Gordon,' the commentator continued, 'is outside Mr Driftwood's Islington home, hoping to catch a few words with him when he leaves for Downing Street.'

Oh, God, thought Hugh. Horrified, he drank in the picture on the TV. The surreal image of his own terraced house filled the screen, with an eager-looking woman standing in front of it.

'Posey, is there any sign of the minister yet?'

Hugh thrust off his duvet and made a dash for the window. She was there all right, clutching a microphone and glaring up at his bedroom. The camera snaked upwards and Hugh sprang back.

'No, Bob, not yet,' said Posey earnestly, 'but Mr Driftwood *is* a notoriously early riser. No doubt he's been working inside on his red boxes for some hours now.'

In other circumstances, such a barefaced lie might have raised a laugh. Hugh knew where it came from, of course. Vanessa. She had been churning out this kind of rubbish in the *Pop* and all the other family newspapers for months. Not for the first time, Hugh cursed his stepmother, and right on cue the phone rang on his bedside table. He grabbed it anxiously. As usual, Vanessa dispensed with any introduction.

'You heard anything yet?' she asked.

'What do you mean?'

'Hugh, honey, what do you think I mean?' Vanessa said with exaggerated patience. Her New York twang, strong as ever, jarred so early in the morning. 'It's all round London. Word on the street says you're getting Transport.'

Hugh's throat went dry. 'I don't know anything about transport,' he protested shakily.

'What's to know?' asked his stepmother. 'Three months ago, how much did you know about sport? And now you're the goddamned Olympic hero. See? It's easy! Sport, transport – only four letters' difference, for Chrissake. You gotta have a bit of confidence in yourself.'

'What I've got,' said Hugh, rubbing his eyes, 'are platoons of TV cameras massing in the street.'

'Hey, that's great!' said Vanessa enthusiastically. He could almost hear her lips smacking. 'The more exposure you get, the better. Just make sure you talk slow; you know how you swallow your words when you're nervous. And say something snappy.

But keep it good and humble.' She gave her usual snorting laugh. 'That shouldn't be too hard for you. Then tell them you're happy to serve the PM in any capacity he chooses. Got all that? You'll be terrific.'

'I don't feel terrific,' said Hugh weakly.

'You're not sick, are you, honey?' said Vanessa, suddenly anxious too. 'You don't look after yourself properly.'

'No, I'm fine, it's just—'

'Which TV is it? Not the shower from Victor Quistling's satellite stations?'

'No,' said Hugh, 'it's the BBC.'

'Good, don't talk to Quistling's lot. They're trash. And listen, Hugh . . .'

'Yes?'

Vanessa's voice softened again momentarily. 'Good luck, honey. Your dad would have been so proud. You're gonna shoot the lights out.'

Hugh smiled despite himself. She'd been using those same words since he was a schoolboy. 'Vanessa, I—'

But such warm interludes never lasted long with his step-mother. She reverted immediately to her usual businesslike tones. 'I guess Number 10's trying to get through now,' she cut in. 'I'll clear the line.'

'Hang on a second, I—'

It was useless. She'd rung off. The phone rang again immediately. Vanessa's predictions were rarely mistaken.

Half an hour later, Hugh was showered and dressed and ready for his close-up. Checking himself distractedly in the hall mirror, he grabbed the newspapers from the inside mat and scanned the headlines. Victor Quistling's *Flick*, which had broken the story of yesterday's scandal and caused this cursed reshuffle, was in triumphant mood today. 'FLICK'S REVELATIONS SPARK ANOTHER GOVERNMENT CRISIS,' it screamed.

Naturally, it made no mention of Hugh or his putative promotion.

Vanessa, on the other hand, had been up to her usual tricks. All the Driftwood family newspapers, the tabloids and the broadsheets alike, had Hugh's picture featured prominently on the front page. 'POISED FOR POWER', the main story in the *Pop* ran. 'A NEW GENERATION.'

As the door slammed behind him, Hugh poised himself for power and tried to gather what was left of his nerves. He smiled for the camera and wondered if he'd remembered to do up his flies.

Chapter 2

In speculating that the TV crew might have come from one of Victor Quistling's satellite stations, Vanessa had for once got it wrong. She should have known that her arch-rival had long ago banned all news from his TV channels. 'News is crap,' Victor had once famously declared. 'And costs too much as well.' As far as he was concerned, it was bad enough having to put the stuff in his newspapers – although he had been working on that one. But when it came to television, no news was definitely good news.

Unfortunately, this meant that on the rare occasions when Victor wanted to know what was going on in the world, he had to rely on the BBC – and he hated the BBC with a vengeance. Still, needs must, and on the day of the Cabinet reshuffle, the VQ Media Corporation's proprietor sat down in front of the giant TV set in his basement office and reluctantly flicked the remote control from one of his own soft-porn channels to the BBC's midday bulletin. His flagship tabloid, the *Flick*, had been gunning for this government ever since its landslide victory at the last election. And, despite its pledges of a new tolerance, it had rapidly refocused its campaign on the incoming Premier literally before the dust from the Euro-Millennium Tower had settled. Now Victor was agog to discover the outcome of his most recent offensive.

It was not one to gladden his heart: 'Hugh Driftwood, the Sports Minister,' the newscaster announced, 'was the main winner in this morning's reshuffle. He takes over at the Department of Transport and becomes the youngest member of Edward Burgins's Cabinet.' The screen showed the lanky, bespectacled figure of the new minister leaving 10 Downing Street, his hair falling awkwardly over his eyes like an Old English Sheepdog's as he waved to a small crowd of onlookers.

Watching this, Victor's podgy face turned to thunder and his eyes bulged behind his own dark-lensed spectacles. As usual his temper sought an instant outlet. He picked up a paper-knife and decapitated a potted begonia on his desk, while the TV report went on to tell him what he already knew all too well: 'The Driftwood publishing company has, of course, been one of this government's staunchest supporters. But Downing Street today denied this had anything to do with Mr Driftwood's promotion. His move is seen by many as the Prime Minister's final attempt to reinvigorate his administration in advance of an election.'

'Bollocks to that,' said Victor, a pioneer of interactive television at its most basic. 'A fucking nuclear bomb wouldn't reinvigorate this commie shower.' With another flick of the knife, he declared war on a peace lily.

'The Premier,' continued the newsreader, oblivious to the carnage he was inflicting on the blameless flora of Victor's office, 'is widely reported to have ordered a top-secret enquiry into the source of the leaks that have bedevilled his administration. This reshuffle was forced by yesterday's resignation of the Trade and Industry Minister, Roger Breech, after details of his personal share dealings were disclosed in a tabloid newspaper.'

That was too much for Victor. '*A* tabloid newspaper?' he exploded, quivering with indignation. '*A* tabloid newspaper? Bastards! *The* tabloid bloody newspaper. Go on, give us the credit for once.'

But the BBC, which loathed him back with an equal, if more discreet, passion, managed to retell the entire sorry saga of the Trade Minister's departure without once giving any free publicity to the *Flick*, to the VQ Media Corporation, or indeed to its proprietor, Victor Quistling himself.

Which was just bloody typical, thought Victor. 'Bastards,' he said again. He searched his desk for further cannon fodder. Two diamanté-studded flamenco dancers – souvenirs from Benidorm – hit the television with a thud and bounced off the reinforced screen installed there by a far-sighted designer, shattering on the floor. Apart from wishing they could have been the BBC chairman's private parts, Victor ignored them.

'The leader of the opposition,' the news report concluded, 'this morning dismissed the reshuffle as the last desperate act of an administration in its death throes.'

'Some hope,' said Victor to himself. This was a cockroach of a government. However hard you stamped on it – and Victor was the leading member of the extermination squad – it kept managing to stagger on. He reached morosely for the remote control and snuffed out the television.

Then he sat and brooded. He brooded long and hard. His tiny eyes, never that far apart, almost merged, cyclops-like, into one as he concentrated on this unwelcome news. The promotion of Hugh Driftwood was the last thing he'd had in mind when he'd told the *Flick*'s editor to break the story of yesterday's scandal. Not, of course, that he knew this Driftwood geezer from a curry puff. But the fact that he was related to Vanessa was enough in itself to send Victor into paroxysms of fury. That woman was getting beyond a joke and something needed to be done about her.

There had once been a time when Driftwood International and the VQ Corporation had coexisted more or less peaceably. Naturally, an occasional skirmish blew up, as was inevitable between two great media empires. But by and large there had been room for them both: Driftwood, the long-established bastion of the patrician centre, its papers fusty and old-fashioned; and the Quistling organisation, its garish tabloids new and brash and with a political stance slightly to the right of Genghis Khan. In one crucial respect, though, they had always been united: their opposition to the left, new or old, and to socialism in any guise.

But that was before Vanessa. Since that woman had taken over the reins at Driftwood International on her husband's death, Victor reflected angrily, she had altered the blasted company beyond all recognition. After one look at the books, she'd hardly paused for breath before dragging the Driftwood Organisation decisively downmarket. Within weeks, she'd transformed its lofty old broadsheet, the *Daily Populist*, into the tabloid *Pop*, introducing, as it boasted itself in its first new-style editorial, 'bigger boobs and better bingo' than any of its competitors.

And that was not all. There was worse, much worse, than that. With an audacity that beggared belief, the woman had forsaken the then government – and the tradition of generations of Driftwoods – and performed a U-turn that would have shamed the most brazen politician, throwing herself into the welcoming embrace of the new left and taking millions of Driftwood's traditional supporters with her.

In this, as in everything else, her timing had been impeccable. When, at the general election which followed, her protégés had swept to power on the crest of a wave, Vanessa had followed triumphantly in their wake, even managing to sneak her own gormless stepson into the slew of new MPs so improbably elected with them.

That had been three years ago. Since then, Victor thought grimly, had come the pay-off. With her new friends firmly installed at Westminster, Vanessa had expanded her empire, jacking up the circulation of her existing papers and launching new ones almost monthly. Whenever necessary, strings had been pulled and favours called in to advance her interests.

Of course, she'd had to swallow hard when the Euro-Millennium disaster had carried off the champions of moderation and the party had reverted, at the drop of a cloth cap, to a former incarnation and was now so far to the left as to be practically invisible unless viewed through the Hubbell on a clear day. Brought in to fill the breach, Edward Burgins – or Buggins, as he was invariably referred to in all the Quistling papers – was a relic of a past government, an elderly firebrand of noble birth whose socialist convictions would have made Lenin gag.

But the country had greeted this change with a kind of bored stoicism, and in any case Driftwood International's interests were now so inextricably linked with those of the government that there was no going back. So Vanessa had gritted her teeth and soldiered on, and only the other day Victor had heard she'd finally been granted a licence to move into satellite television, an area he had colonised under the previous administration and one that he did not intend to surrender without a struggle.

Now came the final straw: this rise to the Cabinet of her blasted stepson, unintentionally assisted by Victor himself. Well, enough was bloody well enough. It was time for the Quistling empire to strike back, and strike back hard. But how? That was the question on which its proprietor now brooded.

Victor could have brooded for Britain and these sessions were rarely unproductive. With enough thought, he could usually come up with a malign scheme to suit every occasion. In time, a smile spread across his face and he reached for the intercom on his desk. 'Brenda?' he said.

'Yes, Mr Quistling?'

'What's the name of that journalist at the *Flick* who wrote the exposé on Roger Breech?'

'Gilbert Falange, Mr Quistling.'

'Yeah, that's the one. Call him and tell him to get down here pronto.'

'But . . .'

'But what?'

'You did agree to channel all communications through the editor, Mr Quistling.'

'Brenda, who owns this shit-heap?' asked Victor dangerously.

'You do, Mr Quistling.'

'Bloody right, I do. So fuck the editor, Brenda.'

'Yes, sir.'

'But first of all, get Falange down here. Oh, and another thing,' Victor added indignantly. 'For Christ's sake have someone to clean up all this *glass*. Before some poor bugger cuts himself.'

His secretary sighed and reached into a well-stocked cupboard of replacement desk ornaments. She was actually called Lavinia but Victor had long ago stopped bothering to remember his secretaries' names. Brenda had left years ago but as Victor's generic title for the species her name lived on.

Far above Victor's own basement office in the building which housed all the VQ publications, Gilbert Falange had been anticipating this call with glee. As Lavinia had correctly identified, it was indeed Gilbert who had yesterday fingered the Minister of Trade and Industry for trading with all too much industry – and under too many assumed names – in the stock market shares which his department was supposed to be regulating.

Today, Gilbert was preening himself. He had propped a

copy of yesterday's *Flick* up on his desk and spent most of the morning expatiating on his favourite topic – himself. 'Good old-fashioned investigative journalism,' he told anyone available, which in this case meant his assistant and secretary who shared his office and so were a captive audience. 'One keeps one's ear to the ground, one follows this lead, one follows that lead, then one day' – he gestured languidly towards the paper – 'another piece of government corruption is uncovered and one can relax . . .'

'That'll make a change, then,' said Stevie Cudlick, his assistant, under his breath.

Gilbert glowered at him. '. . . relax in the knowledge one has served one's country well,' he concluded. Even Stevie was not going to deflect him on this day. 'It's a question of using your brain, Cudlick,' he said airily. 'That's all there is to it. If you tried thinking a bit, instead of foraging around all the time like some over-excited ferret, you too might . . .'

The message that he was wanted in Hades, as Victor's office was unaffectionately known by his staff, came just in time to spare Stevie from Gilbert's critical appraisal, which was a regular feature of the day's routine. 'Ah, a word with our sponsor,' said Gilbert. 'Who can refuse? To offer thanks, no doubt, for yesterday's little coup.' He disappeared with a haste which belied his insouciant tone, and Stevie stuck his fingers down his throat and did a passable vomiting noise for the benefit of Debbie, the secretary, who giggled. Stevie sported a luxuriant ponytail and Debbie thought he was pretty cool.

Stevie would not have disagreed on that score. 'I wouldn't mind,' he complained, 'if he wasn't such a *crap* reporter. I mean, all that stuff about hard work. The oily old git hasn't *moved* off his arse for years. Christ, six months ago he was totally washed up, and now, all of a sudden, he's stumbled across a couple of government scandals and he's prancing around like he's Woodward and Bernstein rolled into one.' Vigorously, Debbie nodded her encouragement as he continued. 'What beats me is where he digs all this dirt from. He wouldn't know a lead if they attached one to his dick and put twenty thousand volts through it.'

Down in Hades, a similar question was puzzling Victor Quistling. Contrary to Gilbert's expectations, he had not been summoned to receive a pat on the back. A monthly salary cheque, as far as Victor was concerned, was more than enough by way of gratitude. What Victor wanted was information, and he wasn't a man to beat about the bush.

'Right,' he said when Gilbert had slumped rather too comfortably in the largest armchair in the office. 'I want to know, once and for all, who's been feeding you all this dope on the government.'

'Dope?' said Gilbert, who deprecated the use of modern slang. For a moment he forgot where he was and continued expansively in his earlier vein. 'Investigation, my dear fellow. Legwork and a bit of good old-fash—' But something about Victor's body language – he'd picked up a paper-knife and was fingering its tip speculatively – sobered him up. Victor knew all too well about the secret source, Gilbert reminded himself. So he fell back on a well-worn formula. 'The identity of my informant must naturally remain confidential between me and the person concerned,' he said. 'To disclose it would be a personal betrayal and, besides, it would contravene my journalistic ethics.' This was not an area Gilbert wished to dwell on, and he wondered how to divert the conversation on to different territory. Since Victor was not volunteering any compliments, perhaps a little fishing expedition was in order. 'You enjoyed my piece on our friend Mr Breech then?' he asked.

Victor gave a non-committal grunt.

Undeterred, Gilbert persevered. 'I did feel I'd captured the public mood in that bit about the leeches of corruption sucking away at the lifeblood of our democracy. Didn't you? Of course—' He stopped and gazed into the herringbone complexion of his boss. The line was disappointingly slack, but he was not easily discouraged. He tried recasting further upstream. 'I hear the circulation hit an all-time high yesterday. I hope, in my own small way, I've contributed to that. Haven't we moved ahead of the *Pop* again? Quite a change since I broke that first story about the Foreign Secretary.'

But the murderous expression just visible through Victor's dark glasses revealed that reliving Gilbert's past successes was the last thing he was interested in. 'What do you know about Hugh Driftwood?' he demanded.

At the Driftwood name, Gilbert suppressed a twitch of recognition. Of course. He should have seen it coming. 'Just been promoted into the Cabinet – Minister of Transport,' he said.

'I know *that*. You think I'm a complete ignoramus or something?' said Victor, regarding him dangerously. 'What I want is the inside track on the bugger. Come on, you're meant to be my bloody political correspondent.'

Gilbert mustered his thoughts. 'Well, he's one of the less unpleasant members of the government,' he said. 'Pretty moderate, which makes a refreshing change with this lot. Quite good-looking in a gangly sort of way, a bit unsure of himself sometimes, but that goes down well with voters. Very earnest but politically a lightweight; his biggest campaign to date was to save some animal protection society. Still, he's popular with the party's grass-roots.'

'And how far do you think he'll go now he's in the Cabinet?' Victor was watching him closely.

Gilbert reflected. 'Hmm. He's only in his early thirties, so he's got there very young. But it's mostly luck and, if you ask me, he's already hit his ceiling. In fact, I'd say he's been over-promoted. He's dedicated, but a bit of a plodder and not generally thought to be too bright. Typical new left education: seven years at Eton followed by three at Millwall Polytechnic. Or university as I suppose we have to call it now. It was only thanks to his family connections that he got the Sports job after the Euro-Millennium disaster.'

As had become customary, Gilbert paused reverentially at the mention of that terrible event. But Victor had no time for such false sentiment. As far as he was concerned, anything that reduced the ranks of the left was a Good Thing.

'Yeah, and now he's in the bloody Cabinet,' he said.

'Well, it's all these recent forced resignations.' The reporter shrugged modestly, but this was wasted on Victor. 'Despite the size of their majority, they're running out of suitable candidates. I shouldn't worry though. Driftwood did all right at Sport, but that was hardly a very demanding job. He won't last ten minutes at Transport. Hasn't got the oomph.'

'But that woman has,' said Victor, almost to himself.

'His mother?'

'Stepmother,' Victor corrected him. 'The American redhead. Bitch. Used to work in television before she married old Driftwood and reckons she knows all the angles. She thinks she can turn him into a contender.'

Gilbert shook his head. 'Not the remotest chance. Take it from me, he doesn't cut the mustard. Besides, Alistair Sloach has got the thing sewn up. He's a shoo-in when the PM goes, and once Sloach is in there there'll be no shifting him for centuries.'

Victor was not convinced. 'Don't underestimate that woman,' he said. 'I've made the mistake too often in the past. Anyway, I intend to be sure.' He lowered his voice. 'Now listen here,' he said. 'I want you to get out there and dig up whatever dirt there is on this Hugh Driftwood. We'll plaster it over the front page of the *Flick* and that should see him off once and for all.'

Gilbert shook his head. 'I doubt we'll get much on him,' he

said regretfully. 'He may not be too clever but he's squeaky clean, by all accounts.'

'There ain't no such thing as a clean politician,' said Victor with conviction. 'There's always sleaze, it's just a question of how deep you dig. How about graft?'

'With all that Driftwood money? Hardly.'

'Well then, sex,' said Victor. 'You know what these old upper classes are like. Perversion, bestiality, incest?' He looked up hopefully. 'Necrophilia, paedophilia, coprophilia?' He might have been reading from the index page of the *Flick*.

'Haemophilia's no use, I suppose?' said Gilbert. 'We could check if that runs in the family.'

Fortunately, Victor was immune to irony. 'Not married yet, is he? Maybe he's queer,' he continued. 'Rear-loading model, eh?' He gave another porcine grunt. 'That's always good for a couple of thousand on the circulation.'

'He's engaged, I believe,' said Gilbert, who was nothing if not well informed, 'to his college sweetheart, Rosemary something. They're getting married next year. Daughter of a left-wing barrister. Couldn't be more respectable. Brainy type, medical researcher. She's away in Australia right now, doing post-graduate research into male impotence. Nauseating, but there you are. No, I think you're flogging an equine corpse there, my dear chap.'

But Victor was losing patience. 'I'm not your dear chap,' he stormed, 'and frankly I don't give a bugger what you think. This geezer, this mole of yours – he's the one I want to hear from. He's obviously got the goods on half the Cabinet. Right?'

Gilbert waved his hand airily. 'Certainly, my contact is at the very heart of government but—'

'No buts. Driftwood should be chickenfeed to him. I've paid him plenty over the last few months, and so far I've just taken what he felt like giving us. Well, this time, you go back and tell him I've got a special request.'

Gilbert looked at him with a pained expression which concealed something rather more akin to panic. 'That's not how it works,' he said querulously. 'I can't approach him as if he's some kind of . . . some kind of political disc jockey.'

For Victor it was the last straw. 'I pay the fucking piper,' he screamed, crashing a plump fist down on his desk. 'I'll say how it works and how it doesn't work. I'm calling the tune now, and that tune is I-get-a-kick-out-of-Hugh-bloody-Driftwood. So piss off out of here and don't come back until you've got the bastard's balls in a nutcracker.' And with that he picked up the remote control and switched the television back on at full volume, indicating that the interview was at an end.

Chapter 3

Unaware of the fatwa which had just been issued against her stepson, Vanessa Driftwood had also watched the BBC's lunchtime news in her headquarters in London's Docklands. She greeted the announcement of Hugh's promotion with a hoot of victory and when the bulletin was over she sat for a while quite still, staring dreamily out of the vast windows over the towers of Canary Wharf. Unlike her rival, Vanessa was partial to daylight and her own office on the penthouse floor of Driftwood House was as airy as an aircraft hangar and only marginally smaller.

At length she snapped her fingers and grabbed the telephone. Her call was picked up by Hugh's voice-mail. 'Busy guy now,' Vanessa chuckled to herself as she listened to his hesitant message. She waited for the tone and boomed, 'Congratulations, honey,' down the line. 'Go in there and knock 'em dead. And don't forget the wicked old stepmother now you're so important.' She chuckled again. The wicked stepmother joke was an old one between them, dating back to their first meeting when Hugh was still a child. Charles Driftwood had been nervous about introducing her to his only son so soon after his first wife's death. But she and Hugh had hit it off immediately. And Charles's own death a few years later had only served to strengthen the bond.

A thought occurred to Vanessa and she replaced the receiver only briefly before redialling an internal number. 'Rowly,' she barked. 'You got a sec?'

Rowland Cranston, her rubicund second-in-command, turned up a few moments later wearing a relaxed grin. 'Morning,' he mumbled, padding across the huge office. He studied Vanessa critically. Her moods were a subject of constant fascination to all the Driftwood staff and Rowland was their in-house Richter, able to assess each temperamental nuance on his own infallible rating system. When something was up, she would remain implacable, her green eyes expressionless and unyielding, and a wise man did his business with her and got out of the office fast. But if she was on good form, those same eyes would radiate a sparkle to every corner of her face and it was not unusual for her to grab Rowland's substantial frame and waltz him around the floor without warning.

That didn't quite happen today, but she was definitely at the positive end of the Cranston scale. Her elegantly made-up features wore a contented expression, and the ashtray in front of her was mercifully empty, suggesting that her most recent attempt to quit smoking had lasted more than the customary twenty-four hours. As usual, she came straight to the point. 'Transport policy, Rowly,' she said. 'What do you know about it?'

'Not a lot,' Rowland admitted. His familiarity with that area extended little further than chauffeur-driven journeys to and from the office, with the occasional trip further afield to Heathrow for an effortless connection to the Driftwood Lear Jet. This, he shrewdly suspected, might not be totally representative of the experience of the average man in the street.

'Yeah, me neither,' said Vanessa. She reached into her briefcase and pulled out a newspaper cutting. 'But there's a guy called Pilltridge who does.'

'Who?'

'Professor at Oxford University. Writes stuff on' – she glared down – '*The Interrelational Interdependency of Modes of Personal Transportation into the Twenty-Second Century and Beyond* and a whole bunch of other crap like that.'

Twenty-five years since she'd left the States, Rowland reflected, and she still talked like a New York cab driver. He sometimes thought she took elocution lessons just to keep her accent fresh. 'Never heard of him,' he said.

'Take this cutting. I want you to get him in here. Full-time. Set him up in a suite downstairs.'

'Is that really necessary? I mean, Hugh will have civil servants to advise him—'

'Which is why the poor mutt will need all the help he can get,' Vanessa cut in. 'They'll run rings round him if we're not careful. No, if Hugh's to make an impression at Transport, we gotta short-circuit those assholes right from the beginning. And that's where Pilltridge comes in.'

'He might not be that easy to secure,' Rowland objected. He was used to dealing with such impossible requests from Vanessa.

'Nonsense. Pay whatever you have to. Say he can bring any research staff he wants. And get him some cute little secretary. That usually does the trick with those academic types. Which reminds me, I fired mine this morning so you'll have to find me a new one too. See if you can get a job lot.'

'What about his contract with the university? We can't just—'

'Sure we can. Offer to buy them a new wing. I never came across a university that said no to one of those. God knows what they do with them. You could fly to Venus on the number of wings I've donated over the years. Anyhow, promise them whatever you have to – just get Pilltridge down here. Tomorrow, absolute latest.'

'I'll do my best,' said Rowland resignedly.

'And in the meantime, have him write an immediate briefing for Hugh. I want it faxed over by tonight. No bullshit. Just the main issues on two sides of A4. Tell him Hugh's not the brain of Britain, so he should keep it simple.'

'Yes, Vanessa.'

'Now, anything else?'

'There is one thing.' Rowland paused. He had good news to impart, and wanted to milk it to best effect. 'I heard from Dick that we got the final go-ahead for the Popviz launch,' he said.

He was not to be disappointed. Vanessa sprang to her feet and let out a whoop, as if her team had just won the Superbowl. 'What date?' she asked.

'Friday, June 9th.'

'Great.' Vanessa's eyes were aglow. 'I'll announce it when I do my spiel at the Brass Monkey Awards in May.'

'You can't do that!' exclaimed Rowland.

'You wanna bet?'

'But the ceremony goes out on the BBC. They'll never let you use their network to launch a satellite competitor.'

'How're they going to know?' asked Vanessa smugly. 'The Brass Monkeys get transmitted live, right?'

'Yes, but—'

'No buts. By the time the BBC find out, it'll be too late. Why waste a captive audience of millions?' And forestalling any other objections, she pushed out her chin and bulldozed on in her usual manner. 'Then there's the question of the launch party,' she said thoughtfully. 'It's gotta be a humdinger. So get out there and book the biggest venue in London. We're going to make a splash like the TV industry's never seen before.

That'll wipe the smile off Quistling's face,' she concluded with a triumphant grin.

When Rowland had left, Vanessa once again sat back in her wide swing chair and stared out of the window towards Canary Wharf. The great tower shimmered in the early spring sunshine. But she paid it little heed. Her thoughts were far away in the past, at a time long before she'd met Charles or Hugh, before she'd even heard of Driftwood International. They were of her first career – of a girl newly arrived from New York in search of a television breakthrough that had eluded her in her own country. She had found it in Britain, all right. In this smaller pond, she may not have been a bigger fish, but at least she was one of a different species, which was exactly what she'd calculated.

She smiled ruefully. After all that, being a quiz-show hostess hadn't lived up to her expectations at all. Sure, she got recognised everywhere, but what good was that if you hardly got a word in edgeways. Four years of purgatory, mouthing platitudes and providing straight lines for Hilton Starr's dire jokes. But it had given her a fleeting fame, and a toehold on the ladder which led to where she was now.

She'd always sworn then that she'd come back one day and show them how a real TV station was run. And now that day was close. She tapped the desk pensively then reached for the phone yet again. There was another call that had to be made. 'I want you to get me Hilton Starr,' she told the receptionist. 'Yeah, that's right, the guy who used to be on TV.'

All this, she reflected as she waited to be put through, and stepmother to the future Prime Minister to boot. Not bad for little Vanessa Zipsky from the Bronx, whose folks couldn't even afford a newspaper, never mind a television set, and whose closest brush with political influence was waving at the mayor after his inauguration at City Hall.

Chapter 4

The putative future Prime Minister awoke the next morning after another night of unwelcome longings, featuring an array of fantasies whose erotic eclecticism took even Hugh by surprise.

He was going to have to do something about these, he decided reluctantly. Since Rosemary's departure to Australia on a year-long sabbatical, his sex life had been distinctly short-staffed and his libido had been kicking its heels resentfully and urging him to take remedial action. In vain Hugh had countered with arguments about faithfulness and chastity, old-fashioned virtues, he accepted, but ones he remained attached to.

His libido was having none of that. It had muttered darkly about the stunning brunette at the Department of Sport who had definitely given him the come-on. Or, failing her, the discreet square not a mile from where he lived, famed for its upmarket clientele and along whose kerbs the tyre marks of crawling Mercedes and Range Rovers practically formed a permanent rut. As a last resort, it conceded reluctantly, it might be prepared to accept a bit of manual intervention, but here Hugh was adamant: his days as a sole practitioner had gone along with his last adolescent pimple and were not coming back, he insisted. His libido would just have to like it or lump it. It had plainly decided to lump it, the result being the unwanted marquee arrangement halfway down the bed.

On top of that, for the second morning in a row, Hugh was suffering from a splitting headache. This time, though, it was from overwork rather than over-indulgence. He had sat up most of the night poring over papers from his new department, and had finally gone to bed at three a.m. with a sleeping pill and a growing sense of terror.

This new job, he was convinced, was going to be a disaster. As Sports Minister he'd rarely had to do much more than entertain the Queen on Cup Final day, hush up the occasional steroids scandal or eulogise some boxing champion at his premature funeral. But the Transport portfolio was something else again. Facts and figures on privatisations, nationalisations, green papers, white papers, integrated transport policies that were disintegrating before his eyes, road-pricing and accident-prevention – or was it the other way around? – all had to be assimilated. They had filled his brain until he despaired of ever grasping any of it.

His first meeting the previous day with the Permanent Secretary at the Department of Transport had not helped one jot. Admittedly the top civil servant was friendly enough, but he'd still managed to make it quite clear he thought he'd got a distinctly duff hand in the ministerial reshuffle. Not that he said anything to that effect; it was just the way he kept shaking his head sadly whenever Hugh ventured an opinion, and, like some latter-day pinstriped Mrs Danvers, took every opportunity to emphasise the effectiveness of Hugh's predecessor.

If it hadn't been for Vanessa, he didn't know what he would have done. Professor Pilltridge had – at the cost of two new wings and a staff gymnasium with integral sauna and massage suite – well and truly come up with the goods. The brief the professor had produced had been a model of no-nonsense concision, putting the reams of official papers with which the department had no doubt deliberately swamped Hugh into some kind of perspective and giving him hope he might after all survive more than a few weeks in the job.

Hugh got out of bed and glanced through the window. This morning, to his relief, the TV cameras were absent from the pavement, although a gaggle of journalists had formed outside. Better get used to that, he thought. The Sports job had been relatively low-profile. But heading up the Transport Ministry meant a seat in the Cabinet and all the accompanying media attention. The very thought gave him renewed palpitations and he dashed into the kitchen in search of caffeine and aspirin. Never had he needed them so much.

Bad as he was feeling, though, he felt a good deal worse after he'd opened the kitchen door. For that was when he discovered that he was not as alone in the house as he'd imagined.

Balanced on a chair with her back to him, foraging in one of his cupboards, was a long-legged girl of about twenty. She had velvety tanned skin and a mane of black hair which hung down almost to the base of her spine. But her most striking feature lay further south, above that stunning expanse of legwork – on her buttocks, to be precise. Each one carried a colourful tattoo. On the left, in large rococo lettering, was an 'R', and on the right an 'S'. Both were surrounded by florid artwork which meandered off up her back and down her legs. Other than these, she was completely and utterly and stunningly naked.

Hugh's body froze over and he stood staring at this apparition for what seemed like an eternity. Finally, he let out a startled gasp, and, alerted to his presence, she half turned around so he was able to drink in the rest of her. For her facade, he discovered, she had eschewed the literary motif in favour of something more functional. At the end of her voluptuous breasts, two brass loops hung from coffee-brown nipples like twin towel rings. Above, a pair of cool emerald eyes stared down on him with interest. 'Don't suppose you've got any pimentos?' she asked. 'Spanish omelette's not the same without them.'

Hugh blinked. Rosemary was away. He had the house to himself. This had to be some form of hallucination induced by his overworked and undersexed state. He closed his eyes and took deep breaths. But when he reopened them she was still there and those legs seemed to be lengthening by the second. 'What . . . ?' He tried to frame a question but his tongue had formed a slip knot somewhere around his larynx.

His visitor had no such problem. She looked him up and down with every sign of appreciation and her own pink tongue darted out of her mouth. Her lips, pillar-box red, pouted as if imminently expecting a letter. 'Yumyum,' she said. 'Whatever you're selling, I'll take the lot. You come with the flat?'

Hugh looked down and realised with dismay that he was as naked as she was. He slept in the nude and, not expecting any visitors, hadn't bothered with a dressing-gown. The blood rushed to his face, which at least stopped it going all too embarrassingly in the opposite direction. For this girl was distinctly sensual, not to say breathtakingly attractive.

Then it struck him with a vengeance, and he felt as if he'd been kicked in the solar plexus. It was a frame-up. It had to be. Of course the girl wasn't a hallucination – she was a plant. Victor Quistling's tabloids were after this government's blood, and if they couldn't get it by honest means, they weren't above contriving a little uninvited photo opportunity.

Her next words did nothing to reassure. 'Don't I know you from somewhere?' she said. She had a cockney accent and a husky, breathless voice. 'Go on, you've been on TV, haven't you?' She reached out, evidently intending to shake his hand, but her toe caught on the edge of the chair and she overbalanced and fell towards him, mouth agape, breasts bouncing heavily against his own bare chest. It was too much for Hugh. Fully expecting a paparazzo to materialise from the waste disposal like some malevolent Grub Street genie, he pulled himself away and fled back through the kitchen door towards the sanctuary of the bedroom.

He didn't reach it. Halfway through the hallway, he collided with a sturdy figure, and together they collapsed on the floor with a crash. Hugh's glasses flew off and, petrified and unseeing, he curled up into a foetal position. In vain he tried to cover his face with his hands. Pictures would be no good to them if he couldn't be identified, he reasoned.

'Jesus Christ, Hugh, hold your horses!' said an indignant voice with a familiar Irish lilt. 'You nearly flattened the life out of me!'

And with that sound, gradually, Hugh's brain began to return to something close to sanity. He'd have known those soft tones anywhere. With a mixture of relief and mounting outrage, Hugh opened his eyes and peered myopically into the baby-blue eyes of Will Cloud. He should have guessed.

'What the hell are you doing here?' he stuttered, as soon as he was capable of saying anything.

'Well now, that's not much of a welcome, indeed it is not!' said Will plaintively. 'Have you no manners?'

'And how in God's name did you get in?'

'Didn't want to wake you up, so I slipped the lock with my credit card,' Will replied with a wink, retrieving Hugh's spectacles and trying them on for size. 'I must say,' he added, 'I don't think much of your security. I thought this place would be crawling with Special Branch folk, now that you're so important.'

'Never mind about me.' Hugh grabbed back his glasses

and glared at him. Will hadn't changed one little bit since their last meeting. He still had the same untidy mop of dark curly hair above a boyish face which conveyed a totally deceptive impression of innocence. 'Just tell me what on earth you're up to?'

'Visit whenever you want, that's what you said. *Mi casa es su casa*, eh?'

'It's been months now. I expected some sort of warning.'

'Well, I'm between jobs. I just finished this conference in Morocco on combating international drug-trafficking. I flew in from Marrakech last night so I didn't have a chance . . .'

Slowly, Hugh got his breath back and his mind round this information. At least it wasn't a press stitch-up, he consoled himself. But the return of Willard Fergal Cloud into his life was an unwelcome development of the worst kind.

In the not-so-distant past, Will and Hugh had attended Millwall University together. Or, to be more precise, Hugh had attended Millwall University while Will had put in the occasional appearance between getting drunk, stoned, laid or arrested – quite often all four on the same day. A Dubliner by birth, Will had chosen London for his studies because, as he'd explained disarmingly on their first meeting, he reckoned its unparalleled opportunities for drunken debauchery surpassed even those of his home town. Against his better judgement, Hugh had rented him a room in the comfortable student flat he'd bought in Docklands, although 'rented' was overstating it, since very little in the way of ready cash ever seemed to change hands. Despite this, he had been drawn to the whimsical young Irishman and they had become firm, if improbable, friends.

But, after graduation, when Hugh just managed to scrape together a mediocre degree in history while his flatmate had astonishingly emerged with a first in modern languages, Will had moved on to a peripatetic career as a freelance interpreter and their paths had diverged. None the less, on his irregular trips back to London Will continued to treat Hugh's home as a permanent hotel. A visit from him invariably spelled trouble and today looked like being no exception.

'I take it she's with you then?' Hugh asked, pointing a trembling finger towards the kitchen.

'Indeed she is!' said Will.

'Who is she?'

Will pondered. 'Well now, there you have me,' he admitted. 'Can't remember exactly what she said she was called.'

Typical. 'I don't suppose the initials RS ring a bell?'

Enlightenment dawned on Will. 'Well spotted,' he said. 'But actually those aren't her initials. It's all coming back to me now. That's her name. She's called Ros. You don't see the "O" till she bends over.'

Hugh recoiled in horror. It was disgusting. 'Let me understand this,' he said slowly. 'Not a dickybird from you for months and now you've broken into my house with some woman you don't know who's got a monogrammed backside and a portable ironmongery hanging off her . . . her . . .'

'Tits,' said Will. 'I think that's a fair summary of the position. I mean, what would you have done?' he added with evident irritation. 'We meet on the plane, see, and I'm chatting her up. And then she tells me she's got nowhere to go for the night. Well, honestly! Who in their right mind would turn down an invitation like that? And even you'd have to admit that she's not half a stunner.'

Hugh looked at him beseechingly. 'There are journalists outside,' he said.

'I know,' said Will. 'They rang the bell earlier but I told them to piss off.'

'You didn't!'

'Well, not in those words.'

'Thank God for that.'

'Actually I told them to fuck off.'

Hugh's face went straight from red to green, like a faulty traffic light. A worse thought struck him. 'They didn't see—'

'Ros? No, don't think so. Does it matter?'

Hugh stared at him incredulously. This was no more than he'd come to expect from Will in their student years, but surely even he had to have grown up since then. Evidently not. With a surge of fresh horror, Hugh sniffed the air. A whiff of blue smoke wafted out from the spare bedroom. 'What's that?' His voice was distraught.

Will shrugged apologetically. 'There was some great stuff going begging at the conference, and when in Morocco . . .'

'Oh, my God,' said Hugh. His head swam with the potential headlines. Sex, drugs, smuggling, self-mutilation. The tabloids would be spoiled for choice.

'Look,' he said desperately. 'You can't stay here. Honestly. I've got my first Cabinet meeting today . . . and as for her . . .' He looked over pleadingly.

'No problem,' said Will. 'I'm only staying for . . . oh, a couple of months at the most. Sure, I won't be any trouble at all. And Ros just came along for the night. Got family somewhere in the Isle of Dogs.' A thought struck him. 'She's looking for a job, so she tells me. Don't suppose you'd know of anything now, would you?'

Hugh's monosyllabic answer was drowned out by the phone ringing in the lounge. Will reached it first and picked it up as if he'd lived there all his life. 'Military tattoos and metalworks,' he said, substituting a broad Belfast accent for his usual mild Dublin burr. 'Aye, hang on. Your man's right here.' He put his hand over the receiver and looked quizzically at Hugh. 'American woman with the voice of Judge Dread?'

'Vanessa,' said Hugh weakly. He took the receiver.

'Who the hell was the mick?'

Hugh gulped. She'd never met Will but knew of him all too

well by reputation. 'It's . . . ah, Rosemary's Irish cousin,' Hugh lied. 'Staying over for a few days.'

'Well, tell him to be careful how he answers the phone,' snapped Vanessa. 'What if I'd been a reporter? Anyhow, forget about that. Did you get the briefing?'

'Yes, thanks,' said Hugh. 'It was a godsend. Believe me, I can't imagine what I'd have done without it. Heaven knows how I'm going to manage anyway.'

'Nonsense,' Vanessa retorted. 'You're as good as any of them. Now, you've got the Cabinet meeting today, right?'

'Yes,' said Hugh anxiously. 'And a briefing with Alistair Sloach beforehand.'

'Good. Speak to me later,' said Vanessa. 'I want to know how you get on.' And she hung up.

Hugh checked the time. 'Oh, God,' he groaned. 'I'd better get moving. Sloach is very big on punctuality.'

Will looked up with interest. 'Sloach? Now that name rings a bell. Isn't he the fella the party once sent to speak at the students' union? Smug oily type. Small in stature but big in self-importance, even though he couldn't have been more than a few years older than us at the time. Had a conker the size of St Paul's, if I remember rightly.'

'That was Alistair,' said Hugh. 'He's changed a lot since those days, though,' he added loyally, but without conviction.

'Nose shrunk back to Albert Hall proportions now, has it?'

'No, I meant—'

'If I recall, he talked a whole lot of baloney about the moral rectitude of the new left.'

'He *is* a bit on the puritanical side,' Hugh admitted. 'But very sincere.'

'Honestly, Hugh. You would have defended Stalin as a bit over-enthusiastic but with his heart in the right place. So how come you've got to see the man?'

'He's my new boss,' Hugh replied dolefully.

'Jesus!' said Will, helping himself to an apple from the bowl on the table and lounging back on the couch. 'You certainly know how to pick 'em.' He examined the apple critically then took a healthy bite. 'But how does that come about?' he went on. 'I thought you were in the Cabinet now. So isn't his nibs the PM your boss? Old Buggins?'

'Burgins,' Hugh corrected him automatically. He sighed, wishing it could be that simple. 'I *would* report direct to the PM,' he explained, 'if the last leader – may he rest in peace – hadn't brought Transport and Environment under one umbrella. So although I get a seat in the Cabinet, my immediate superior is the Minister of the Environment, and that's Alistair Sloach.'

Will tutted sympathetically. 'You have my condolences,' he said. 'Still the same pompous little pipsqueak, is he?'

Hugh grimaced but avoided the question with the skill of a seasoned politician. 'I'm sure he'll be fine once we get to know one another,' he said with a confidence he did not feel. 'The trouble is I once made an accidental speech at party conference denouncing his Victorian values crusade.'

'Now there's an interesting one,' said Will, with that look of indulgent mystification which transported Hugh back to interminable student discussions in which Will always got the better of him. 'I hope this isn't a daft question, but how on earth can anyone make an accidental speech?'

'Oh, *I* don't know!' Hugh replied distractedly. 'Somehow I managed to pick up the wrong papers, and I was halfway through reading the bloody thing out before I realised it wasn't my appeal to ban fox-hunting at all. It was Roger Breech's coded attack on Alistair's Moral Millennium Campaign. But I'd have looked a right prat if I'd stopped mid-flow and admitted it was a mistake. And I could feel the audience was with me, so I just carried on. It was the only standing ovation I've ever had, as a matter of fact.'

Will took another bite of the apple and observed his friend pityingly. 'I don't even like to ask what happened to Roger Breech.'

'Ah, that was slightly unfortunate,' Hugh admitted. 'Seems he'd been on a bender the night before and didn't realise what had happened either. So he went on and delivered my thing about foxes. A very good speech it was, too,' he added with some indignation. 'I'd sweated buckets on it. Not that the committee of the Quorn appreciated it coming from old Breech of course. Apparently they called him in the next day and broke his riding crop over his head, or whatever it is they do to the Master when he turns bad. Poor man's never really recovered. Anyway,' Hugh concluded with a tremor of anxiety, 'I think Alistair Sloach still holds the whole affair against me.'

'Settle yourself, Hugh,' said Will soothingly. 'Sure, you always were such a worrier. He'll have forgotten about it ages ago.'

'I hope so.' Hugh ran a hand through his hair. 'He certainly seemed to be very pleased by my appointment, and he's someone to keep on the right side of. Ever since he was the PM's spin-doctor in the leadership campaign he's been very influential. They say he's the person to watch and when Burgins goes, he's a cert to—'

He broke off as he looked at his watch again. 'Damn. I'd better get my skates on.' He dashed towards the bathroom, stopping only to glare back reproachfully at Will. 'I'll talk to you when I get back,' he said. 'In the meantime, for pity's sake be careful. Don't let Miss – your friend – near the windows until the press have gone. Oh, and you'd better keep her away from the tin-opener,' he added as an afterthought. 'It's magnetic – she might do herself an injury.'

Chapter 5

Hugh was quite wrong to believe that Alistair Sloach had been pleased with his appointment. In fact the diminutive Environment Minister – or the Macclesfield Machiavelli, as one journalistic wit had dubbed him in honour of his birthplace – was distinctly displeased.

Not that he disliked Hugh *per se* – at least no more than he disliked the rest of his colleagues, whom he held in a kind of generalised contempt. No, Alistair thought to himself as his car dropped him at work that morning for his usual seven o'clock start, he had no strong feelings about the man either way, despite that speech at the conference in which he'd had the impudence to criticise the Moral Millennium Campaign.

Nor, he reflected sourly as he sipped his first coffee of the day, did he even object to the fact that Driftwood was clearly mentally subnormal. That, after all, was par for the course with this government, which had undergone a dumbing-down of hideous proportions since the Millennium disaster had carried off its brightest members. Anyway, Alistair had been in politics long enough to know there were some real advantages to having an incompetent subordinate, not the least of which was the excuse it provided for automatically overruling any decision he was presumptuous enough to make.

No, Alistair's real objections to his new Minister of Transport went much deeper: they were rooted in the very existence of such a post at all. This reshuffle, he was convinced, would have been the ideal opportunity to have abolished the position of Transport Minister entirely. There was absolutely no need for it when Alistair was perfectly willing, indeed eager, to do both jobs simultaneously.

In the hours before the changes were announced, he had told Edward Burgins this in no uncertain terms. 'Really, Prime Minister,' he'd maintained, 'I'm perfectly capable of representing both Environment and Transport at Cabinet level on my own.'

But for once his arguments had fallen on deaf ears. 'I'm quite sure you are, Alistair, my dear chap. But we ought to give Driftwood a chance. New blood and all that. And I think you'll find he's surprisingly reliable.'

Certifiable would be more accurate, Alistair had thought malevolently, but when he had pressed his case further, the PM had said with a glint in his eye, 'I *am* capable of making some decisions on my own, you know, old chap.' And in the end there was no option but to drop it.

This in itself, Alistair mused moodily, was an ominous sign. As Hugh had noted, Sloach had been the Prime Minister's campaign manager in the leadership contest earlier that year. But he had been much more than just that. In the aftermath of the Millennium disaster, Alistair had kept his head when those around him were losing theirs faster than the Bourbons on a bad head day. With a political adeptness which had astonished everyone, he'd plucked Edward Burgins, the elderly left-wing aristocrat who had been a long-serving minister in a past government, from the obscurity of near-retirement on the backbenches and propelled him virtually single-handedly to the very top. In return, when the new Premier had formed his first Cabinet, Alistair had been rewarded with the Environment portfolio and since then had become accustomed to Burgins hanging on his every word and acting on his every recommendation.

Recently, though, the PM had begun displaying worrying signs of wanting to break free from this cosy dependency. Driftwood's appointment was not the first time he had failed to consult Alistair on some key decisions, and on one occasion he'd not even bothered to return an urgent telephone call. This was a tendency, Alistair was resolved, that must be stamped on at the very earliest opportunity. And so too must Hugh Driftwood if Alistair was to take full control of the ministry and pursue his masterplan to its conclusion.

For, as had been plain to everyone except Burgins himself, Alistair's move in championing him as leader had not been remotely altruistic. Like everything he had ever done in his life, it was all part of a grand strategy – the Sloach agenda. From his escape from the stifling confines of his working-class roots, to his migration to London as a minor party official, to his marriage to the spinsterish daughter of a former leader and subsequent not-unconnected ascent up the hierarchy, it had all been with but one destination in mind – and that destination was Number 10 Downing Street.

The Millennium disaster, however, had not formed part of this blueprint at all. It had struck from nowhere and for a brief moment it had wrong-footed Alistair Sloach. Not that he unduly mourned the disappearance of the last Cabinet, for their passing had left the field gratifyingly open for new aspirants.

But it had come at the wrong time for him. He was becoming a force in the party, certainly. He was gaining in reputation. He had even, through his book on public morality, begun to enjoy a certain appeal among the more puritanical elements of the electorate. But *The Human Sewer – A Respite from the Cesspit* had only recently been published, and he needed a longer run-in before he was ready to launch his own bid for the leadership.

Hence Alistair's decision to promote Burgins, one of the party's most senior surviving MPs, as the ultimate compromise candidate. That the man was the most incompetent dolt ever to have held high office had been clear to him – if to nobody else – from the outset. But that was precisely the point. Burgins could be counted on to make a complete hash of the job within months, Alistair reckoned, providing him with a God-given opportunity to thrust the man aside and finally realise his own destiny.

That moment was coming closer. Sloach could feel its approach, sense it like the rumble of distant thunder. Since taking over, Burgins had suffered one humiliating scandal after another and, with his administration fast sinking into a quicksand of sleaze and corruption, there could be only one candidate of sufficiently upright character to step in and rescue the party from imminent disaster. And that, it was surely clear to all, was Alistair J. Sloach.

Now, as he reached his endplay, the Macclesfield Machiavelli did not intend to allow anyone to stand in his way, and certainly not a nonentity like Hugh Driftwood. The abolition of Hugh's role was a vital part of the grand plan. It would, he calculated, enable him to raise his profile one notch further without having to make the next obvious, but desperately dangerous, move – to the wastelands of the Home Office. A transfer there, Alistair was convinced, would be political suicide. For, as a close student of political history, he knew that few Home Secretaries had ever survived the experience to move to the premiership. No, he had to avoid that poisoned chalice at all costs and stick comfortably to an expanded Environment Ministry until he could make an easy transition to Number 10 when fortune beckoned.

Which left one question unanswered: how to get rid of

Driftwood? And that was the problem that was occupying Alistair as he awaited impatiently for Hugh's arrival. It had to be fast. It had to be sharp. And it had to be done in such a way that the PM would see the error of his ways in not trusting Alistair in the first place. Finally, it had to be a cataclysm so complete that there would be no question of a replacement.

Such a challenge might have baffled many a brain, but not the pentium-chipped model belonging to Alistair J. Sloach. Thoughtfully, he glanced through the agenda for the day's Cabinet meeting and his eye alighted on a small item near the bottom. Yes, he thought. Oh, yes. That would do very nicely indeed. But he had to move quickly.

He summoned his press secretary, Joe Duggery, who was the spin-doctor's spin-doctor and had often carried out sensitive assignments for him. Joe was absolutely sound, even if he did look like he'd been cloned from one of the less prepossessing members of the weasel family. 'Tell me about this top-secret proposal to renationalise the London Underground,' Alistair demanded, settling back in his chair and placing his fingertips together contemplatively.

As usual, Joe had an encyclopaedic knowledge of everything going on in the joint departments of Transport and Environment. 'Well, Minister,' he began, 'it was initiated by Mr Driftwood's predecessor, in keeping with the government's new thinking on privatisations. Provided it's done sensitively, I see no real difficulty with it from a PR point of view.'

'And if it's done insensitively?' asked Alistair, his expression impassive.

Joe regarded him with some curiosity. 'Ah,' he said. 'The consultative paper for today's Cabinet envisages three options. The most extreme of them is frankly barmy, but either of the other ones should do the trick.'

'Tell me about the barmy one,' said Alistair, stroking his bulbous nose thoughtfully.

'Compulsory purchase of all shares with zero compensation? An absolute no-brainer, Minister.'

'Take me through it all the same.'

'But it would cause pandemonium!'

'Humour me, Joe,' Alistair insisted quietly but with a certain menace in his voice.

'If you say so, Minister.' Joe knew Sloach was already perfectly familiar with the proposals but his was not to reason why. 'As you are aware, your own predecessor privatised the Tube, line by line, giving free shares to regular passengers and staff. It was a very popular move at the time. But of course one of the conditions was that trading in the shares wouldn't begin until next year, so they couldn't be sold until then.'

'Go on.'

'Ever since, there's been quite a healthy competition – almost a rivalry – between the lines. A great deal of brand loyalty's developed, even to the extent of dedicated user groups forming around each of the Tube companies and passengers going into stations as volunteers to help clean graffiti off walls and tidy up trains. As a result, the quality of the service has improved immeasurably and the likely market value of the shares has shot up. Of course, it varies company by company but in some cases it's increased nearly tenfold. So heaps of people are sitting on enormous unrealised profits and there's a vested interest in continuing the status quo. If you try and renationalise without compensation, you'll effectively be confiscating their windfall. It would be asking for trouble.'

'You don't say!' said Alistair, drumming his fingers on the desk. 'Well, Joe, it may interest you to hear that the new Transport Minister is minded to do exactly that.'

'If you'll forgive me saying so, Minister, he must be bonkers. The passenger action committees will eat him alive. Not to mention the City and the Tube workers unions.'

'Quite,' said Alistair. 'But, on the other hand, don't you think we must allow Hugh some rope . . . or rather leeway, to make his own decisions?'

'But, Minister! I would strongly advise you to persuade him—'

'No.' Alistair held up his hand. 'My mind is made up. Far be it for me to stifle the enthusiasm of youth. We must give Hugh his head.' He paused and a delphic smile played across his face. 'None the less, we wouldn't want to rush into this without a proper public debate. Perhaps you might just like to sound out some external views?'

'Ah,' said Joe. He was beginning to see where the minister was coming from. 'So you want me to leak it?'

Alistair raised his eyebrows in mock horror. 'My dear chap! Certainly not. There's no question of leaking. It's simply a matter of nurturing the channels of communication with those who put us in power; a little democratic irrigation, so to speak.'

'So you want me to irrigate it, then?' said Joe without changing his tone.

'With such a vital issue at stake, I do think the public should always be kept informed, don't you?' Alistair replied with practised blandness. Then, fleetingly, his expression acquired something of the night. 'Just make damned sure it's not attributable,' he said balefully.

Joe made for the door, but paused as he reached it. 'Is Hugh Driftwood really in favour of this?' he asked with a shrewd glance back.

'He will be in half an hour's time,' replied Alistair.

As Joe left, Sloach checked the great antique clock on his wall. His press secretary was a quick worker. With a bit of luck, the rumours would be all round London within minutes of the Cabinet meeting beginning. Then, if the reaction was as rapid and as violent as Alistair confidently expected it to be, the fat should well and truly reach the fire about halfway through. In all probability, Hugh would get pulled out early to sort it all out. And Alistair knew how much the PM *hated* people leaving in the middle of Cabinet meetings. He could never be sure that they weren't flouncing around outside the doors of Number 10, trashing him to the press before announcing their resignation.

The Macclesfield Machiavelli put his arms behind his head, lounged back comfortably in his swivel chair and awaited the arrival of his new subordinate with quiet satisfaction.

Hugh was approaching the meeting with a good deal less equanimity. Sloach's reputation as the Cabinet's chief predator was legendary, and since that ill-fated speech he was never quite sure where he stood with him. He was to be pleasantly surprised, though. Alistair seemed perfectly well disposed towards him today, even vaguely friendly, his expression warm and affable.

Perhaps he wasn't going to be difficult to work with after all, Hugh thought with some relief. 'What . . . I mean . . . are any important Transport issues likely to come up at today's meeting?' he asked with as much nonchalance as he could muster once they had settled into the comfortable armchairs in the corner of Alistair's plush office.

'Nothing you can't manage, Driftwood, old chap,' said Sloach expansively. 'Transport bores the rest of the Cabinet out of their wits – such as they are.' His lips turned up in a grim smile. 'Just my little joke.' Then, casting his eye over the agenda, he said, 'The spending plans are due to be finalised over the next few weeks, but that shouldn't be raised today. In any case, they were put to bed by your predecessor and merely need to be rubber-stamped.' He paused. 'There *is* one tiny thing I wanted to talk to you about, though.'

'Yes?'

'This paper on the renationalisation of the Underground. Which option do you think we should recommend?'

Hugh did his best to summon up the facts from his briefings. There had been so many papers on diverse subjects that they all seemed to have merged into one soggy mass in his mind. 'I didn't think we had to come up with a recommendation yet,' he said in some panic. 'It's just a consultative document, isn't it?'

'Absolutely,' Alistair reassured him. 'But I rather thought this might be an opportunity for you to be bold and decisive. Show your mettle. You know, a new brush . . .'

'Oh,' said Hugh.

'So it would be best to produce a clear preference.'

'But which one?' asked Hugh anxiously.

Alistair waved a hand in the air. 'Far be it from me to second-guess your views,' he said. 'But, if I might just be permitted to give you a tip, I believe the PM is very averse to all these fat cats making fortunes out of Tube privatisation. Can't be fair, eh?' Alistair paused. 'So what about . . .' – he glanced down at his papers – 'option three?'

Hugh racked his brains. 'Return to the public sector without compensation?' he asked doubtfully.

'Precisely. What's your view on that?' Sloach's eyes narrowed.

'Eh, well, I . . .' Hugh tried to recall the professor's aide-mémoire. He was sure he had cautioned against this. 'Don't you think it might be a bit unpopular?'

Sloach shrugged his shoulders. 'My dear chap, if all we want to do is court public popularity, then we're in the wrong jobs, eh? Surely we must consider what is right, rather than what is popular.'

'Yes,' said Hugh, scratching his forehead. 'Quite.'

'And of course, it's all top secret, and at a very preliminary stage, so nobody but the Cabinet will be privy to our thoughts.' Alistair smiled urbanely. 'Besides, my private sources tell me that opinion in the party is very much in favour.'

'Really?'

'And it's surely in keeping with the PM's more . . . ah . . . firm approach to the private sector since he's taken the helm.'

'Perhaps I just ought to consult my officials,' said Hugh. He took off his spectacles and pinched the bridge of his nose. He was getting another headache.

'In due course, certainly,' said Alistair smoothly. 'But there's no time right now. We can provide Cabinet with a provisional recommendation, and it won't be as if you can't go back on it later, of course.' He looked across the desk with a hint of impatience.

Hugh blinked. If Alistair was so keen, then he had better go along with it, he reasoned. Moreover, this was a man who had the PM's ear and would be sure to know his thinking on the matter. It was a pity he wouldn't have time to discuss it with the civil servants, or even Professor Pilltridge, but, after all, he ought to be able to make some decisions on his own. 'Very well,' he said at length. 'We'll go for option three then.'

'Good.' Alistair raised a bony finger. 'There is one last thing. Since this will be your first Cabinet, it's best if I allow you some elbow room. Let you show you're your own man.'

'That's very considerate,' said Hugh gratefully.

'So what I suggest,' Alistair continued, 'is that you lead this discussion. I'll take a back seat. In fact, I may even pretend to be rather against it. That way you'll come across as fighting your corner, which won't do you any harm at all.'

'Fighting my corner,' said Hugh. 'Yes. Thank you, again. I do appreciate it, ah . . . Alistair.'

'Not at all. The least I can do. Now you'd better be heading over to Number 10, eh? Doesn't do for the new boy to be late on his first day. I've just got one or two things to finish, then I'll follow on in my own car.'

From his office window, Alistair Sloach watched Hugh's ministerial Jaguar depart just as he might have watched the *Titanic* pulling out on its maiden voyage.

He was going to enjoy running the department on his own, he thought to himself.

Chapter 6

Joe Duggery was a first-class press secretary. When he was told to leak, he leaked. Or rather, he irrigated. And so, within an hour of his early morning meeting with Alistair Sloach, news of the decision to confiscate all shares in the privatised Tube began to trickle, and then to gush, through the usual channels. And by nine thirty the story had achieved near-Niagara proportions which were inundating the Tube network itself.

As the morning rush-hour approached its tail-end, a frenzy of Chinese whispers passed between commuters, jumping from train to train and from line to line with breathtaking speed. Soon, the news had been published on the Internet sites of the various Underground user groups, alerting an even wider audience to the impending disaster. And they, intent on protecting their cherished investment at all costs, opted for immediate action. They decided to call an impromptu demonstration at Westminster Tube station, on the very spot where the first announcement about Underground privatisation had been made by the then Environment Minister some years earlier. From there they would march on parliament itself to lobby their MPs against this abominable policy reversal.

And passenger action groups were not the only ones to hit on this idea. Another more clandestine body was thinking along precisely the same lines. The cross-company carpetbaggers were a syndicate of canny capitalists who, just before the share issue, had systematically remortgaged their homes and invested everything they owned in season tickets for all the Underground lines, in the certainty of cleaning up with multiple share allocations. With these vast sums of money at stake, the carpetbaggers' consortium had grimly participated in an emergency conference on their own World Wide Web site. Now they too headed towards central London in militant mood.

Last but not least came the financial services contingent: the City of London had been monitoring the new administration's policies with increasing alarm, but this further example of socialism gone berserk was the last straw. At the time of privatisation, in what was then considered to be a cunning ruse, the merchant bankers had waived tens of millions in underwriting fees in return for a small percentage of the Underground's total market capitalisation when shares finally commenced trading. But their post-dated cheque was about to come skidding back with a vengeance, and from their secret crisis centre near the Bank of England they debated how to respond. One suggestion – the establishment of military-style cells with a view to launching a series of immediate terrorist attacks – was narrowly voted down in favour of an only marginally less violent model of direct action. A strike committee was elected and a group of flying pickets dispatched to Westminster. Its mission: to demonstrate the City's implacable opposition to the latest government madness by preventing all passengers from entering or leaving the area by Tube. Makeshift barricades were gathered from building sites around the area and loaded into the boots of Jaguars and Mercedes, together with placards on which the word 'scab' had been carefully printed in neat copperplate to discourage would-be strike-breakers. Thus equipped, the procession of belligerent suits set off on their capitalist crusade along the Thames.

The passenger groups were the first to reach the Houses of Parliament. At around ten o'clock, representatives from all – or almost all – of the various Underground lines started crowding into Westminster in their thousands, shouting obscenities about the government, chanting partisan slogans and threatening bona fide Tube travellers, who today largely consisted of Japanese tourists on a day trip to the House of Commons. These cowered back in fear as the militant commuters rampaged along the platforms, defacing posters and vandalising chocolate machines at will.

The visitors were spared the gangs' full xenophobic ire, however, by the belated arrival of an even more attractive target. Since privatisation, a rigid hierarchy had developed among the ranks of the newly enfranchised Underground groups, based on the likely value of the shares in their respective lines. And in this new caste system, one section had instantly emerged as the Untouchables of the entire network, their rolling stock having long since spectacularly crashed on the grey market: when the despised Northern Liners finally descended on Westminster – long after the others, as engineering works at Camden Town were causing severe delays – their advent proved the final straw. With long repressed tensions bubbling to the surface, all hell broke loose and each of the factions turned on the other in an orgy of internecine strife.

Casualties mounted rapidly, not least because, after their early tactical retreat, the Japanese tourists were now fully seized of the situation and had begun to regroup. Dividing themselves into two crack units, they sent one off on a mission to halt the influx of opposition reinforcements by throwing themselves on the rails in front of arriving trains, while the other established a bridgehead in the ticket hall and, armed to the teeth with the station's fire extinguishers, mounted small but deadly forays into the warring masses.

Finally, into the mêlée marched the City of London pinstripe brigade. They were met with glee by the commuter battalions, who were faring worse than expected under the Nipponese onslaught and welcomed what looked like a soft target from the nearer-East. But the City suits also proved more robust than they'd at first appeared. Demonstrating that the playing fields at Eton had lost none of their winning ways, the assorted bankers and stockbrokers formed into a rugby scrum and surged forward.

Finally, as hara-kiri tourists, rioting commuters and militant merchant bankers all threw themselves into the fray, so too did the police. With Scotland Yard not two hundred yards from the scene of the action, it was inevitable that they'd be quickly on the scene, and indeed it was scarcely more than an hour before officers in riot gear began gathering incredulously by the station's entrance, truncheons at the ready. In they waded, hitting out with practised discrimination. Tipping their plastic helmets to the City gents, they alighted on the foreign tourists as the most likely cause of trouble, and set about weeding them out and dragging them up to street level.

This opened up a new front at the very foot of Big Ben itself, inviting further ranks of overseas visitors to join in enthusiastically in the belief that they were taking part in some ancient British pageant.

With the battle escalating rapidly, the Metropolitan Police Commissioner's decision to call in the army was all but a foregone conclusion. For some reason, though, the helicopter gunships and armoured personnel carriers which soon converged on Parliament Square had the opposite effect from that intended, adding to the atmosphere of crisis and spurring the demonstrators on to even greater manifestations of their fury.

So, as the entire area descended into a seething mass of anarchy that threatened to engulf much of central London, the police and the army finally opted for a change in tactics: they sealed off the area, withdrew to the sidelines, and left the remaining combatants to slug it out among themselves.

Oblivious of the carnage that was going on not far away, the Cabinet began its meeting in good spirits. Expectantly, Hugh took his place at the table. He'd never dreamed, when he'd joined the junior branch of the party at the age of fifteen because it supported his campaign to save a local animal sanctuary, that it would lead to all this, he reflected with awe.

Indeed, unlike most politicians, he'd never even aspired to high office. In those early days one thing had led to another and he'd ended up as a party foot soldier, pushing leaflets through doors and doing his bit for the good of all. Then, over the years that followed, opportunities for advancement had fallen into his lap as if by magic, and it had seemed churlish to disappoint all those people who were prepared to place their faith in him. Now here he was, a member of the highest executive body in the land, and agog to discover how the really vital decisions of state were arrived at.

He was to be quickly disillusioned. This was their first gathering since the *Flick*'s scandalous revelations and the Trade Minister's resignation, and Hugh's colleagues were much more interested in scavenging around the carcass of their former colleague than discussing anything as banal as the running of the country. The meeting rapidly degenerated into a quarrel about government leaks. Victor Quistling was not the only person anxious to know the identity of the mole who had been providing the *Flick* with the inside track. In the Cabinet, suspicions were rampant and the air was thick with low-flying insults.

'It's got to be an insider,' said the Chancellor of the Exchequer, looking around balefully. 'We might as well invite Victor Quistling to sit in on Cabinet in future and cut out the middle man.' He glowered at his colleagues. It was not long since the *Flick* had revealed that he himself was living in sin with an attractive model thirty years his junior. He had narrowly survived that scandal, but the headlines still stung.

'Insider?' said the elderly Home Secretary, who was not good in the mornings – or for that matter in the afternoons or evenings. 'Must be that fellow Roger Breech. Trade and Industry. He's an insider. Said so in the *Flick* the other day. Where's he gone, anyway?'

'He resigned,' said the Chancellor, gritting his teeth, and stifling his surprise that his colleague was a reader of the *Flick*. For the rest of the Cabinet, it came as a revelation that the Home Secretary could read at all. 'Besides, he was a different kind of insider. He was buying shares which he knew were going to go up.'

'Well, there's no point in buying them when you know they're going to go down,' observed the Home Secretary, who was a socialist of the old school. 'When I was young, that was what a chap had a stockbroker for.'

Nobody bothered to explain. 'In any case,' the Chancellor continued, 'Roger would hardly have leaked something about himself. So he's ruled out. And so am I,' he added complacently, 'since I've also suffered one of these appalling intrusions into my personal life.'

'Yes, how is your little *enfanta*, old chap?' asked Alistair Sloach, relieved to have someone to get his teeth into after the strain of having to be pleasant to Hugh Driftwood. 'Delighted you've been taking our commitment to youth opportunities so seriously; or perhaps I should say childcare?'

The Prime Minister, Edward Burgins, who could rarely get a word in edgeways at Cabinet, intervened before actual bodily harm could ensue. 'Gentlemen, gentlemen,' he said soothingly. 'And ladies' – he nodded nervously towards the formidable Defence Secretary – 'or rather, *women*, of course.' She was a vocal supporter of political correctness at Cabinet meetings. 'This is getting us nowhere. We've got to remain calm.'

As usual, the Cabinet ignored him. The Chancellor, keen to retaliate but afraid to pick on the formidable Alistair Sloach himself, searched around for another target for his retribution and alighted upon Alistair's new subordinate, who did not appear to be listening.

'I wonder what our up-and-coming new Transport Secretary thinks about this crisis?' he asked nastily.

'Well, I, ah . . .' Already bored by the political infighting, which was not what he was expecting at all, Hugh had been sitting picking fluff out of his trouser turn-ups and had indeed let his concentration lapse. He was daydreaming guiltily about Will's tattooed girlfriend with the pillar-box lips. He dragged himself back and racked his brains for a view. 'I can't believe any of us would deliberately set out to harm a colleague,' he said finally, oblivious to the looks of incredulity which this remark elicited.

Having had his attention drawn to Hugh, the Prime Minister realised he had been remiss. 'I've forgotten to greet the new recruit to our . . . ah . . . happy little band,' he said brightly. 'Now that Joe has stepped into the breach to fill Roger Breech's . . . ah . . . breeches, Hugh Driftwood here has taken over at Transport. Welcome, welcome, welcome.' He nodded benignly to nobody in particular.

The Cabinet regarded its new member with a jaundiced eye, and allowed itself a tepid murmur of greeting. Other than promoting Hugh, the Prime Minister had avoided upsetting the delicate equilibrium of his team with a wide-ranging reshuffle. Instead, to replace the multiple-dealing Trade and Industry Minister, he'd switched over the former Secretary of State for

Transport, whose chief qualification for the job was that he was a dedicated socialist of such immense wealth that other people made all his personal investment decisions for him.

'Coming back to the question of the press,' continued the Prime Minister, 'I'm sure we'd all like to pass on, through Hugh, our appreciation to his stepmother for the admirable support the Driftwood newspapers have given the government over this recent crisis.' This met with a more enthusiastic chorus of hear-hears and the Prime Minister beamed. That day, the Driftwood *Pop* had carried an editorial strongly condemning Victor Quistling's wilful scandalmongering. 'It's at times like this you know who your true friends are,' the PM added. 'And now,' he said, digging into the large stack of papers in front of him, 'we've got a very full morning, so perhaps we'd better get started.'

As the agenda moved through the Estate Agents (Nationalisation) Bill and on to the National Lottery (Abolition) proposals, the new Industry and Culture Secretaries took centre stage and Hugh again allowed his thoughts to roam. And they wandered inevitably back to that girl. In fact, she had been tenaciously occupying a most secret corner of his mind ever since the morning's encounter. As she'd stood on that chair and licked those stunning lips, there had been a sexual charge in the atmosphere Hugh had not known for years. Rosemary was a wonderful woman and Hugh had no doubts about his love for her. But their sex life together, never exactly tempestuous in the first place, had subsided into the perfunctory early on in their relationship. Now the promise of Ros's sensuality had awakened deep and long-repressed fantasies. The tattoos and nipple-furniture, far from repelling him, had heightened the sense of the exotic which even now was stirring in Hugh sensations quite at odds with the august surroundings of Downing Street.

This was all Will Cloud's fault, Hugh thought bitterly. There had been a period in their student years when most things that went wrong in his life were the Irishman's fault, but he'd unwisely assumed those days were long gone. But now he was well and truly back, and promising to cause as much havoc as ever. Well, he'd have to go and cause it somewhere else. The last thing Hugh wanted was to be stuffy about his new responsibilities, but it was not as if he had only himself to consider. Ever since Alistair Sloach had published his tome, *The Human Sewer – A Respite from the Cesspit*, this administration had been pinning its hopes on trying to out-moralise the opposition. And Alistair's Moral Millennium Campaign had gone down surprisingly well with the electorate, making up some of the leeway lost during the recent series of resignations. With its emphasis on some spurious Victorian value system, it was not something Hugh himself had any time for, but you couldn't argue with the opinion polls and the one thing the government could do without was a further scandal.

And scandal was something Will could provide in spades, Hugh reflected. The years when they'd shared the student flat in Docklands were still etched, with a mixture of sheer horror and sneaking admiration, on Hugh's consciousness. There was the time when Will's pot fumes set off the neighbour's smoke alarm two doors away. The fire brigade had alerted the police, who'd tried to press charges. Vanessa managed to hush that one up, even though Hugh was in the university library at the time and couldn't possibly have been implicated. 'It's still your apartment,' she warned. 'And one day when you're running the country, the whole thing could be dredged up and used against you.' In vain Hugh had protested that he had no desire to run anything more complex than a bath, and even that only with assistance. But in the end he'd humoured her as always.

Then there were Will's women. With his lyrical Irish charm and boyish good looks, the man seemed to act as a magnet towards the opposite sex. Hundreds of them, probably thousands over their university years. Every shape, size, race, religion and sexual orientation had been represented, for Will was an equal opportunities employer and was nothing if not eclectic. They'd passed through his bedroom without touching the sides, evidently enjoying the facilities he provided, then – infuriatingly – remaining friends with him even as he moved on to his next conquest.

The only woman to have passed through his own bedroom, then as now, Hugh thought wistfully, had been Rosemary. And she hadn't exactly passed through; rather, she'd sunk foundations on day one and become an immovable fixture ever since. Her recent departure on sabbatical to Melbourne was the first time they'd been apart.

That was another thing about Will's visit. Rosemary. Thank God she was away. She'd always frowned on Will at university and she wouldn't take kindly to the news that he was back. Of course, she might have mellowed towards him since those days. But Hugh didn't hold out much hope. His suggestion that Will be his best man at the wedding, if he could be tracked down, had met with an arctic response. 'Won't do your political career any good,' she sniffed. 'Besides, Daddy would hate it. After all, the man's an ex-convict.' Hugh's protests that thirty days for the possession of cannabis did not make Will a criminal had met with no more than a frigid smile.

Hugh resolved to tackle Will as soon as possible. The girl – Ros – would be more than enough excuse. Perforated nipples and rear-end artwork were all very well, in their time and place. But, regrettably, that time was not now and that place was not in the home of a Cabinet minister in a government with a precarious hold on power. Despite himself, Hugh felt another frisson as Ros's image once again filled his mind, consigning the Cabinet and its affairs to insignificance. But not for long.

'Now,' said the Prime Minister. 'We move on to the consultative document on the renationalisation of the Tube. The Transport Secretary.'

Brought back to reality with a jerk, Hugh became aware that everyone was staring at him. 'Em ... I ...' said Hugh, desperately riffling through his papers like an errant schoolboy. Finally, he managed to find the place and began speaking, aware that his voice was coming out as a high-pitched squeak. 'Em ... the ... ah ... consultative document was circulated with your Cabinet papers,' he said. 'Naturally this plan is at its very earliest stages and still highly confidential.' He looked up and Alistair gave him an encouraging nod. 'I would refer you,' Hugh continued, slightly more confidently, 'to option three, the zero-compensation route.' He just hoped the Environment Minister was right about this one. He had tried to reach Pilltridge on the car phone on the way over to Downing Street, but his line had been busy, so he was on his own. 'I would advise you that, after some considerable deliberation, this is the path that we ... that is I ... am currently minded to take. I would naturally welcome your input.'

A stunned silence reigned around the Cabinet table. Everyone looked down and seemed to be waiting for someone else to speak. Then, suddenly and unexpectedly, the Prime Minister chimed in. 'Well, Hugh,' he said, and to Hugh's immense relief his voice was brimming with enthusiasm, 'I think that's a thoroughly sound suggestion, and I must say I'm all in favour of it. I'm delighted to find some really radical thinking being brought to the Transport Department at last.'

A strangulated sound came from the direction of the Environment Secretary, but Hugh hardly noticed. 'Thank you, Prime Minister,' he said, taking a deep breath. 'I know it may be slightly unpopular, but of course we're not here to do what's popular, we're here to do what's right.'

'My sentiments exactly,' the Premier beamed. He held up his

hand as a minion entered the room and handed a sheet of paper to the Cabinet Secretary. Then, once the door had closed again, he resumed. 'Now what does everyone else think?' For once, though, his colleagues appeared to be devoid of opinions. There was a fit of coughing among the ranks and everyone began examining their fingernails. 'Alistair!' said Burgins, turning abruptly to the Environment Secretary. 'I assume this has your backing?'

'Well,' began Sloach. He was looking uncharacteristically confused. 'Up to a point, PM,' he blustered. 'Naturally, I have to discuss the matter with Hugh here at greater length but, all things being equal, I ... that is ... we ... support ...' Then, however, as the Cabinet Secretary scribbled something in the margin of the recently delivered note and slipped it to the Prime Minister, Alistair regained his composure. 'Naturally,' he said, 'I would not want to overrule my enthusiastic young colleague, but I do feel I have to warn you of the potentially grave consequences of pursuing this route.'

'Oh,' said the Prime Minister, absently reading the memo. 'And what would those be?'

'Well, civil disobedience for one, maybe even serious public disorder, if it were not handled very carefully.'

'Ah,' said Burgins, finally looking up and glaring around the table. 'A very valid point, Alistair. Very valid indeed. And how does the Secretary of State for Transport answer that, eh?' That his tone had suddenly acquired an edge was clear to all around the table. All, that is, except Hugh. The PM had just undergone one of those mood swings for which he was notorious, but Hugh, drunk on the heady brew of Prime Ministerial approval, was oblivious to it. In fact, he was just getting into his stride. Alistair had been right all along. He should not have doubted him. 'I think that would be rather overstating the dangers,' he said airily, throwing a complicit smile across to the Environment Secretary. 'Naturally, there would be some opposition, but nothing we couldn't counter with rational argument.'

'So,' said Burgins acidly. 'You'd say that the chances – to pluck a random example out of the air – of dispossessed shareholders rampaging violently through the streets of Westminster would be fairly minimal, would you?'

'Absolutely,' Hugh breezed. 'Quite out of the question.'

'No likelihood whatsoever,' continued the Prime Minister, stubbing his pencil viciously on the table, 'of the police and army having to be called out to quell rioting by mobs of rabid merchant bankers?'

'N . . . no,' said Hugh, becoming rather less sure of his ground.

'Or' – the Prime Minister looked down at the memo in some astonishment – 'groups of Japanese tourists attempting to throw themselves under Circle Line trains in protest?'

By now Hugh was thoroughly confused, wondering what the hell the PM was on about. 'I . . . I . . . wouldn't have thought so . . .' he stammered.

'Well, I suggest you think again,' snarled Burgins, hurling the note across the table. 'It looks like you've overestimated the fair-mindedness of the British people, Mr Driftwood. We seem to have a virtual revolution on our hands, ladies and gentlemen.' He glared across at Hugh. 'And I suggest that, since the Transport Secretary got us into it, we'd better ask him to go out there pronto and get us out of it.'

As Hugh hurriedly gathered up his papers and made for the door, he could feel the eyes of the entire Cabinet boring into his back and a wave of despair swept over him. They could recognise a humiliation when they saw one, and they were looking at one right now. This was an inauspicious start and he knew it. He could have wept into his red box.

Once outside, there was a worse gauntlet waiting to be run. Dashing through the front door of Number 10, his mind reeling, he was confronted with the mass of reporters who had gathered there with breathtaking speed. He ignored the microphones being thrust at him and jumped into his waiting car. And as it screeched out of Downing Street and took a detour to avoid two struggling figures who bore a worrying resemblance to the Metropolitan Police Commissioner and the Governor of the Bank of England, apparently trying to bash each other's brains out, he again cursed Victor Quistling and the *Flick* for putting such a sudden and unwelcome end to his sojourn at Sport. But for their revelations about Breech, Hugh would still be happily immersed in nothing more intricate than the badminton championships.

The ultimate villain, though, was not Quistling. Malign though he was, he was just trying to sell his newspapers, an activity Hugh was not unfamiliar with, having grown up in a publishing family. No, the real culprit was this worm somewhere in government who, by feeding Quistling these confounded leaks, was so deftly manipulating the revolving door at Number 10. But who could that be?

A thought suddenly struck him and he sat up straight. Might it be – could it possibly be – Alistair Sloach? After all, this terrible business about the Tube had got out very quickly and he and Alistair were the only ones who had known about the decision in advance. But surely not! Not Alistair of all people. At length, Hugh dismissed the idea as absurd. Whatever his faults, Alistair was an honourable man and everyone knew he was fiercely loyal to the Prime Minister. He would never intentionally embarrass the government in such a way.

Ultimately, Hugh decided with a sigh of resignation, speculation about the identity of the leaker was futile. Instead he concentrated on his own immediate problem; he buried his head in his hands and wondered what he was going to do about these dreadful riots.

*   *   *

In the event, it was Vanessa who saved the day. Alerted to the unfolding disaster by a frantic message from her stepson, she immediately mobilised Professor Pilltridge. And once again her secret weapon proved his worth. Being of a less trusting nature than Hugh, he quickly established the origins of the morning's rumours through his own contacts and launched a whirlwind campaign to counter-brief the transport correspondents, union bosses and City analysts whom he numbered among his personal friends.

It was an uphill struggle, not helped by a continued flow of disinformation emanating from 'sources close to the Environment Minister'. But with the help of his contacts the professor eventually succeeded in turning the tide. Soon, all the media, including local radio stations, had adopted his new spin on events, refuting the earlier reports and carrying stories of a shocking plot within the Government to smear one of its own members. As the crowds around Westminster tuned in to hear that they had merely been the victims of an evil rumour, they truculently dispersed and some semblance of normality returned to the area.

Indeed, by nightfall, a backlash in favour of Hugh Driftwood had begun to make itself felt. The late editions of the *Evening Standard* carried broad hints about 'Machiavellian' forces at work and even praised the new Transport Minister's speedy response to the crisis, concluding that he had come through his first major test with flying colours.

It was after midnight before Hugh finally arrived home exhausted. There was no sign of Will Cloud. His kit, though, was scattered all over the flat, and an ashtray filled with a suspiciously sweet-smelling substance had been left smoking on the dining-room table. Sellotaped on to it was a note:

Gone out clubbing. Don't wait up. Ros evicted, as

instructed. She didn't half fancy you, though. Apparently she gets off on powerful men – and I didn't disillusion her about you!

I renounce all claims to her body. You should give her a whirl some time before you enter into the bonds of eternal Rosemary. Promise she won't disappoint. Her number's attached.

Will

PS Judge Dread called again. Phone her back. She asked me how Rosemary was. How the hell should I know? It's at least five years since I last spoke to the woman and not a day too long.

Hugh was not disappointed that his heart-to-heart with Will would have to wait for another day. He really wasn't up to it tonight. For a few moments he stood staring at the scrap of paper with Ros's telephone number on it, and, his earlier excitement resurging within him, he felt a terrible longing. Then, quickly, before he could change his mind, he ripped it up into tiny fragments and consigned them to the toilet in the cloakroom off the hall.

Chapter 7

Victor Quistling was a man used to getting results. Like any self-made dictator, when he issued a disposal order, whether it related to the broken glass on his office floor or to a Cabinet minister's career, he considered it as good as done. Such delegation was the secret of his not inconsiderable success.

So the downfall of Hugh Driftwood was a *fait accompli* as far as Victor was concerned, and he put the whole Driftwood family firmly to the back of his mind – not, admittedly, a very long journey. There they might have stayed had it not been for a chance remark from the head of the VQ satellite TV company.

'I hear the Driftwood TV venture's coming on apace,' he said at one of their weekly meetings. 'Vanessa's planning to make a big announcement about it at the Brass Monkey Awards next month.'

'Bugger that woman,' said Victor, vivisecting a zebra plant with a stab of his paper-knife. He had been following the rumours about Vanessa's broadcasting ambitions but it came as a jolt that she was getting so close. 'Why the Brass Monkeys?'

'Driftwood are sponsoring the whole awards ceremony this year. Vanessa gets to hand over the final award for a lifetime's achievement in TV. And the entire ceremony's going out live on the BBC. Couldn't be a better opportunity for her to make the announcement, not that the Beeb'll be too happy when they find out.'

But even the prospect of the BBC being upstaged at their own event did not cheer Victor. 'So what are we doing about it then?' he asked belligerently.

The satellite head presented him with a typed sheet of paper. 'We did draw up some contingency plans, if you recall.'

Victor glanced at them and smiled grimly. 'Fine,' he said. 'Go for it.'

It was then it struck him that, despite his diktat, no revelations about Hugh Driftwood had yet hit any of the Quistling presses. Not a single picture of him kerb-crawling in King's Cross, no scandal about share-dealing irregularities in an offshore tax haven, not even a tiny item in the gossip columns linking his name obliquely with a minor mafioso or toe-sucking starlet. Admittedly there had been a gratifying glitch a few days ago when that riot had broken out on the London Underground, but Hugh had managed to overcome that little local difficulty with disappointing ease. In fact his firm handling of the situation had, if anything, enhanced his reputation. Moreover, in all other respects, he seemed to be proving quite a success in his new Cabinet job, parrying parliamentary questions and renationalising airlines with an energy rarely seen before in the sleepy reaches of the Department of Transport.

As soon as he'd got rid of his satellite man, Victor recalled Gilbert Falange to his office. 'Well?' he demanded.

'Nothing,' said Gilbert wearily, dispensing with any pretence that he didn't know what Victor was talking about. 'Naturally, I consulted my source as you suggested, but it's like I told you already. The guy's squeaky clean.'

Victor looked at him acutely. Years in the business had furnished him with an in-built mental lie-detector. He knew instinctively when he was being deceived and he had no doubt he was being deceived right now. Gilbert, he was sure, had not even raised the subject with his informant. This, he thought angrily, was the trouble with dealing with the monkey rather than the organ grinder. The only way he would get anywhere was to obtain direct access to Gilbert's mole. As his mind developed into a regular Noah's ark, he was about to throw Gilbert out without further ado, but thought better of it. Ultimately, he knew the sort of language Falange understood. 'Okay,' he said resignedly, 'how much?'

'I beg your pardon?'

'How much do you want for this geezer's name? Tell me who he is and I'll negotiate direct.'

'I told you, I couldn't possibly . . .'

'Five hundred?'

'Journalistic ethics—'

'A grand?'

'Certainly not.'

'Five?'

Gilbert shook his head with what appeared to be genuine regret. 'No sum would induce me to compromise my—'

It was no use. As Gilbert might have put it himself, Victor was flogging an equine corpse. He regarded the journalist in some puzzlement. Falange's venality was a company legend and he had been quietly confident that this approach would finally deliver the goods. But, incredible as it seemed, Gilbert's recent successes appeared genuinely to have imbued him with some modicum of professionalism.

Reflecting that it was a sad day when he couldn't even bribe one of his own journalists, Victor dismissed the *Flick* reporter with a curt nod, and settled down to pondering other ways of getting at the Driftwood family. For get at them he would, of that he was sure.

Gilbert was also in a pensive mood as he left the office. Five thousand pounds was a lot of money. If only he could have put Victor in touch with his contact, he would have done it in a flash, and bugger ethics. But the truth, which he was certainly not going to admit to his proprietor, was that he had no idea who the informant was.

Earlier that year, at a time when his never very promising career in journalism had reached an all-time low, an unmarked brown envelope had arrived on his desk by post. It contained a series of mouth-wateringly salacious accusations about the then Foreign Secretary's private life; and not only that, it was accompanied by ample evidence of times and places to back them up. Of the sender's identity, though, there had been not a single clue.

Naturally – for however lazy he was as a journalist Gilbert was no slouch when it came to lining his own pockets – he'd gone straight to Victor Quistling and told him that he needed some slush money to secure a serious political scoop. Victor had been generous for once: his hatred of the government knew no bounds and the story was calculated to weaken its already precarious hold on power. So Gilbert had not only lodged a small fortune in his own personal safety deposit box, but when the Foreign Secretary had later resigned in disgrace, he had basked in national glory as a new political giant-killer.

And that was not the end. Over the coming months, enve-lopes from the unknown benefactor containing more revela-tions about government ministers had appeared regularly in his postbag and Gilbert's little nest egg had grown almost as fast as his reputation. For a while, he'd spent idle hours speculating who might be behind these leaks, but he'd eventually tired of that. Some disgruntled civil servant, perhaps, or a frustrated junior minister. As long as they kept the supply going – and so far there was no sign of a let-up – what did Gilbert care?

Back in the chief executive's office, it wasn't long before Victor again grinned to himself. He spoke into his intercom. 'Brenda, find out the name of Falange's assistant, the spotty kid with the earring and the ponytail, and get him in here. And don't let Falange find out.'

Stevie Cudlick was duly summoned and stood nervously in front of Victor's desk, expecting the worst. Gilbert Falange had had it in for him since the day he'd started, but at that time Gilbert was held in such low esteem that his word counted for nothing. With his immediate boss's new rise to prominence, Stevie feared for his own future. He need not have worried.

'I've just been talking to Falange,' said Victor, eyeing the ponytail with distaste. 'All this success seems to be going to his head. He's getting complacent, and I don't like that in a journalist.' Stevie concentrated on looking suitably uncomplacent. 'I expect a young chap like you could run rings around him,' Victor continued. 'You see, the trouble with Gilbert is that he's not hungry any more. How about you? Are you hungry?'

Fervently hoping he was not about to be offered a job as restaurant critic, Stevie indicated that his appetite knew no bounds.

'Good. I've got an important piece of investigation that needs doing,' continued Victor. 'A bit of undercover work. Ever heard of Hugh Driftwood?'

The ponytail wiggled up and down. 'New Minister of Transport.'

'That's the one. I want you to put together a profile on him. An in-depth. Along the lines of the thing we did the other morning on Roger Breech. Get the picture?' Stevie got the picture. 'It won't be that easy. Geezer's supposed to be clean. But there's always something there and I'll bet you can find it.

You get me a good story on Driftwood,' said Victor, 'and you can have Falange's job. I'm fed up with the pretentious little sod anyway.'

Stevie, who had long harboured hopes of displacing Gilbert, tried to keep the glee from his face. Mostly restricted to the office up until now, he was convinced he had the makings of a great investigative journalist if only he had the chance. And here was a task he could really get his teeth into.

'One other thing,' said Victor. 'I want you to keep an eye on Falange. Find out where he's getting all this dope on government ministers. If you're lucky, you might be able to use the same source and save yourself some work.'

Stevie left Victor's office in a state of high excitement. After long months of sitting around while Gilbert preened himself, insulted him and deprived him of any credit for his work, he was at last going to be given his big break. Things were beginning to move and he did not intend to waste a second.

Chapter 8

Chandhi Sittar ran a laundry. It was a very unusual laundry. It might have been anywhere but it happened to be on the outskirts of Bombay.

And that was a good location, because the Indian police had more basic things to worry about than the activities of a quiet young man who spent his days in front of a computer screen in a nondescript suburban office. For Chandhi's cleaning establishment did not have a single washing machine or tumble drier in sight. In their place were nothing more than an IBM mainframe and a couple of PC servers.

What Chandhi ran was a virtual laundry; what he cleaned were computer messages. His was a handy location on the Internet, providing a service known in the trade as 'remailing'. And it was a godsend for anyone who wanted to communicate anonymously on the global superhighway.

And, in Chandhi's experience, lots of people wanted to do just that. The trouble with the Internet, he had long ago discovered, was that it was rather too transparent: it revealed a great deal about its users which its users might not always want to have revealed about themselves. As a result, a number of profitable businesses like Chandhi Sittar's had now grown up which specialised in receiving computer messages, cleaning them of anything which might lead back to their point of embarkation, and then winging them anonymously on their way.

Every day thousands of messages passed through Chandhi's virtual hands from all over the world. Of these, most arrived and left in microseconds without ever appearing on his screen. But, human nature being what it was, occasionally Chandhi would sit at his keyboard and flick through a couple of the E-mails at random. He liked to think of this as his own form of market research.

Sexual deviancy was the most common motive for anonymity and Chandhi had seen some pretty sick things over the years. Some of them made his stomach turn, although they never failed to fascinate. In other countries, police had sometimes taken legal action to force remailers to surrender their clients' identities. But not, much to Chandhi's relief, in India. The business was, after all, a very lucrative one, and that was without even taking into account the sideline income: Chandhi was not above exploiting his unique position for a bit of long-distance blackmail when the opportunity arose.

Late one morning Chandhi was doing his usual trawl of the morning delivery. He was halfway between a child molester from Germany who was spilling his heart out to a New York psychiatric researcher, and a Swiss embezzler negotiating with the Geneva police from her secret hideout (which Chandhi could have told them was not half a mile away from their own headquarters). Suddenly he came across a message which seemed worthy of a second look.

It was the name of the recipient that first caught his attention: Driftwood, Vanessa. He was not unfamiliar with that name, for his wife had once been an editorial assistant at the *Bombay*

Morning Echo, Driftwood International's Indian flagship paper. Chandhi called up the rest of the message and read it swiftly. And he had to admit it was novel.

> Vanessa,
>   This is your last warning. You are destroying all that I worked for. There are enough trashy television stations around without your adding another. Give up your plans to launch Popviz, or else! If you go ahead with your announcement at the Brass Monkey Awards, you'll make television history in a way you never intended. This is no idle threat – proceed at peril of death.
>   Yours sincerely,
>   Lord Reith

This was strange indeed, thought Chandhi. Lord Reith, as he recalled, had been the founding father of the BBC, but he was pretty sure he was dead now. And while the reach of the Internet was miraculous, it was not *that* miraculous. With considerable curiosity, his gaze darted to the top of his screen which displayed the true identity of the sender. What he saw there made his eyebrows shoot up and brought a low whistle to his lips. Well, well, how extraordinary, he thought. He would have to ask Gita about that when she got home.

Meanwhile, though, he had a service to provide. Still shaking his head gently in wonderment, he clicked his mouse on the re-send icon on his computer. And almost instantaneously the message disappeared as, impeccably laundered, it departed on its onward journey.

Chapter 9

The anonymous E-mail arrived at its destination within micro-seconds, but, technological activity being well ahead of the human kind, it had to wait to be read until Vanessa Driftwood turned on her PC and consulted her E-mail in-tray the next morning. Even then, Chandhi Sittar might have been disappointed by her reaction. Perusing the message with nothing more than a slight frown, she earmarked it to be printed and immediately passed on to more important matters.

She glanced at her agenda for the day, left neatly typed on the desk the night before by the new secretary that Rowland had found her. As ever, there was a busy schedule to get through, beginning with her regular early morning appointment with Rowland himself.

He turned up a few moments later with his customary breakfast – two bacon sandwiches and a beaker of black coffee – balanced precariously on top of a file. 'Morning, Vanessa,' he muttered, effortlessly taking in her distracted expression and a small worm-like pyramid of cigarette ends in the ash-tray on her desk. A five or possibly a six, he decided. This was not a day for getting anything wrong. 'Any news?' he asked.

'Nope,' she said tensely. 'The Candy-Courtesy deal's going through, and I want to talk to you about Popviz later on. Otherwise all quiet on the western front.'

Rowland took a healthy bite out of one of his sandwiches. He had a good idea what was preoccupying her. 'How's Hugh settling in the new job?' he asked. 'The professor living up to his reputation?'

Aware she had been seen through, Vanessa smiled grimly. 'The professor's doing a great job. The guy seems to have an auto-detect mechanism for civil service bullshit. He sees Hugh once a day and cuts through it like a guillotine. Then Hugh takes all the comments back to the department and they don't know what's hit them. Apart from that problem with the Tube, which Pilltridge managed to sort out, I guess Hugh's doing just fine.' But in her voice there was a rare note of uncertainty. 'What's the word on the street?' she asked.

Rowland reflected. 'Seems pretty positive,' he said cautiously. 'Hugh's certainly getting better name awareness ratings now. But Transport's not exactly at the forefront of public interest.'

'Exactly,' said Vanessa with sudden force. 'You hit the nail on the head. Transport is the pits, professor or no professor. And the sooner we get Hugh outta there, the better.'

'But you only just got him in there,' Rowland objected.

'Listen, Rowly,' said Vanessa. 'We've got to get a move on here. This PM's dead in the water. It's only a matter of time before the guy goes phut, and between you and me, good riddance to him. But we have to be prepared for that day. Transport's just not got a high enough profile. Hugh needs to be running something grown-up by the time of the leadership contest if he's to stand any chance.' She stood up and began pacing around the office with her customary gait, nose pushed forward, hands clasped behind her back, looking every inch like a helicopter about to take off. 'I want to start moving things along faster.'

'What about yesterday's Cabinet meeting?' asked Rowland. 'Anything for us out of that?'

Vanessa shook her head. 'Not a thing. I called Hugh last night to check.' She held up her hand, anticipating his protest. 'Don't worry, I didn't give the game away. I was real subtle. You'd have been proud of me. But that's another thing. We've got to ease off with these leaks – it's getting danger—' She broke off mid-syllable as a young woman entered the room carrying a pile of post. 'You've met Rowland Cranston, haven't you, Miss Flato?' asked Vanessa.

'Yes, indeed,' said Miss Flato demurely. 'It was Mr Cranston who recruited me.' She smiled at Rowland and deposited the papers on Vanessa's desk.

Rowland eyed her retreating back appreciatively, recalling a most satisfactory first meeting. She was still just as attractive as he remembered, with a deeply tanned complexion and jet black hair pulled to the back of her head in a fashionable chignon. 'How's she making out?' he asked and at once regretted his choice of words.

'Just as well as she did at the interview, I imagine,' Vanessa ventured shrewdly. 'But it's a bit too early to trust her with anything confidential, don't you think? Now, where was I?'

'Leaks.'

Vanessa's brow furrowed. 'Oh, yeah, we gotta start being careful with the leaks. It's getting dangerous. They're launching all kinds of investigations and one of these days someone's going to get wise. God bless him, even Hugh's going to put two and two together eventually.'

'Don't worry,' said Rowland soothingly. 'We've covered our backs completely. The closest they can ever get is Gilbert Falange and then they hit a brick wall. Anyway, as a matter of fact, I've come up with something new – and from a completely different source this time.' Vanessa raised an auburn eyebrow as Rowland threw a folder on her desk. 'Matthew Potts,' he said triumphantly.

'What, the Chancellor? Love's young dream again?'

'Precisely.'

But Vanessa looked disheartened. They had both been dismayed when their previous revelations about the Chancellor's affair with a woman nearly half his age, carefully leaked through the unwitting good offices of Gilbert Falange, had failed to have much effect. Instead of revulsion, the public's attitude had generally been one of indulgent admiration. If the elderly Lothario was up to it, they seemed to feel, then who were they to object, and although he had little hope as a Prime Ministerial candidate, his tenure at 11 Downing Street still appeared secure. 'I hope it's better than the last time,' said Vanessa. 'Is the girl still living with him?'

'Not half,' said Rowland. 'And listen to this. It appears Matthew's a lot more careful with his own purse strings than he is with the public's. In fact, he's notoriously stingy and it seems he's let his young lady's personal borrowing requirement get out of control. And she, being unemployed and evidently two seats short of a majority in the brains department, decided to take up her God-given entitlement to a job-seeker's allowance. So she popped down to the Social Security and signed on.' He regarded Vanessa expectantly and was not disappointed. An ecstatic smile had filled her face. 'She signed on quite innocently, under her own name, and gave her address as Number 11 Downing Street, SW1. Apparently it seemed the most normal thing in the world to her, so she didn't think to mention it to anyone.'

'And the Department of Social Security has happily been sending a weekly giro along to her at the Chancellor's official residence?' Vanessa asked.

'Fortnightly, actually, but yes, that's the gist of it.'

'Don't tell me no one at the DSS even noticed?'

'Not at first,' said Rowland. 'Each office deals with thousands of claimants and Downing Street's not such an unusual address. But then it was spotted by some sharp-eyed clerk who happens to live next door to one of the *Pop*'s reporters, and one thing led to another. Of course I've fed them a story about holding off till the right moment, so that should keep them quiet for now . . .'

Vanessa's green eyes had lit up. 'Wonderful,' she said. 'The Chancellor's history this time, for sure. Even the great British public will have to draw the line at welfare fraud by the head of the country's finances.' Then she frowned again. 'But let's just think it through. After this, the Chancellor's brushing bits of Downing Street off the seat of his pants, right?'

'Right.'

'So where's that leave Hugh?'

Rowland sucked in his lower lip. 'There'll be another reshuffle of course, and the PM's running out of options. Provided he's doing okay at Transport, and we've no reason to think he isn't, there would be a fair chance he would get a further promotion. But it's difficult to say where. What d'you reckon?'

Vanessa's demeanour took on the usual distant look which indicated she was thinking hard. She snapped out of it after a few moments. 'Anything's better than Transport,' she declared. 'Besides, time's too short to pussyfoot around. I say we go for it.'

'Fine,' said Rowland. Then he hesitated. This seemed as good a time as any to raise a subject that had been worrying him intermittently. 'I've been meaning to talk to you about one thing,' he ventured. 'I just hate the thought of giving another scoop to Victor Quistling. The *Flick*'s pushing ahead of us. And it's beginning to hit our bottom line.'

'Tell me about it,' said Vanessa. 'Olympic committees don't come cheap nowadays, you know.'

'Exactly. So couldn't we run with this one ourselves and give the *Pop* a circulation boost?'

But Vanessa shook her head emphatically. 'No way,' she said. 'I hate it as much as you do, but it's the price we've got to pay. We can't be seen to turn on the party now, just as Hugh's moving up. Nope, we have to play fairy godmother to Gilbert Falange one more time.'

And before Rowland could marshal any other arguments, she moved the agenda on to more conventional business. 'What progress from Dick Tockin?' she asked, visibly changing mental gear.

'Full steam ahead,' said Rowland, pulling the file on the Driftwood satellite venture from his bundle. 'Some problems with the American network contracts but nothing they can't handle. On schedule to go live on June 9th. Are you still planning to make the announcement at the awards ceremony next week then?'

'Sure thing,' said Vanessa. 'But I've had another weird ... well, let's talk about that in a minute. I want to bounce an idea off you first.'

'Bounce away.'

'The weekly chat show, *Livewire*.'

'Yes? Don't tell me you changed your mind about Hilton Starr hosting it?' he said hopefully. Rowland had been against that idea from the beginning. As far as he was concerned, Vanessa's chosen candidate was a has-been who had never really been much cop in the first place. He might have been a blast from Vanessa's eventful past, but it was unlike her to let sentimentality cloud her commercial judgement.

'Certainly not,' said Vanessa, tossing her hair back stubbornly. 'In fact Hilly's coming here later in the week to finalise the details. No, I was thinking more about who we get to guest on the inaugural show.'

'And you had an idea?'

'A humdinger,' said Vanessa. She paused for effect. 'What would you say to the PM, if we could swing it?'

There were quite a lot of things Rowland would have said to the Prime Minister, none of them repeatable outside a City boardroom, but that was clearly not what she meant. He weighed up her suggestion. It was not what he'd been expecting. He'd assumed they would fly over some Hollywood superstar as the big attraction for the new station's first night. But this idea was certainly novel. 'You know the PM's refused to do any more TV interviews?' he reminded her. With a chuckle, he recalled the time when Edward Burgins had last appeared on television. It was the *Panorama* special where he'd been tackled unexpectedly on the vexed subject of his wife's private business. He'd tied himself in so many knots that it would have taken a troop of boy scouts to disentangle him, and since then he had refused to go within a hundred miles of a television camera. 'He hasn't been on the box for ages.'

'Exactly,' said Vanessa. 'Which is why he'll be all the more of a draw. Think of the rarity value. A coup for Popviz on its first night.'

'You'll never get him to agree.'

'Why not?' asked Vanessa. 'The election's not that far off, so he'd better get back into the swing of things fast. And after all, we're not the BBC. We'll promise him an easy ride – no politics. Just a whole lot of stuff on his cutsey grandchildren and his favourite breakfast cereal and what he said to the President's hamster last time he was in the White House. It'll make the old fool look Prime Ministerial, the Lord help us. Do wonders for his image.'

Why not indeed, thought Rowland. The idea was growing on him rapidly. It was a typical example of Vanessa's lateral thinking. 'It might work,' he admitted. 'I'll run it by Dick and see what he says.'

'Well, he'd better think it's good,' said Vanessa. 'Because I've already asked Hugh to put it to the PM next time he gets the chance.' She tapped her nose. 'There've got to be some advantages in having a contact in the Cabinet, after all the work we've done.'

It was only as Rowland was about to leave that she raised the subject of this morning's anonymous correspondence. 'One last thing,' she said. 'It's hardly worth mentioning, but I've had another of those goddamned threatening notes.'

'Not again! Who's this one supposed to be from?'

'Lord Reith apparently.'

Rowland grinned. 'At least he's getting a bit more original. Those ones from the Pope and the President were a bit on the obvious side. How did it arrive?'

Vanessa pointed to her computer screen. 'Internet.'

'Aha!' said Rowland triumphantly. 'He's slipped up there then, whoever he is. E-mail messages are easily traceable.'

'I guess so,' said Vanessa. 'Although it beats me why some guy in India should have it in for me.'

'India?'

'Look at the top.' She collected the sheet of paper from her printer and handed it to him.

Rowland wiped his greasy fingers on a handkerchief, dug a pair of half-moon spectacles out of his top pocket and read it through. 'You're right,' he said. 'Bombay, of all places. Well, they must have just as many nutters there as we have in Britain. Maybe someone with a grudge against Driftwood India. Shouldn't be difficult to get the police there to track him down and warn him off.'

Vanessa nodded pensively. 'Normally I wouldn't bother. The only thing that concerns me is how he knows.'

'Knows?'

'He mentions the announcement at the Brass Monkey Awards and I've done my damnedest to keep that under wraps. Just in case the BBC gets wind and tried to put the kibosh on it.'

'That is worrying,' Rowland admitted. 'I'd better have a word with the police here, just in case.'

'I guess so,' said Vanessa reluctantly. 'It would be kinda boring if I got murdered right now.' And she let out one of her famous snorting laughs.

'I'll get on to Scotland Yard right away,' Rowland promised, gulping down the last remnants of his breakfast and heading for the door.

Chapter 10

Alistair Sloach had been somewhat disappointed with the effect of his first strike against Hugh Driftwood. True, the Transport Minister had been forced to rush from the Cabinet room in order to quell the crisis, which the PM had not liked one little bit. But on the other hand, Driftwood then seemed to have brought it back under control with surprising speed and a dismaying show of political acumen.

Perhaps he had underestimated Hugh, Alistair conceded with some irritation, as he sat one evening in his office at the House of Commons, a glass of Scotch at his side and his ministerial boxes piled high in front of him. It looked as if it would be necessary to step up his campaign, to open up a second front, as it were. And this time, he must be more careful to avoid implicating himself: too many people for his comfort had suspected him of having a hand in Driftwood's first débâcle. The next offensive must be seen to come from a different source entirely.

And Alistair had no doubts as to who that source should be. There was only one other man in the Cabinet with the gumption to put paid to Hugh Driftwood once and for all. This time, Alistair would throw Hugh well and truly to the wolves, or, rather, to the wolf, in the genuinely lupine shape of the Chancellor of the Exchequer, the Rt Hon. Matthew Potts MP.

Nothing could undermine a minister more effectively than having his budget slashed from underneath him. And although next year's Transport spending plans had to all intents and purposes been put to bed, that did not preclude their being dragged smartly back out, kicking and screaming if necessary, should the opportunity arise. Right up until the day of his Budget speech, the Chancellor would be on the prowl for any chance to shave a few more million off next year's spending. This year, Alistair Sloach intended to provide him with the kill of a lifetime.

Over a number of days, he had consulted his confidential briefings and compiled a list, which he had typewritten personally, of the areas where the axe could easily be wielded, together with all the likely arguments the Transport Department officials would come up with to protect their bloated spending plans.

First, there was the proposed Land's End by-pass, tucked craftily away in an obscure corner of the roads programme; a complete waste of money, as far as Alistair was concerned. Well, that could go, for a start.

And then there were the extra road lighting provisions. If they were really so important in the fight against crime, then the Home Office could bloody well pay for them themselves. Alistair added those to his little list.

And the air traffic control inspectorate's annual bash in Bermuda. This year they could direct themselves to Skegness, reflected the Environment Minister grimly.

Finally, there was that horrendously expensive scheme to dismantle the M25 and turn it back into a series of country lanes, following the great traffic reductions brought about by the renaissance in public transport. The environmentalist lobby were fighting the proposal tooth and nail on the grounds that it would endanger countless species of wildlife which lived off the waste from motorway service stations, not to mention the damage to the countryside that would be inflicted by whopping great juggernauts carrying off billions of tons of rubble. Well, Alistair resolved with a smirk, the Greens could keep their precious motorway. That whole project could be put off for a good long while.

Bit by bit he mixed a lethal cocktail of spending reductions – death by a thousand cuts, he chuckled to himself – which, if implemented, would deliver a body blow to Hugh Driftwood and put a decisive end to his future career prospects.

Now how to disseminate this information? Alistair debated with himself at length, but eventually came to the conclusion that there was no point in behaving any differently to everyone else in the Cabinet. With the government leaking like a colander, he may as well join the shower party. And with that thought in mind, he took out a large envelope, placed the typed list inside and carefully addressed it on the front to Matthew Potts, Chancellor of the Exchequer, The Treasury, marking it 'STRICTLY PRIVATE AND CONFIDENTIAL – TO BE OPENED BY ADDRESSEE ONLY'.

Excellent. He would slip the letter into the post room off the Members' Lobby and then nip down for a few quick ones in the Strangers' Bar; Alistair's attachment to Victorian values did not extend to abstinence from Scotch whisky, for which he had an inordinate fondness. Later on, he would come back up and finish off his boxes.

Hugh Driftwood was sitting in the Central Lobby as Alistair passed by clutching his envelope. He nodded briefly to his Cabinet boss but did not speak to him. Prompted by Professor

Pilltridge, even Hugh was now coming round to the view that the Environment Secretary might not have been totally unconnected with his recent setback. He was determined to tread very warily with Alistair from now on.

He glanced at his watch. As usual, Will Cloud was late. He was supposed to be there at ten, and it was already twenty past, which was typical. Anxiously, Hugh scanned the faces of people coming up the hallway from the St Stephen's entrance.

It was now two weeks since Will's unexpected arrival and Hugh had still had no opportunity to tackle him on the date of his departure. They had been playing Cox and Box in the house in Islington: when Hugh left for the DoT in the mornings Will's door would be firmly shut with only a faint whiff of blue smoke escaping from underneath to bear witness to his – and very probably someone else's – presence within. And when Hugh returned home from work exhausted late each evening, Will would already have left to pursue his ongoing research into London's infamous club scene.

Finally Hugh had decided to bring matters to a head by inviting Will to the House of Commons for a drink and what he hoped would be a man-to-man talk. Although he had to admit that, since the departure of the tattooed and beringed Ros, Will had been little trouble and there was now hardly any pretext for asking him to leave.

Such a thought, though, was a temptation which fate could not resist. Suddenly, from the direction of the St Stephen's entrance, Hugh heard a distant commotion and the sound of a raised voice with a familiar lilt to it. With a heavy heart he made his way down to the security station by the door in St Stephen's Porch. Just in time.

'Jesus,' Will was complaining good-humouredly to a constable, playing up the Irish accent with his most mischevous grin. 'Just because I'm from the Emerald Isle, it doesn't mean I carry the ould Semtex everywhere I go, does it now?' The policeman looked at him stony-faced but Will blithely pushed on. 'Now, if it has to be a strip-search, how about enlisting the help of that young policewoman over there? She can delve wherever she likes.' The law still did not seem amused, though, and Hugh cut in.

'I can vouch for this man,' he said wearily. 'He's an old friend of mine.'

The policeman swivelled round but relaxed when he recognised Hugh. 'Of course, Minister,' he said. But he still insisted on a further search before allowing Will through the checkpoint.

'Come along and have a drink before you cause any more trouble,' said Hugh once they'd arrived back in the Central Lobby.

'Trouble, is it?' said Will. 'I thought this was the Mother of Parliaments. The cradle of democracy? You'd have thought . . .'

Hugh did not want to hear what Will would have thought. Taking his arm, he propelled him rapidly along through the Lower Waiting Hall and down the stairs to the Strangers' Bar. Not all that long ago, this bar had moved and was now on the former site of the lady members' toilets, prompting much ribald humour from its regular clientele. As always, it was packed with MPs and Commons officials entertaining journalists and other guests.

Anxiously, Hugh sat his friend down in a quiet corner where he might be out of harm's way for a while. Only then did he begin to untense a little. 'What can I get you?' he asked.

But Will held up his hand in protest. 'I won't hear of it,' he insisted gravely. 'You've been kind enough to put me up all this time, so this round's on me.'

That was a refreshing change, Hugh reflected as he watched Will slip off to the bar and, predictably, begin chatting up the barmaid. Not that he'd ever been tight with money. Far from it – Will was invariably generous beyond his means. But throughout their university days he had been constantly broke and Hugh had been the lender of first resort. It was difficult for Hugh to make the mental leap to this new Will. On the other hand, though, now that he came to think of it, freelance interpreting was not a badly paid profession so things could well be looking up.

'Translation business going well, is it?' Hugh asked when Will returned with a couple of pints in one hand and the barmaid's telephone number tucked away in the other.

'Not bad,' said Will. 'But if truth be told, I've mostly given all that up now. Sure, I do a couple of days a month to keep the hand in. And I tipped up at the Marrakech drugs conference because I fancied a bit of sunshine and . . . eh . . . recreation.' He lounged back in his seat, hands behind his head and legs askew as usual. 'But it's so bloody boring,' he continued, 'sitting in a booth translating other people's speeches on wine mountains and butter lakes. No mental challenge at all.'

'So what exactly do you do with yourself, then?' Hugh asked.

Will looked away evasively. 'This and that,' he said, taking a healthy gulp of his drink and glancing round the bar-room. 'This and that.'

An awful thought struck Hugh. 'You're not some kind of dealer, are you?' he asked, horrified. 'I mean, Marrakech and all that . . .'

Will laughed uproariously. 'Jesus, no!' he said with delight. 'What do you take me for – a complete eejit? No, I don't deny I've a fondness for the weed, but I'm only a conspicuous consumer, definitely not a supply-sider. And I don't go in for the hard stuff either, before you ask. Just the occasional joint for relaxation purposes, same as always.'

'I remember,' said Hugh, with feeling.

'Honestly, Hugh, you should give it another go yourself,' Will urged. 'I know it took us days to clean up all your vomit that time, but it's often like that when you've not tried it before, and you should have persevered. It would stop you being so bloody uptight.' Hugh did not reply and Will shrugged. 'Suit yourself then, but you don't know what you're missing. Anyway, as far as work goes, I've found myself a great little niche. Something entirely legal,' he added reproachfully, 'and it gives me a fine living.' He grinned. 'I'll tell you about it some other time. Now,' he continued, 'what was it you got me in here for? Time to evict me, I suppose?'

Hugh had indeed been determined to tell him he would have to leave, but the evening was turning unexpectedly mellow and as Will had proved a surprisingly undemanding house guest, he decided to relent and give his friend the benefit of the doubt for a bit longer, despite the little incident at the St Stephen's entrance. 'Look,' he said, 'you can stay for another few weeks. But you'll have to be gone when Rosemary comes back.'

'I certainly will,' said Will, an expression of mock panic overtaking his features. 'No question of that. You won't see me for dust once the ould ball-breaker shows up again.' He ignored Hugh's glare. 'Where is the . . . where is Rosemary anyway?'

'She's finishing her thesis at the University of Melbourne,' Hugh replied coldly.

'Is she now?' said Will. 'Well, long may it continue. And while we're on the subject,' he said, smiling his most innocent smile, 'how did you get on with Ros?'

Hugh shook his head silently. He had been hoping they could keep off the subject of Ros. She had been intruding with unseemly regularity into his fantasies and he didn't want to provide his libido with any further ammunition.

'You didn't phone her?' asked Will incredulously. 'You passed up the opportunity of a lifetime?' He looked at Hugh in despair. 'Honestly, I give up on you sometimes. She was a sitting target, that woman, really had the hots for you after she caught you in your pelt the other morning. Didn't you get my note?'

Hugh reddened. 'I flushed it down the loo.'

It was too much for Will. He smacked his glass down on the table and gazed over in disbelief. 'You're a bigger fool than I took you for, Hugh Driftwood! Do you know what her nickname was? The Human Blowtorch. Honest, swear to God. Told me straight out. I mean, she did, God didn't, if you get my meaning. And what's more, she lived up to the reputation one hundred per cent, I can tell you.'

'Careful,' hissed Hugh. 'Keep your voice down.' A young man with a ponytail had sat down with a junior government minister a few tables away and seemed to be taking more interest in their conversation than in his companion's. 'Look.' Hugh lowered his own voice. 'I don't deny I found her attractive. But I'm engaged to Rosemary and I couldn't possibly . . . I just couldn't . . .'

'Sure you could!'

'No, honestly . . .' But his voice tailed off helplessly, for even as he said the words, his libido was kicking in to launch a rearguard action and he began wondering if it was really so impossible. Why not? Why not ring her? One last fling wouldn't be the end of the world. And, after all, Rosemary was a very long way away. Could he pull off a quick U-turn, he wondered? Why not, his libido prompted gleefully, you're not a politician for nothing . . .

'Tell you what,' he said, as casually as he could. 'I wouldn't want to be rude to her. Why don't you give me the number again, and I'll at least call her up for a chat. No harm in that, eh?'

But Will soon put paid to this idea. 'Too late now,' he said, pursing his lips stubbornly. 'You've thrown away the only copy I had of it. Wouldn't have a clue how to get hold of her. No two ways about it – you've blown it, which is more than she'll ever do for *you* now.'

Hugh's heart sank. 'There must be a way of getting in

touch. Didn't you say she was looking for work? Maybe I could help.'

'I did say that,' said Will primly. 'But, sure, you didn't seem very interested in helping at the time, if I recall.'

'I've changed my mind. What sort of job was she looking for?'

'What are you going to do? Scour every Jobcentre in London with the woman's discarded knickers, searching for a perfect fit? Forget it. Just accept that you screwed up good and proper, and put it down to experience.'

But having once given way to his basest instincts, Hugh found it difficult to rein them back in. He looked disconsolately at Will. 'You must have some idea where I should look,' he said.

Will smiled a distant smile. 'Where you'd least expect, Hugh, where you'd least expect.'

And before Hugh could press him any further, they were interrupted by a House of Commons messenger. He approached carrying a green card which Hugh accepted with a grimace. It was one of the forms that constituents filled in when they'd come to visit their MP. If you were anywhere in the House, the messengers would track you down and Commons tradition dictated you had to make yourself available to be lobbied. 'Damn,' said Hugh. 'Listen, I'll be back in ten minutes. In the meantime, just sit there quietly. And try not to get into any trouble.'

'What would I be doing that for now?' asked Will, as if such a possibility were the remotest thing in the world. 'I'll just stay here and have a quiet smoke. Can't be any harm in that, can there?'

Absently, Hugh shook his head and took off back upstairs. The bars were among the few places left in the Palace of Westminster where smoking was still allowed.

In the Gothic splendour of the Central Lobby, where the petrified statues of former Prime Ministers looked down with ill-concealed contempt on their successors, his constituent was waiting for him impatiently. Hugh could usually assess from a quick glance what his visitors would want to talk about. This one had an angry concerned expression and Hugh put her down at once as either a Nature Conservator, a Greenpeace Co-ordinator or a Rapist Castrator – they generally shared the same demeanour, he'd found.

He was in the right general area. It turned out she had an urgent petition to put before him on the clubbing of baby seals. As this was a cause close to Hugh's heart, he gave her his full attention. So it wasn't until she was well into her diatribe that the full thrust of Will's last remark finally hit home with a sickening thud.

'The government must intercede at once,' the constituent was saying stridently, poking her finger at him.

Will never smoked tobacco.

Suddenly Hugh felt like he'd just been clubbed over the head himself. 'Absolutely,' he said faintly.

Cigarettes were disgusting, Will had always maintained, and carcinogenic to boot.

'And we must ask our European partners to protest as well,' she insisted.

'Indeed we must,' Hugh agreed distractedly.

Ipso facto, the quiet smoke Will had in mind was of a quite different substance.

'You will take action, won't you, Minister?'

Christ! Will was sitting smoking dope surrounded by half the top politicians in Britain.

'Yes, of course I will.' Hugh's smile was as forced as sunflowers in Siberia.

He had to get back there before the shit, or at least the smoke from it, hit the Strangers' Bar fan in a big way.

'Good. So you promise to do your best to save the poor seals?' the constituent concluded, satisfied.

If he could only get her to go away, Hugh would have promised to fly personally to Norway, rehabilitate the bloody things and provide them with intensive counselling to get over the trauma. But it took another ten minutes of bland assurances before she finally departed and Hugh was able to race back down to the Strangers' Bar. He anticipated the worst and his fears were more than justified.

In the corner, an altercation had broken out between Will and a short saturnine man. With a further sinking feeling, Hugh realised it was none other than Alistair Sloach.

'This is the smoking area!' Will was maintaining heatedly. 'Look up there. It says so on that sign.'

Alistair, his oversized nose out of joint in the most literal sense, was having none of it. He sniffed the air with a suspicious squint. 'The smell is distinctly odd,' he said nastily. 'Surely that's not . . . is that . . . is that marijuana you've got there?'

'No,' said Will, cheerfully stubbing out what remained of his roll-up and slipping it into his pocket. 'But if it's some you're after, I know a good place you can get it.'

Sloach looked as if he was about to explode. 'How dare you!' he spluttered. 'I've never been anywhere near drugs in my life.'

'Aha!' countered Will triumphantly. 'How would you know what they smell like then!'

But Alistair had already had enough. 'I will not be cross-examined in this of all places. No doubt one of the policemen will be better acquainted with such intoxicants and will know exactly what to do with the likes of you!' A thought occurred to him. 'Who brought you in here in any case?' he demanded.

This was Hugh's cue. Nervously, he stepped forward and coughed. 'Hello, Alistair,' he said as casually as he could. 'Is there a problem? This gentleman's with me, actually.'

Sloach turned on him with a vengeance. 'Is he now?' he said through clenched teeth, 'I should have guessed,' written all over his face. 'Well, Driftwood, I strongly suspect your guest here of smoking an illegal substance.'

For once Hugh managed to think on his feet. 'Ah,' he said. 'I think I know what might have happened. You see ... eh ... Will's a ... an asthmatic! He smokes menthol cigarettes to, ah ... to ease his, ah ... breathing. Don't you, Will?'

From his corner, Will wheezed encouragingly. 'Exactly,' he spluttered. 'Menthol cigarettes. That's what they are. My asthma.' He slapped his chest by way of illustration.

'So that's what you must have smelled, Alistair,' continued Hugh earnestly. 'Quite an understandable mistake really.'

Alistair did not look convinced. 'I've never heard of such a thing.'

'No, honestly,' said Hugh desperately. 'I was at college with Will here. He was a founder member of the Millwall University "Just Say No" campaign. A complete drug-free area, aren't you, Will?'

'Definitely,' Will agreed, trying to douse something in his pocket which appeared on the verge of reigniting. 'Disgusting stuff, pot. Wouldn't touch it with a bargepole.'

Alistair looked a little less sure of himself, but he continued to bluster. 'I have the gravest doubts,' he said, 'and you, Driftwood, should be careful who you defend, even if you did attend some minor ... some minor borstal with this thug. However, as a Cabinet colleague I am bound not to doubt your word.' He addressed himself to Will. 'Just make sure you don't cross my path again,' he said. 'I never forget a face.' And with that, he turned on his heels, muttered something about being tough on crime and tough on the causes of crime, and stalked off with a scowl.

When he was certain Alistair was gone, Hugh mopped his brow and collapsed on to a chair. 'Bloody hell,' he said, in a passable imitation of his friend's Dublin accent. 'Bloody hell,

Willard Fergal Cloud. You'll drive me to suicide one of these days, so you will.'

Alistair was still scowling when he reached his office a few moments later. Slamming the door closed, he helped himself to a whisky from the mahogany cabinet by the window to supplement the two he had just disposed of in the bar, and sat down at his desk to think.

This most recent scene had confirmed his worst suspicions about Driftwood, he thought gloweringly. He had always known the man was a complete imbecile, but now it was plain that he was highly dangerous as well. If those were the kind of people he associated with, layabouts and junkies, then he posed an even more serious danger to the government – and in particular to Alistair's Moral Millennium Campaign – than he had even thought in the first place.

The discovery lent a messianic self-righteousness to his already firm determination to get rid of the man once and for all. Grimly, Sloach's thoughts turned back to the envelope which was even now winging its way to the Chancellor. When he saw the contents of that list Matthew Potts would know exactly what to do, he reflected with a malevolent glint.

By the end of next week, Driftwood would be history.

Chapter 11

A few tables away in the Strangers' Bar, sitting listening to a junior agriculture minister spouting on about milk quotas, Stevie Cudlick had observed the incident between Alistair Sloach and Hugh Driftwood as far as possible. Although not close enough to follow the cause of the fracas, the very fact there had been an altercation between the two Cabinet ministers was useful in itself, and he would be sure to pass it on to the diarist at the *Flick*.

None the less, he realised with some disappointment, it did not constitute the political scandal which Victor Quistling had charged him to come up with. Indeed, Stevie was beginning to despair of ever doing so.

He nursed his beer restlessly and nodded automatically as the minister passed happily on to mad cows. He was getting fed up with this whole Driftwood project, he decided. Every avenue seemed to lead nowhere. He had been stalking Hugh for nearly two weeks now without catching him with even so much as a parking ticket. His hopes had soared for a while when he'd discovered that Hugh's fiancée was

away and he was currently sharing his house with this hand-some, slightly rakish-looking Irishman who was now in the bar with him. But his suspicions of latent homosexuality did not seem very probable and anyway had finally been dis-pelled by the highly polished, and irrefutably straight, way that Hugh's house guest had been trying it on with the barmaid.

Stevie had taken a multi-track approach to his assignment from Victor Quistling. As a first line of enquiry, he had trawled every database of press extracts he could lay his hands on in search of some previously undisclosed titbit from Hugh Driftwood's past. But if it was there, it was very well hidden. Every source told the same sickening story. From his birth into the Driftwood publishing dynasty, through his education at a minor public school and his unspectacular record at Millwall University, followed by his engagement to the daughter of a top left-wing barrister, Hugh's life had been every inch that of the typical upper-class socialist.

The premature death of his mother had been one of his few encounters with adversity, and even that only resulted in the arrival on the scene of Vanessa, who had clearly shaken the family up good and proper. Reading between the lines, Stevie reckoned that without her ambition on Hugh's behalf, his surprise entry into parliament and subsequent meteoric ascent up the political ladder would have been most unlikely. And ever since then, the man had been the very epitome of a con-cerned, caring politician, painfully diligent, and frustratingly well-behaved. How boring could you get? Stevie wondered.

His researches into Hugh's history having dismally failed, tailing the Transport Minister in person had been Stevie's second tactic. He had followed him daily from his house in Islington to the Ministry of Transport and caught up with him again in the evening, when the likelihood of trapping him in some vaguely illicit activity seemed greater. But Hugh's

nights, it turned out, were mostly spent at tedious official func-
tions, making interminable speeches about road-sign reform or
bicycle-pump harmonisation.

Nor were the weekends much better. The previous Saturday
Stevie had spent many mind-numbing hours trailing Hugh
round his Sussex constituency to church bazaars by day and
working men's clubs by night. And all to no avail; none of his
efforts had yielded even the tiniest peccadillo. If his life had
been as dull as Hugh Driftwood's, Stevie would have topped
himself long ago.

So everything now depended on the third front: Gilbert
Falange. Stevie had already moved on this by conducting a
thorough search of Gilbert's office at the *Flick* to see if he
could glean anything on the identity of the mystery government
informer. Of highly placed contacts, however, there had been
no trace.

It did not occur to Stevie to go through Gilbert's incoming
post. Not that he had any scruples about doing so, but he had a
weakness for spy novels and was convinced that any transfer of
privileged information would take place in a basement car park
somewhere, or in a remote country pub; certainly not through
such prosaic channels as the Royal Mail.

So Stevie did not notice the anonymous buff-coloured envelope which arrived for his superior the morning after his
encounter with Hugh and Will in the Strangers' Bar. What
he could not fail to see, though, for he had made it a point of
observing Gilbert closely, was the gleam of anticipation with
which the *Flick*'s star reporter pounced on this particular letter,
and his look of near-ecstasy upon reading its contents.

The story which appeared in the *Flick* early the following week confirmed Stevie's conviction that there was a link
between that envelope and Gilbert's inside track on government scandals. Falange had gone to town on the episode of
the 'Downing Street Dole-Scrounger', and a picture of the

Chancellor leaving his official residence with his girlfriend on his arm and a hangdog expression on his face filled most of the front page. On page two, Gilbert related how he had painstakingly pieced together the details of this shocking episode through months of investigation, and on page three there was a feature on older men in history brought to their knees by younger sirens. In an editorial, also penned by Gilbert, the *Flick* declared that the hour when the Chancellor joined his young lady on the dole queue could not be far off, adding that he would hopefully be followed in short order by the Prime Minister, Edward Burgins, and the rest of this sorry excuse for a government. These, it concluded, were extra unemployment statistics which the country could well afford.

Stevie read the article in the certain knowledge that, far from having been on the case for months, Gilbert had come on this story very recently indeed. If only he could lay his hands on one of those packages, it would surely not be difficult to establish the sender's identity and then at least one of his tasks for Victor Quistling would be out of the way.

From now on, Stevie resolved, he would subject Gilbert's postbag to the minutest scrutiny. Fortunately, with his new celebrity status, Gilbert had taken to arriving ever later in the morning, and often did not put in an appearance until well after lunch. Stevie would have ample time each day to pursue his new tactic.

The Chancellor obligingly fell on his sword just in time for the lunchtime news and, in the inevitable reshuffle, Hugh was one of the last to receive a summons from Downing Street. The delay gave him food for thought. However well he'd recovered, his eclipse at Cabinet over the Tube renationalisation fiasco was sure to be still fresh in the PM's memory. So he was not optimistic about surviving this further upheaval. Which was a great shame, he reflected dejectedly, because with Professor

Pilltridge's help he'd just begun to get to grips with Transport policy. He even seemed to have established a good working relationship with the Permanent Secretary, which would now all be for nothing.

Ted, his official driver, was usually the best source of information on the Prime Minister's intentions, but today he had little to offer on Hugh's fate. 'Old Higginbottom's being kicked upstairs though,' he told Hugh conspiratorially, as he drove him the short distance from the offices of the Department of Transport to Downing Street.

This was news to Hugh but not all that surprising. The Home Secretary was a relic of a bygone era who could have gone under the hammer at Christie's without an eyebrow being raised. On the other hand, though, his departure meant that the reshuffle was going to be far more wide-reaching than expected, and that did not bode well for Hugh.

He sat in the little ante-chamber outside the PM's study and prepared himself. The trouble with Edward Burgins – one of the many troubles, in fact – was his unpredictability. He cultivated an air of vagueness, but beneath lay a demented cunning which it was always a mistake to underestimate. Like some benevolent, slightly scatty headmaster, he was friendly up to a point, but quite capable of turning on you if he imagined you'd overstepped the mark.

Even knowing how to address him was a dilemma. When appointing new ministers, the PM always insisted that all formality be dropped. A toff turned populist, he prided himself on being a man of the people. 'I'm a blunt fellow,' he would say. 'Can't be bothered with all this bowing and scraping.' This usually lasted until he came off the loser, which he invariably did, in some intellectual skirmish with the minister in question. Then, he would pass word through the Cabinet Secretary that he was 'the Prime Minister, after all', and expected to be addressed as such by his more junior colleagues.

Today, the PM was in jovial mood. He was sitting with a bundle of coins in front of him, making them into piles on the table. His blithe lack of concern about the crises which had rocked his government never failed to amaze Hugh. In this case, though, the PM had clearly perceived a silver lining in the cloud, namely the departure of a Chancellor of the Exchequer who had long been a thorn in his flesh.

'Good afternoon, Prime Minister,' Hugh said.

'My dear fellow, how many times do I have to tell you, do call me Edward,' the PM beamed. 'Now I want you to know how much I've appreciated the fine job you've been doing at . . . ah . . .' – he glanced down theatrically at his papers – 'Transport. Very . . . enthusiastic. Yes. Enthusiastic is the word.'

Damned by this distinctly faint praise, Hugh gulped. It wasn't looking good. 'Thank you, sir, eh . . . Ed . . . eh, Prime Minister. I've found it a great challenge—'

'Quite so. Do let me finish. You're getting like one of those Radio 4 presenters, always interrupting,' said Burgins tetchily. He rearranged the pennies on the table into two piles and formed a bridge between them with his pencil. Then he sat back to admire this, one of the more ambitious construction projects of his premiership. 'Now what was I talking about? You've made me lose my drift.'

'What a fine job I've been doing at Transport, Prime Minister.'

'Have you now? Isn't it up to me to be the judge of that?'

'No, that was what you were saying.'

'Was I? Well anyway, I expect you have; but because of this unfortunate . . . ah . . . incident . . . I'm now planning some very considerable changes in the Cabinet. Very considerable changes indeed.' He beamed again, his good humour restored at the thought of his colleague's fate. 'Sad though it was to lose Matthew, it has given me an opportunity to freshen things up. Now about this department of yours. Alistair Sloach

keeps pestering me to abolish the post of Transport Minister completely and amalgamate the whole thing into Environment. And, y'know, it's not such a bad idea.'

Hugh's heart sank. Alistair was going to win, it seemed, and Hugh's final legacy to his ministry would be to consign it to oblivion. 'The two departments are ... ah ... inextricably linked,' the PM continued, glancing once more at his briefing paper. 'Car pollution and the environment and ... motorways ... and ... ah ... all those sort of things.' It was not for nothing that Burgins was known as a big-picture Premier.

Hugh gathered his wits for a last stand on behalf of his ill-starred department. His own fate was almost academic now. 'I *must* ask you to reconsider, Prime Minister,' he said. 'I mean, just because I've not come up to scratch there doesn't mean that someone else couldn't succeed. And I don't have to remind you that the tradition of an independent Transport ministry goes back a long way. Are you absolutely sure this decision is wise?'

But his pleas fell on deaf ears. Looking distinctly unimpressed by Hugh's rhetoric, Burgins indicated his mind was made up and, after a few more attempts, Hugh determined he might as well be magnanimous in defeat. 'Well,' he lied nobly, 'if I must pass this on so soon, I can think of no safer pair of hands to take it on than Alistair's.'

'Eh?' said the PM.

'Alistair Sloach, I'm sure he'll do a fine job.'

'I doubt it,' said the PM. 'Home Office is a bugger, you know.'

'Is he going to run the Home Office as well then?' asked Hugh in confusion. Why didn't they just merge the whole bloody government into one amorphous mass and let Alistair get on with it?

It was the PM's turn to be confused. 'As well as what?'

'Transport and Environment.'

The PM tutted with some impatience. 'He won't be doing that, you silly idiot,' he said. '*You* will. I'm moving Alistair over to run the Home Office.' He drew closer to Hugh and lowered his voice, although they were completely alone. 'Home Secretary's going to the other place, don't you see. Nobody knows it yet. He's accepted my offer of a seat in the Lords. Eh?' He looked at Hugh expectantly, evidently relishing the effect of what he fondly imagined to be a bolt out of the blue. That it was already under discussion at every taxi rank in Greater London did not enter his head, and Hugh did not enlighten him. 'So Alistair Sloach's moving to Queen Anne's Gate,' the PM continued. He allowed himself a malevolent little chuckle. 'That'll wipe the smile off his smug face.' Then he put his hand on Hugh's back. 'And I want you, old fellow, to take on the new Department of Environment and Transport. Won't half infuriate Alistair. Not, of course,' he added hurriedly, 'that that's got anything to do with my choice. No, you're the best man for the job, I have no doubt. So what do you say?'

What was there to say? 'I'd be honoured,' said Hugh, a flood of gratitude welling up inside him. 'I promise I won't let you down, Prime Minister.'

'Jolly good. That's settled, then,' said Burgins. He looked pointedly at his watch. 'Ought to get on now.'

But Hugh had just remembered his task from Vanessa. This seemed as good a time as any to bring up the question of the television interview. He had to approach it carefully, though.

'Can I raise one other matter, Prime Minister? On a completely different subject,' he added hurriedly, noticing that Burgins appeared to have developed a repetitive wrist disorder. 'I know it's been your policy of late not to give television interviews, but—'

'It's been my policy to maintain the dignity of my office,' the PM interrupted a trifle frostily. 'I may be Prime Minister, but that doesn't mean I'm prime-time fodder for some right-wing

reactionary from the BBC whose only intention is to misrepresent me to the public and confirm his own preconceived . . . ah . . . preconceptions.'

'But what if you had an opportunity for a cosy interview, say, on a subject of your choice, with someone sympathetic, and all the questions agreed in advance? A chance to reach out directly to the public over the heads of the media spin-doctors. It might give your popularity just the boost it needs. Not, of course, that it needs any boosting, but we aren't far from an election and . . .'

There was a pause while the PM mulled it over. 'It's a good idea, Hugh, but the answer would have to be no. I wouldn't trust them an inch. Not those buggers at the BBC or the rabble on the other side either, come to think of it. And as for Victor Quistling's channel . . .'

'And if it were none of those?'

'I don't get you.'

'You may not know that Driftwood International is about to launch a satellite television station.'

'Ah.' The PM allowed a penny to drop off the edge of the table and then picked it up. 'Your esteemed stepmother. A charming lady, and always very supportive. I see what you're getting at. Just when is she due to begin broadcasting?'

'June 9th. They expect to reach a record audience. And they were hoping you might appear on the opening night.'

By his facial contortions, Hugh gathered the PM was weighing this up. 'It may be possible,' he said. 'Yes, yes, I could certainly think about it. Tell me, who is to host it? I can't be doing with any of those Dimbleforths.'

Vanessa had not briefed Hugh on this. But he promised the Prime Minister he would find out as quickly as he could and come back to him. And with that he rose to leave.

'One last thing,' said Burgins, opening the door for him and putting his arm on Hugh's shoulder. 'I'm sure it's not necessary

to tell *you* this, but I've been warning everyone today as a matter of course. The *Flick* is well and truly on the rampage now. Muck-raking.' His face puckered in disgust. 'Digging around for all sort of dirt. So it would be well to be extra vigilant about your private life in the coming months. How is . . . ah . . .' He groped for a name.

'Rosemary?'

'Yes, that's the fellow. Rosemary. How is she?'

'She's on a sabbatical in Australia right now, doing post-graduate research in—'

'Good, good,' the PM cut in. Beyond establishing that she was not masterminding any major social security frauds – which seemed reassuringly improbable from so remote a location – he manifestly had no further interest in Hugh's fiancée. 'Well, as I said, I'm sure it doesn't apply in your case. But just be sure to keep your whistle clean anyway.'

Hugh phoned Vanessa from the car to relay the news of his promotion.

'What did I tell you?' she exclaimed excitedly. 'I said you'd shoot out the goddamned lights, and shooting them out's exactly what you're doing. Now I know you'll be busy, but you've got to find time for a celebration. Lunch next Thursday, and that's an order.'

Hugh promised he'd do his best. 'And it's looking good for the TV interview too,' he added. 'I asked the PM, and he seemed pretty favourably disposed. Wants to know who the interviewer is, though.'

'He's going to be here to sign his contract on Thursday,' said Vanessa. 'Come along and you can judge for yourself.'

Chapter 12

Nick Claretis was one of the last in a dying breed of artisans. From premises in London's Knightsbridge, he ran a highly successful niche operation catering mainly to the export market, in which – as his glossy brochures put it – 'years of craftsmanship have been melded with state-of-the-art technology to create a product of distinction, proving there is still one field in which Britain leads the way'.

Conveniently located a stone's throw from Harrods, his tiny workshop attracted a select and loyal clientele. So successful was he that one customer had even suggested nominating him for a Queen's Award For Industry. Nick had found that very amusing; the idea of attaching the royal coat-of-arms to the anodyne-looking packages he dispatched around the world appealed to his sense of irony. As it happened, he would have laughed heartily at the remark in any case, as it had been made by a Spanish terrorist leader far more at home with Semtex than small talk and such people were notoriously volatile and prone to take violent offence at any perceived slight.

For Claretis & Co. (established 1976) was a bespoke bomb-maker, supplying handcrafted devices to the very elite of the terrorist world. Of course most of Nick's clients had their own in-house ballistics operations. Any self-respecting outfit had the capacity to manufacture a perfectly acceptable bomb for normal, everyday use. These were fine for taking out the president of a minor banana republic, or maiming a bunch of tourists with something quick and dirty stuffed in a trash can. But Claretis & Co. had long ago shunned such mass-market products. Rather, it was a bomb boutique, and for something for that special occasion there was nothing to beat it.

It was not Nick's style to solicit new clients. Very rarely would he even accept a commission from anyone outside the tightly knit community of international terror, for his was a precarious profession and a relationship of trust was essential.

On occasion, though, an offer would reach his desk which presented such an interesting challenge that he would waive this rule – provided, of course, that the prospective client came with the right references and a suitably filled case of unmarked notes.

The oriental-looking man now sitting before him had come with just such a commission.

'We normally go out to tender for our bigger orders nowadays,' he said in a perfect Oxbridge accent. He had a wispy grey beard, and as he spoke, he tugged gently at one strand of hair after another, lifting up the skin on his chin into a series of pinky-white peaks. Nick waited in vain for one of them to twang painfully out of its follicle, and fingered his own neatly trimmed moustache protectively. 'You know,' the man continued petulantly, 'these devices have gone up by far more than inflation in the last few years. I don't know what you chaps are up to.'

Nick shrugged non-committally. What did he expect, a bloody government enquiry?

'But this is a special order, so we're bypassing the usual channels. It's quite a sophisticated device that's needed. Of course, I recommended the client to you *at once*.' The visitor smiled ingratiatingly. Obviously a good cut was to be had from this one. 'So what do you think?'

Nick studied the sketch in front of him. 'It's going to have to be pretty small to fit,' he said. 'Quite a challenge.'

'I thought it would appeal. But remember, it must be to the client's exact specification. It's got to do precisely what's required of it – nothing less – and definitely nothing more. That's a *sine qua non*. No other injuries than the one intended.'

Nick glanced at the neatly typed specification. 'This is very unusual,' he commented pensively. 'Very. The device will have to be carefully calibrated to produce such a precise explosion. And you're asking for a lot of functionality in a confined space. When would I have access to the . . . ah . . . the receptacle?'

'By this weekend at the latest.'

Nick scratched his head. 'Well, it can be done, and I am probably the only person who can do it. But, of course, perfection doesn't come cheap.'

'My client is aware of that. What figure would you suggest?'

'Fifty thousand.'

'Pounds?'

'We invoice in guineas, actually.'

The man smiled again. 'That's perfectly acceptable. Half on delivery, half after a satisfactory conclusion.'

'I hardly think that's necessary. I haven't failed you yet.'

'This is a particularly demanding client.'

'Very well. The usual arrangements?'

'Yes.'

After his visitor had left, Nick sat staring at the drawing on his desk for a good half an hour. This was going to require some real ingenuity, he reflected, and several days' hard slog. But fifty grand was fifty grand. And with green fees what they were, it couldn't have come at a better time.

Chapter 13

Vanessa Driftwood and Rowland Cranston were having one of their rare arguments. Hilton Starr, Vanessa's choice to host the evening chat show on her new satellite TV channel, Popviz, was due at Driftwood House to sign his contract, and the head of the Driftwood TV operation had asked Rowland to intercede one last time to try and talk her out of the appointment.

'It's a big mistake,' Rowland warned her. 'Hilton's a has-been – an alcoholic too, by all accounts, and a philanderer. He's worse than the bloody Chancellor, been bonking one young girl or another for years. Now he's shacked up with some blonde bimbo from children's TV and he's never out of the gossip columns. I'm telling you, the man's bad news. This is a new channel and *Livewire* is our showcase; we should find some fresh talent to present it.'

But Vanessa was adamant. 'Hilton's the guy for the job,' she said. 'It's a new channel all right, and that's why people will be reassured by a familiar face.'

Rowland stared at her curiously. 'You don't owe him anything, you know. He was all washed out long before you dumped him for Charles Driftwood.'

She turned on him furiously. 'I didn't dump Hilton. I . . . it was over between him and me long before Charles ever came on the scene.'

Rowland backed off at once. He'd never known her get so angry so fast. 'Sorry, Vanessa, I'd just heard that—'

'What did you hear?' she snapped.

'After you quit his show, it went downhill pretty fast.'

She relaxed a bit. 'Yeah, well, I wasn't like the other girls he'd had in that job. Up until me, all they had to do was stand there looking dumb and be the butt of his jokes. So I came along and gave him as good as I got, and the audience loved it. And I got the Brass Monkeys to prove it.' She glanced behind her at the row of awards which lined her bookshelf.

'And after you went, they couldn't find anyone else?' asked Rowland. He had often wondered about that period in Vanessa's life, for she rarely discussed it.

'Not like me,' she replied with some pride. 'They sure tried. They must have auditioned a hundred sassy American redheads. But the show never worked the same . . .'

'Which is why you think you owe it to Hilton to help him make a comeback,' Rowland concluded.

Vanessa shook her head. 'I don't owe anyone anything,' she said. 'I'm giving him the job because he's right for it. I can sense it. The time's ripe for a revival of that whole seventies kick and we're going to be out at the forefront.'

Rowland gave up. Maybe she was right. Certainly Vanessa had shown herself to be an inspired judge of public taste in her newspaper career. He still wasn't convinced, though. There was more to this than met the eye but he valued his job too much to delve any deeper, so he changed the subject. 'I'm seeing an Inspector Ffelcher from Scotland Yard this afternoon about your anonymous E-mails,' he said. 'Are you around, if he wants a word?'

Vanessa shook her head, her temper abating as fast as it had flared. 'Nope. I'm having lunch with Hugh. And Hilton's coming in to sign the contract.' She glared at him defiantly. 'Immediately after that I've got to leave for the airport to catch Concorde to New York. They got problems with the Candy-Courtesy deal and they need Vanessa there.' As often, she encased her own name in verbal quotation marks, as if referring to some entity which went far beyond her own mortal flesh. 'You'll have to handle the inspector on your own. I'm back tomorrow night if he really needs to see me in person. But take it from me, there's nothing in those threats – just some jerk getting kicks at our expense.'

Rowland nodded, relieved to have escaped unscathed from the subject of Hilton Starr. In future, Dick Tockin would have to do his own dirty work.

For Hugh, the week following his new appointment had been a hectic one. There were many decisions to be made about how the combined Ministries of Environment and Transport would be integrated, where the new entity would be located, and how the staff would be reorganised. And in the meantime, the work of each area still had to be done, with the usual series of minor crises demanding his attention on a daily basis.

One rather more thorny problem arose mid-week. Frogmarch Construction, builders of the new Channel Tunnel between Folkestone and Boulogne, had never been very stable financially but in recent months their difficulties had escalated. By Wednesday afternoon their huge mountain of debt had begun to develop fault lines and was threatening to shift and engulf the company completely.

The directors had approached Hugh demanding a state bail-out and, with an election not that far off, massive job losses were the last thing the government needed. On the other hand, the new Chancellor was trying to rein public expenditure back in after the renationalisation spree the new administration had indulged in since taking over, so a massive injection of public cash was out of the question.

Transport Department officials had worked on this conundrum through the night and by Thursday morning they were able to announce a rather ingenious solution. It was Hugh's job to present it in the most favourable light to the financial press, who had been following events avidly.

He spent the morning giving interviews, which he felt went quite well in the circumstances. Communicating with people had always been one of Hugh's strongest suits, and when well prepared he was more than capable of handling reporters efficiently and politely without giving much away.

At noon the office was still under siege, and Hugh thought of cancelling his lunch appointment with Vanessa. On second thoughts, though, he decided that the break would do him good. So he merely called her to shift the timing back and was finally able to escape to Driftwood House only an hour later than scheduled.

It was always relaxing to visit Driftwood International's building in Docklands, in a way like returning to his youth. Indeed Vanessa's huge glass-walled office was virtually his own personal museum of childhood. On his father's death, when Vanessa had finally taken full control of the company after running it unofficially for years, she'd moved the whole operation from its original Fleet Street headquarters into a monstrous Lego-like building overlooking the Thames. And on its twelfth floor, with a curious nostalgia for an era she'd never known, she had recreated the chief executive's office exactly as Hugh remembered it from the distant past, right down to the massive musty-smelling oak desk under which he used to play as a child. She'd even brought the old portrait of his grandfather shaking hands with Baldwin. For want of an opaque wall, it hung incongruously in the centre of the room, suspended from the ceiling by two thin wires and surrounded by glass cases full of Vanessa's old television awards.

When Hugh arrived she was on the phone as usual, her figure framed against the back of a large swivel chair, the receiver cradled between her shoulder and her folds of auburn hair as if it had been grafted on at birth. She blew Hugh a silent kiss and waved him into a chair while she finished her conversation. It was evidently becoming heated.

'Listen, Dick,' she was saying. 'Nobody is saying you're not in charge of the station. But just remember who put you there, okay?' Her demeanour grew increasingly flushed. 'Vanessa's the goddamned editor-in-chief,' she shouted. 'And don't you forget it.'

Hugh listened with half an ear. Vanessa's abrasive manner of doing business was legendary and he was quite used to it by now. Besides, his interest in the family media empire had always been minimal. His father had once harboured fond hopes of his only son following in his footsteps, but Hugh had always preferred politics and it had come as a huge relief to him when Vanessa had seized the reins. Hugh was more than happy for her to continue. His father had left him comfortably off, with a legacy which included a sizeable shareholding in Driftwood International. And, under Vanessa's able stewardship, the value of his stake had multiplied many times over.

'No, I don't think Hilton Starr's a goddamned has-been,' Vanessa continued, clearly coming to the end of her fuse. 'But if you come out with that one again, that's exactly what you'll be.' And she slammed the phone down.

Hugh looked at her questioningly. 'Popviz?' he asked.

'Yeah, Dick Tockin. He's my head honcho there. Till now, at any rate.'

'But?'

'It's this chat show, *Livewire*,' said Vanessa, lighting up a cigarette.

'The one the PM's going to appear on?'

'Right. The choice of the host is turning into a real pain in the ass. Everyone's thinks they know better than me. I'm telling you' – she grimaced – 'the next call's gonna be the goddamned tea-lady wanting to get her two bits' worth.'

'Well, who do you want to do it?' asked Hugh.

Vanessa paused mysteriously. Then, without warning, she started making little cupping movements in the air with her hands, like a black and white minstrel on speed. 'What would you think,' she asked, 'if I said Twinkle, twinkle?'

Hugh stared back mystified. 'I'd think you'd gone barking mad,' he said.

'Twinkle, twinkle – Hilton Starr,' she repeated impatiently. The movements of her hands became more insistent.

Finally there was a faint stirring in Hugh's memory. 'You mean ... the fellow who was on TV years ago, the one you used to work with?'

'You got it,' said Vanessa.

'Oh,' said Hugh, thinking back.

Several decades earlier there had been no more famous British TV personality than Hilton Starr. As a teenager, Hugh had watched his show most nights while doing his homework. A tiny egregious Northener, he'd started out as a disc jockey before turning with astonishing success to presenting a nightly TV quiz show. His programme was most memorable for its nauseating introduction: 'Twinkle, twinkle,' a disembodied voice would shout. 'Hilton Starr,' the studio audience would scream back inanely, and then the man himself would come bounding out on to the set, maniacally imitating a twinkling star by opening and closing the palms of his hands.

There was something else which marked out the show. At

Hilton's side, always, there had been an attractive young 'assistant', who had done little other than exchange some light banter with him before accompanying his guests down a glittering staircase on to the set. And it was as one of the so-called 'Twinkle Girls' that Vanessa had first come to England, before marrying Hugh's father and moving on to better things.

What had happened to the *Hilton Starr Show*? Hugh wondered. For a while it had been the BBC's number one attraction, but at some point it had simply disappeared without trace. It was a very seventies kind of programme. It must have been dropped soon after Vanessa left, and since then little had been heard of its host. 'Is Hilton still around then?' he asked.

'Sort of,' Vanessa replied. 'He gets the occasional commercial and guest appearance on nostalgia programmes and retrospectives. And I'm fixing it for him to get an award for a lifetime's achievement in television at next week's Brass Monkeys ceremony. Just to get his face back before the public. He hasn't done any real work for a while though.'

'But why him?'

Vanessa shifted uncomfortably in her seat. 'Hell, not you as well!' she exclaimed in exasperation. 'The guy's right for the job. Besides, he's hit on hard times and deserves a break. What do you think about him interviewing the PM?'

Hugh considered. 'Well, nobody could accuse him of being hard-hitting,' he said, recalling the mindless drivel which had characterised Hilton's old programmes. 'Burgins might even manage to outwit him, which would be a novel experience.'

'Great,' said Vanessa with satisfaction. ''Cos it's all settled. Hilly's going to be here to sign the contract before we head out to lunch, and if Dick Tockin doesn't like it he can damn well lump it. I'll get my secretary to give you Hilton's biography so you can show it to the PM.' She pressed a buzzer on her desk and a few seconds later a young woman came into the room. 'Rosalyn,' Vanessa said, 'could you dig out Hilton Starr's précis and run off a copy for Hugh?'

'Certainly, Mrs Driftwood,' replied the young woman. 'By the way, Mr Starr is in reception. Also, Mr Driftwood's office at the ministry telephoned. They didn't want me to interrupt your meeting, but asked if he could call back as soon as possible.'

'Okay,' said Vanessa. 'Why don't you let Mr Driftwood into the conference room. He can call them from there while I deal with Hilton. Okay, Hugh? . . . Hugh?'

But her stepson's attention was far away. Mouth agape, he was staring in front of him as if he'd seen a vision. With a mixture of rising excitement and utter bewilderment, he gazed at Vanessa's new secretary and wondered whether he was dreaming. For, although her long hair was now tied up at the back of her head and she was smartly attired in a blue two-piece business suit, there was no mistaking those emerald eyes for a moment. Mesmerised, Hugh's gaze shifted further down. Through the thick material it was impossible to detect any sign of them. But that the nipple rings were there he knew beyond a shadow of doubt.

Hugh dealt with the query from his office in a virtual trance. Would he be able to do an interview for that evening's nine o'clock news about the new Channel Tunnel finance initiative? He agreed without thinking, unable to drag his mind away from a far more pressing question. What in God's name was Ros – Rosalyn – doing working in Vanessa's office? Could Will Cloud really have sent her here for a job? It was almost unimaginable that he could be so stupid, but Hugh had to believe the evidence of his own eyes. With equal distraction, he dealt with a number of other questions from his private secretary at the DET, as it was now called, then drifted back towards Vanessa's office, still thunder-struck.

There, Vanessa's meeting with Hilton was under way and apparently not going very well. The sound of raised voices could be heard through the closed door. Evidently it was Vanessa's day for heated argument.

'You *cannot* be serious!' Vanessa was shouting. 'I'm doing you a favour, for Chrissake. Have you any idea how much flak I'm getting here for giving you the goddamned job?' There followed a quieter interlude during which Hilton's more measured tones could be heard saying something indistinct. Then there was a further explosion from Vanessa and the door of her office crashed open and she burst out.

'Just forget it,' she shouted back into the office. 'I'm going to lunch, and if that contract's not sitting signed on my desk when I get back, then the whole goddamned deal's off. Got that?' She turned away dismissively and addressed herself to her stepson. 'You ready, Hugh honey?' she said. 'I'm just gonna powder my nose then we're outta here.'

As Vanessa stormed off, Hugh peeked into her office. The diminutive figure of Hilton Starr, familiar from all that time ago, was standing looking at the bookcase. His back was to the door, but for an instant he half turned around and Hugh was able to glimpse his face. It was quite a shock. The intervening years had not been kind to Hilton. His features had lost much of their old vigour and he looked haggard. Yet he was still clearly identifiable as the same Hilton Starr who had once smirked out of the box when Hugh was a boy. Hugh smiled, but Hilton gave no acknowledgement. He just seemed to stare straight through him.

In any case, Vanessa returned before they could exchange any words. 'Let's go,' she said. Under her breath, she told Rosalyn, 'Get Hilton to sign the goddamned contract if he wants the job. Otherwise, throw the asshole out.'

'What on earth was all that about?' asked Hugh over their appetiser at The Meet Joint, one of the smart restaurants which had sprung up in Docklands to cater for the new media arrivistes.

'I can't believe that guy,' said Vanessa, lighting up another cigarette while picking viciously at a plate of olives. 'I give him a chance to make his big comeback. I even fix it for him to get a goddamned Brass Monkey award and all he can think about is what kind of billing he'll get and how big his dressing room's gonna be. How's that for gratitude?'

She remained preoccupied by the subject of Hilton throughout lunch, although that did not prevent her questioning Hugh closely on his new job and his current popularity rating with the Prime Minister.

'It's the *next* Prime Minister I've got to worry about,' said Hugh. 'Alistair Sloach has really got it in for me now that I've moved into his office at Environment. Not that he's done so badly out of the reshuffle. Being Home Secretary may be pretty thankless, but you couldn't get a better platform for a leadership bid.'

'You reckon he'll challenge?' asked Vanessa, her interest reawoken.

'First chance he gets,' said Hugh gloomily. 'It's just a matter of picking the right moment. And when he does, he's a racing cert to win.'

Evidently this gave Vanessa food for thought, for her eyes assumed that familiar pensive look. Hugh took advantage of her unaccustomed taciturnity to try, as casually as he could, to elicit some information about Ros.

'Miss Flato?' said Vanessa absently. 'Don't know where Rowly got her. I guess from the agency, like all the others. No, wait, I think she approached him direct for a job. Fine references, though, so I thought I'd give her a try. Seems to be pretty efficient, so far. Why do you ask?'

Hugh made up some lame excuse about wanting a new secretary in the constituency, but he needn't have bothered. Vanessa's mind was elsewhere.

It was late afternoon before they returned to Driftwood House. Vanessa had to pick her briefcase up from her office before her onward journey to Heathrow Airport. Although his car was waiting for him, Hugh accompanied her to the twelfth floor, ostensibly to collect the PM's copy of Hilton Starr's biographical note. Secretly, though, he was also hoping for one further encounter with Ros. He swore to himself he wouldn't speak to her, much less ask her out. He just wanted a last glimpse of that sensational body to refuel his memory for the increasingly rabid fantasies she had been provoking in him.

In the event, the detour was opportune, for Hugh had forgotten to turn his mobile phone on and there was yet another urgent message to ring the DET. 'Use the phone in my office, honey,' said Vanessa. 'I gotta go or I'll miss my plane.' She took her leave of him with a customary bear hug and disappeared back towards the lifts.

Hugh rang his office to be told of a further interview request. BBC Radio had been trying to track him down to appear on the *PM* programme in only a few minutes' time. 'Can you get over to their Westminster studio?' his private secretary asked.

'I don't think so,' said Hugh, checking his watch. 'If they want me, they'll have to do it down the line from here.'

It was arranged that the BBC would ring him back on Vanessa's private number. Hugh replaced the receiver and began to compose himself, all thoughts of Ros dispelled for the present. These interviews could be daunting, and it was as well to be mentally prepared. He ran his hand through his hair as he rehearsed some of the probable questions in his mind.

When the telephone went, he let it ring twice before picking up. 'Yes,' he said, 'this is the minister. Fine. When will I be on?

Very well . . . yes, I'm quite ready.' Sitting down on the side of Vanessa's desk, he closed his eyes to concentrate.

So preoccupied was he that he was scarcely aware of the door of the office opening and of Ros sidling in. He did not see the curiously hypnotic expression which filled those emerald eyes as she stood observing him. Nor was he aware of the snake-like swaying of her body as the Human Blowtorch moved towards the desk and sank to her knees in front of him. The first he knew that all was not as it should be was when he sensed a strangely warm sensation in the very last place he would have expected.

'What the . . .' he said, opening his eyes in astonishment and closing them again in haste. 'Miss Flato! Ros! What do you think you're . . . ?'

But the unformed question was left hanging because it was pretty obvious what she was doing. And anyway, it was too late to do much about it. On the line, the minion had disappeared and someone else had come on. 'Yes,' Hugh replied, trying unsuccessfully to keep a rising tone of sheer unadulterated panic out of his voice. 'Yes,' he repeated. 'I'm – I'm still here . . . oh, God . . . oh, God . . . Oh, good afternoon, Mr Dimbleforth.'

Vanessa's chauffeur tapped on the screen which separated him from the passengers' compartment.

'What is it, Mike?' she asked.

'I just been listenin' to the radio,' mumbled the driver. 'Thought you might want to know that Mr Driftwood's goin' to be on the *PM* programme in a minute, something about this new Channel Tunnel.'

'Great, Mike. Thanks. Do me a favour and switch it through here, will you?'

Vanessa sat back in the cream leather upholstery with a smile of satisfaction. This kind of exposure could do nothing but good for her ambitions for Hugh and he generally performed well on the radio. The result of the recent reshuffle had exceeded her best expectations and his career was going exactly according to plan. Shame about Alistair Sloach getting the Home Office, though. She would see if Rowland Cranston had any ideas on that.

The item on Channel Tunnel refinancing was number three in today's running order and they reached it at ten past five. 'Following this week's cash crisis at Frogmarch Construction, the Department of Environment and Transport today announced a new initiative aimed at rescuing the company,' said the newsreader. 'The solution is claimed by the government to be entirely privately financed, but the leader of the opposition has condemned it as yet another example of a return to the old socialist ways. On the line to discuss it is the Secretary of State for Environment and Transport, Hugh Driftwood MP. Are you there, Minister?'

'Good afternoon, Mr Dimbleforth.'

Back in the office, Hugh was trying to focus his brain on the interview and ignore the heady attentions he was receiving three feet lower down. Holding the telephone in a vice-like grip with one hand, he feebly attempted to ward Ros off with the other. The main thing was to avoid getting aroused, but it was easier said than done. His lower portions appeared to have teamed up with his libido and declared UDI, determined literally to milk this experience for all it was worth.

'Now, Minister,' said the interviewer. 'What's all this about bailing out the second Channel Tunnel?'

'Eh?' Hugh gurgled, concentrating hard. 'Ah . . . it's not a question of a bail-out at all. It's just . . . it's merely . . .' He summoned every nerve to carry on. You can do it, he told himself. Hang in there. But this imagery proved counter-productive and as his gaze dropped down he lost his thread completely. 'It's . . . it's . . . it's . . . not . . .' he stuttered.

'The opposition says it is,' his inquisitor cut in smugly, taking advantage of Hugh's unexpected hesitancy. 'And, I should warn you, they're going to make the most of it. Yet another regression to the nanny state, they claim. Back to the interventionism of the 1960s. Looks like they've got the bit firmly between their teeth on this one, doesn't it, Minister!'

They were not the only ones. Ros's head was bobbing up and down like an Olympic swimmer's. 'The whole thing's being blown out of all proportion,' Hugh maintained shakily, conscious that something not dissimilar was happening to himself. 'We . . . we . . .' He stopped abruptly and a low moan escaped his lips. 'Don't!' he said. 'Please, don't!'

'I beg your pardon, Minister?'

Hugh stared panic-stricken at the ceiling. He had to pull himself together. 'Please don't . . . ah . . . be taken in by the other side's knee-jerk negativity,' he managed lamely. 'As usual, they've got completely the wrong end of the . . . ah . . . stick. There's no question of government intervention.'

'That's not what your opponents think. They reckon it's the taxpayer who'll foot the bill.'

'Non . . . non . . . nonsense,' Hugh babbled. 'Look,' he added, trying desperately to regain his composure. 'Of course . . . *of course*, in a sector as vital as transport, the government's bound to take an interest. But . . . but . . .' It was no use. Ros was warming to her task. Worse, not content with her initial manoeuvres, she was widening the field of operation. 'But I must stress that the ball's firmly in the private sector's . . . ah . . . mouth . . . I mean . . . court.'

'Not according to the leader of the opposition, it's not. He says all this talk of private finance is just a smokescreen. No more than lip-service were his words.'

'What?' squeaked Hugh. 'Nothing of the kind.'

'State funding through the back door!'

'Back door?' Hugh was beginning to feel quite faint. 'Certainly not. This is a revolutionary new approach to . . . ah . . . guaranteeing a major infrastructure project which will not cost the taxpayer a penny. Of course, it is just an experiment and we'll just have to ah . . . ah . . .'

'Suck it and see?' the interviewer prompted.

'. . . judge how it goes in the fulness of time,' Hugh snapped weakly. 'I do wish you wouldn't put words in my mouth.'

But in that department, words were the least of his problems. Sensing his level of arousal, Ros had redoubled her efforts. And overtaken by some form of penile dementia, Hugh was powerless to resist.

'Minister, the cross-Channel ferry operators say if this new tunnel goes ahead their business will suffer terminal damage. That could mean thousands of their staff on the dole. What do you say to that?'

'There are no . . . no guarantees,' Hugh stammered, 'but naturally, I'll do my level best to prevent any . . . expulsion . . . I mean . . . dismissal . . .' He was practically shrieking now. '. . . or rather discharge . . . of seamen . . . oh, God . . . that's to say . . . of sailors . . . I mean, ferry workers!'

'Come, come, Minister!'

Never had an interviewer's exhortation been taken quite so literally. 'I . . . I . . . I . . .' Hugh stammered.

'You know as well as I do . . .'

'Ahhhh!'

'Sorry?'

'Ahhhhhhhhhhhhh!'

'I think we may have a problem on the line, Mr Driftwood.'

Hugh was certain of it. 'I'm coming,' he panted desperately, and his body arched backwards and shuddered as he matched action with words.

'I beg your pardon?'

'I have come,' said Hugh, and no politician could ever have been more truthful, 'to the . . . ah . . . conclusion that it's impossible to do anything in this country without a whole lot of carping and cavilling. Sometimes I think we're just a lot of moaning minnies . . .'

'So you're relaxed about the project?'

'Relaxed?' Hugh gasped, collapsing against Vanessa's desk. 'Relaxed? I'm totally bloody drained. I mean, yes, I think you could say that I'm relaxed about it. Utterly relaxed.'

'Thank you, Minister. There we must leave it. That was Hugh Driftwood MP, Minister of Environment and Transport. Now, it's time for Thought for the Day, with the Reverend Lester Pinkerton . . .'

Still reeling, Hugh listened as a BBC operator thanked him for his contribution. Then he replaced the receiver with a final groan and looked down at Ros, more in sadness than in anger.

And he wondered distractedly whether this came under the PM's definition of keeping his whistle clean.

Back in her car, Vanessa reached forward and turned down the volume with a frown.

That had been an uncharacteristically hesitant performance from Hugh, she reflected with some concern. And he was usually so good on the air. She just hoped he wasn't losing his touch. She made a mental note to send him back to the media training specialist who had done such a good job with him when he'd first started in politics. Now that he was on the very threshold of greatness, perhaps he could do with a refresher course.

Outside the Driftwood headquarters, the ponytailed driver of a car rather less grand than Vanessa's also switched off his radio. Stevie Cudlick had been waiting in bored frustration for some hours now, having followed Hugh there earlier that day. He was not normally a listener to Radio 4 but this latest assignment had awoken in him a belated interest in more upmarket current affairs. He had caught the end of Hugh's interview and was as unimpressed as Vanessa. If this bloke Driftwood carried on like that, there wouldn't be any need for Victor Quistling to dispose of him through the newspapers. He would just shrivel up and disappear of his own accord.

Stevie stared up at the huge building. The minister was still in there, he was sure of it. He'd watched Vanessa and Hugh come back from lunch, and had then seen Vanessa leaving alone in her sleek black limousine. He had been expecting her stepson to follow behind. But the ministerial Rover remained firmly parked by the entrance, the chauffeur leaning against the side enjoying a sly cigarette.

This shadowing lark was turning out to be a dead loss, thought Stevie irritably. He'd been following him for nearly three weeks now, with not a sausage to show for it. God knew what Driftwood was up to in that building, but if his recent record was anything to go by, it wasn't going to make a Sunday-school teacher raise an eyebrow, much less fuel a tabloid scandal.

Nothing to be gained from hanging around here any longer, he concluded. May as well throw in the towel for the day. Thoroughly disheartened, he started up the engine of the battered old Golf, and as he drove off he cast a last withering look back towards Driftwood House.

'Boring old sod,' he muttered to himself.

Chapter 14

On the eleventh floor of Driftwood House, nestling among the boilers and air-conditioning ducts at the opposite end of the building from Vanessa's office suite, there was a small room known as the 'special security unit', whose existence was known to only a very few of the organisation's staff.

The room had been an integral, but secret, part of the design of the new headquarters, and had been constructed to Vanessa's strict specifications when she moved the company here from its outmoded premises in Fleet Street some years before. Expertise and machinery had been flown in covertly from the United States, and specialist workers brought to the site at dead of night to instal the complex cabling and heavy equipment the room required.

Like the tentacles of some giant octopus sitting on its roof, the wires which spread forth from here permeated every crevice of the Driftwood building. For this was Vanessa's own personal surveillance centre, a sophisticated spying operation with a mass of listening devices and video-monitoring equipment which permitted her and two of her most trusted staff to keep tabs on virtually every employee, meeting, whispered conversation and incipient plot in any part of the London office. Nobody in the place could as much as burp without Vanessa finding out about it and wanting to know what they had had for lunch.

It was in this room that, on the same afternoon when Hugh Driftwood had been the object of Ros Flato's unsolicited attentions, an elderly man sat slumped at a console, his head buried in his hands, his mind in turmoil. The man's name was Reg Diggle and he was one of the staff who ran the special security unit. And what he had just seen had shocked him to his very core.

Reg had joined the Driftwood Press Corporation, as it had been called then, at the age of fourteen, when Fleet Street was still at the heart of the British newspaper industry, and had worked his way up from junior messenger in the print room to become premises manager in charge of the old building. But when the move to Docklands took place, exactly forty years to the day after he'd first arrived at the company, he was considered too old to master the intricacies of running of a modern intelligent building, from elevated floors with endless miles of fibre-optic wiring to sophisticated air-conditioning ducts criss-crossing the ceilings like spaghetti. A younger man was recruited to take his place, and the threat of redundancy had hung over Reg for a while.

Then, one day, Vanessa summoned him into her office and, while he sat petrified on the edge of a chair, explained precisely what was meant by 'special security' unit. He and one other colleague were to be offered the chance to work there. If he accepted, he would report directly to her and must carry out certain tasks precisely as she specified. Above all, confidentiality would be paramount, in recognition of which he would receive a special cash bonus over and above his weekly wage, to be handed to him by Vanessa personally. Reg had accepted the new position with alacrity, as the alternative was an early retirement which he would have loathed, and from then on he had served Vanessa with a devotion bordering on the fanatical.

But in the hours that followed Hugh Driftwood's organ-blowing experience on Radio 4, it was revulsion rather than devotion which dominated Reg Diggle's thoughts. He had been going about his daily activities in the usual way, monitoring the surveillance screens, changing cassettes in the video recorders and making notes for Mrs Driftwood of anything which might turn out to be of interest, when he happened to tune into the hidden camera monitoring the chief executive's office. Naturally, this camera did not remain permanently on like all the others. Vanessa had the ability to guarantee herself a privacy she did not extend to the rest of her staff by flicking a switch under her desk, so cutting the office off from her own spy network. At all other times, though, the camera's output was monitored by Reg and John like every other in the building.

It was the scene that Reg had witnessed during Vanessa's absence that afternoon that was affecting him so deeply. Not a prurient man by nature, he had followed events involving Mrs Driftwood's stepson and her new secretary with a growing sense of nausea and outrage. More than once he had gone to turn the screen off, but was prevented by an intense curiosity for which he berated himself even as he succumbed to it.

However, soon after the radio interview ended, he did finally reach for the off switch. Not just the one controlling the camera in Vanessa Driftwood's office, but the master switch. With a disgusted cry, directed at himself as much as those in the picture, he snapped it decisively down, causing all the machinery in the room to grind to a cacophonous halt. Reg was left alone in the unaccustomed darkness, lost in his thoughts.

It was nearly half an hour before he stirred again. He looked at the time. Soon John, his colleague, would be arriving to take over the evening shift and allow him home for his tea. Reg pulled distractedly at his remaining tuft of grey hair. What should he do? That was the question that was plaguing him.

It went without saying that he had to do something. He could not stand idly by and allow such wickedness to go unchecked. That would be like dancing with the devil. But how could he, Reg Diggle, no more than a humble security guard at Driftwood International, administer a telling-off to someone as elevated as the boss's stepson, and a Cabinet minister to boot?

He needed time – time to think. And in the meantime nobody must know that anything out of the ordinary had happened, least of all John. Abruptly, Reg returned the master switch to the 'on' position and watched the video screens as they cranked back into life, resuming transmission of the everyday scenes of Driftwood staff winding down for the night. If only he could be as carefree as they appeared, as carefree as he himself had been only a few hours earlier. But Reg now faced a dilemma compared to which Hamlet's little problem was like a day at the races.

Automatically, he set about the regular evening task of changing the videotapes. These were carefully labelled and stored for a minimum of two months, in case Vanessa needed to check up on anything later, and indeed she would occasionally come down to the room and ask Reg or John to locate some incident in which she had an interest. All she had to do was specify the place and approximate time and it could invariably be traced.

That was another thing, thought Reg, aghast. What if Mrs Driftwood came across that tape? What if she wanted to view something and ended up seeing her own stepson engaged in that filthy, disgusting act in her own office? Reg could not even bear to think about it. Mrs Driftwood, to whom he owed so much, must at all costs be spared exposure to such moral turpitude.

There was only one option, Reg abruptly concluded. Acting on impulse, when he reached the chief executive's office tape, he did not label it and add it to the neat shelves with the others as he should have done. Instead he pulled it from the machine and quickly slipped it into the Sainsbury's carrier bag he'd brought his lunch in. Then he laid the bag beside his coat. It went against all Mrs Driftwood's instructions, but desperate times call for desperate measures. He would decide what to do with it later.

With a heavy heart, Reg sat down again and waited to be relieved.

That evening, in his council flat in the south London suburb of Caustwick, Reg Diggle continued to wrestle with his dilemma. He could not settle for a moment. He got up and strode around. He turned on the television and watched twenty seconds of his favourite soap, then turned it off and stared at the damp patch on the wallpaper for a while. Tormented, he examined every possible course of action.

How could he ensure that nothing of this sort ever happened again? And what should he do with that tape, which was even now radiating its evil from his lunch bag and polluting the atmosphere of the living room. He could destroy it, of course. But that would solve nothing. A young man like that who had gone wrong would just carry on the same unless shown the error of his ways. And next time Reg might not be around to save Mrs Driftwood from finding out.

He sighed. Mr Hugh used to be such a nice young man. Reg remembered him from years ago, when Mr Driftwood Senior was still alive. Mr Hugh was his only son and the lad often came in to work in the office during his college holidays. He had once asked old Groatsy, the head messenger, if someone could wash his car for him and Reg Diggle had volunteered. When he handed the keys back later that day, Mr Hugh gave him a pound and patted him on the back, and said, 'Thank you very much indeed.' Beautifully mannered, he was. A credit to the family. And now so high in the government too, right up there hobnobbing with the Prime Minister and the Queen and goodness knew who else. He was the Minister of Environment and Transport, building all those new roads and running the train service and the buses. Come to think of it, the number three had been coming much more regularly since he'd taken over, so he couldn't be doing too bad a job.

Reg's attitude softened a little. Maybe Mr Driftwood wasn't really that bad, just misguided, led astray by lust and lechery, which could happen to anyone. What he needed was a good talking-to by someone who understood right from wrong, who could put him back on the path of morality double-quick. But Reg kept coming back to that same question: who?

If only his late wife, Gladys, God rest her soul, had still been there, she would have known what to do. She always had a way of finding solutions to the tricky problems of life. Not that he would have said what he had seen. Not to her. The thought of even discussing those revolting acts with Gladys made him shudder. But he could have told her of the wickedness without telling her the details and she would have come up with an answer.

Or what if he confided in John, his colleague in the surveillance room? No, that was out of the question too. Despite all Vanessa's exhortations, John could have a big mouth sometimes and would not understand the need for secrecy. He would go blabbing around the office about it, and maybe he would talk to the wrong person and it would get into the papers or something. Into the yellow press. That was the last thing Reg wanted. Not that any of the Driftwood publications would ever print anything like that, of course. But there were others around who would like nothing better than to drag the Driftwoods through the gutter. Whatever happened, that had to be prevented.

Exhausted with this mental torture, Reg looked around the room for something to take his mind off his predicament for even a moment. His eyes alighted on the *Caustwick Examiner*, the free local paper, which had come through the letterbox earlier and was sitting on the mantelpiece. He picked it up and skimmed through it, not really reading, just passing the time. And suddenly an item almost leaped out of the page at him, like an act of God, he decided afterwards, or perhaps a signal from Gladys from beyond the grave.

All at once, he knew. He knew with total certainty: that was what she would have done, and that was what he must now do. With a feeling of blessed relief as if a heavy burden had been lifted from his back, he checked the address and time in the newspaper advertisement and began laying his plans.

Chapter 15

Candida Blitz was the little blonde bimbo from children's TV that Hilton Starr was living with. She was certainly blonde, but contrary to the rest of Rowland Cranston's description to Vanessa she was in reality not very little, being a willowy five foot ten, and her days as a bimbo had long since come to an end. Indeed, as she had been told that very day by her new producer, she was getting 'a bit long in the tooth' for children's television.

It was this conversation which was bearing on her mind as she waited for Hilton to come home from his meeting with Vanessa Driftwood. Candida did not like the new producer. He was pushy and far too young. He must have been at least ten years her junior. And that was part of the problem. 'Candida darling,' he'd said on meeting her, and she didn't appreciate the instant familiarity one little bit, 'I'm a fan. I was weaned on the *Jolly Roger*. Watched you all the time when I was a kid. I even used to make all those bloody plant holders out of old washing-up-liquid bottles. But I ask you. Times have moved on, darling. Kids nowadays want to know how to hack into the

Pentagon's central defence systems. Making useful Christmas gifts out of discarded kitchen refuse went out with the ark.'

Candida did not agree. It was true that the *Jolly Roger* had begun slipping in the ratings against new programmes with names like *Thwack* and *Cop It* and *Worm-eating for Beginners*. And that was no doubt why the BBC had brought in this brash young parvenu to shake things up. But Candida knew instinctively that these were just a passing craze. Kids, or children as Candida still preferred to think of them, were the same now as they'd always been. She had been chief presenter on the *Jolly Roger* for over fifteen years. She was a national institution. And she had the awards to prove it.

She'd pointed this out to Chaz as he sat in her office stroking his stupid goatee beard, but he'd looked sceptically at the rows of cups and plaques proudly arrayed on her desk. 'Sure,' he said, 'but check out the dates on them. I mean, we're talking pre-history here. Let's face it, it's yonks since you've won anything. Past glories, darling. You can't go on living on them.'

'It's not so long,' said Candida, almost in tears. 'Besides, I still get nominated. It's just that . . .'

'It's just that you don't win,' said Chaz brutally.

'I'm up for a Brass Monkey for best children's presenter this year. And everyone says I have a good chance.'

Chaz looked at her. He was not without compassion, but he'd been brought in here to do a job and he'd made up his mind he couldn't do it with Candida still around. There was no point in pouring old wine into a new bottle. 'Tell you what,' he said. 'I'll make a deal with you. You win that award and we leave everything more or less as it is. Sure, I'll make a few changes here and there, but we'll stick to the old format. But if you lose, we do it my way.'

'Meaning?'

'I'll give it to you straight, darling. It means you start

looking around for something else. Something more suited to your ... ah ... age-group. Not necessarily at once, but soon. Say within six months. That's fair, isn't it? I mean there are heaps of things you can present. You know, quiz shows, holiday programmes for pensioners, that sort of stuff. Don't you fancy sunning yourself on a beach in Malaga and getting paid for it?'

Candida did not. She *was* the *Jolly Roger*. Presenting it had become her life. She thrived on children who had walked backwards from John O'Groats to Land's End to raise money to save baby hippos. And the thought of giving it all up filled her with despair.

As ever, back in the safety of the house she shared with Hilton Starr in Hampstead, she confided the whole thing to Zoë. Zoë had been her constant live-in companion ever since those very first days on the *Jolly Roger*. She had come with the job. Aged fifteen, with yellowing teeth and mangy skin, she was largely retired now but she still made the occasional TV appearance and, unlike Candida, Zoë had retained her drawing power. Audience figures would shoot up whenever she was scheduled to be on the programme.

'They're trying to dump me, Zoë,' Candida told her tearfully. 'What am I going to do?'

Without for a moment taking her wizened eyes off the banana and nut supper Candida was preparing for her, Zoë set her head to one side and listened. The chimpanzee had long ago discovered that this was all that human beings expected of her and had developed a range of expressions to cope with most situations. They gave people, Candida not least, the quite mistaken impression that she understood their every word. It was not for nothing that Zoë had become the most successful animal in British broadcasting history.

Candida sighed. 'Oh well,' she said, 'I'll just have to make sure I win that award.' Ever the optimist, she brightened at the thought. That was the solution. She had her contacts, she could still pull a string or two. She would canvass for votes like a politician. Maybe Hilly would be able to help. Between them they knew an unrivalled cross-section of the broadcasting establishment which was responsible for electing the Brass Monkey winners. And Vanessa Driftwood had fixed it for Hilly to get this special award for a lifetime's achievement in television, so she must have some pull there.

If only she could confide a bit more in Hilly, but he'd become ever more moody and self-obsessed of late. There had been a time at the beginning of their relationship when he'd at least shown a little interest in her career. Recently, though, he seemed to think about nothing but himself and his so-called comeback. Not that even that prospect had made him very happy. Quite the opposite, in fact. For the last few days he had been in a foul mood, throwing things around the house and even, once, trying to kick Zoë, although she'd dodged out of the way in time. And he kept shouting obscenities about Vanessa Driftwood, which did not make sense to Candida at all. She knew that he and Vanessa had once been lovers, but that was years ago. Now Vanessa was being kind to him, and you'd think he would be grateful instead of being so horrid about her. No, there was something very strange about Hilly's behaviour, Candida decided, and in his current state he was the last person she could talk to about her problem. She'd have to get through it on her own.

Right on cue, the front door banged and Zoë scuttled off under the kitchen table. Hilton stormed in, looking as furious as Candida had ever seen him. He slammed his briefcase down in the corner.

'Well,' she said, fearing the worst. 'How did it go with Vanessa Driftwood?'

'How do you bloody well think it went?' he asked, stamping

over to the drinks cupboard and pouring himself a large gin.

'Wouldn't she give you the contract then?'

'Of course she gave me the frigging contract. It's all signed and sealed. But what good's it going to do me?'

'I don't know what you mean,' said Candida. 'At least you'll be on the telly again, and people will recognise you in the street and you'll get invited to places on your own account, instead of just because you're with me.'

Candida realised too late she'd made a mistake as Hilton pounced on the remark. 'Oh, yes,' he shouted. 'Just rub it in, why don't you! Remind me how famous you are compared to me.'

'That's not what I meant at all, and you know it,' said Candida, on the verge of tears for the second time that day. 'Besides, I don't suppose it'll be true for much longer.' Perhaps he would ask what she meant by that, she thought, and then she could unburden herself. But as ever he was too immersed in himself to pay any attention.

'What good's it going to do me?' he repeated. 'Don't you realise, it's too fucking late!'

'Language, Hilly, language! And in front of Zoë too!'

As usual when he was in this mood, Hilton alighted with glee on her slight speech defect. 'In fwont of Zoë, in fwont of Zoë!' he taunted. Then, completely losing control, he began to shriek. 'Can't you get it through your thick skull, you daft bitch? Zoë's an animal. She doesn't understand a frigging word you say!'

'Well, at least she *tries* to listen,' sobbed Candida. 'Which is more than you ever do.'

'Oh, Christ.' Hilton gulped his drink down. 'You're unbelievable. That's right, turn on the bloody waterworks. That solves everything.' He banged down his empty glass and picked up the gin bottle and his briefcase. 'I'm going up to my study.

I've got work to do.' He stopped at the door, swaying slightly, and stared back at Candida Blitz, her head buried in her hands on the kitchen table, with Zoë curled up at her feet. 'You both make me sick,' he said.

Chapter 16

However much he tried, Hugh could not get Ros Flato out of his mind. The excitement of those moments in Vanessa's office, the sheer intoxicating danger of the situation and its mind-blowing climax, lingered for days and played havoc with his concentration as he went about his ministerial duties.

His constituency secretary, Annette, who had been with him long before his rise to Cabinet level, noticed how tense he was when she came into the ministry with some local correspondence. 'Is there anything wrong?' she asked, after a series of uncharacteristically curt responses from him.

'Wrong?' said Hugh, crossly. 'What on earth could be wrong?'

'Just asking,' she said. 'There's no need to jump down my throat,' and was taken aback when that seemed to make the situation even worse.

But it was not only the incident itself which dominated Hugh's thoughts. What was really preoccupying him – no, obsessing him – was the conversation he'd had with Ros after it was all over, and the almost unbelievable suggestion she'd made. He replayed that conversation over and over again in his mind. She couldn't be serious, he told himself. And even if she was, he must have been mad to have agreed to it. It was absurdly dangerous, indescribably reckless. Just because he'd survived the radio interview – and by the skin of his teeth, at that – didn't mean . . .

She had left him her number and this time he'd kept it safe. He would just have to ring her up and make it clear that the whole thing was impossible and she must knock it on the head, as it were, before they got too carried away.

He made the call with a trembling finger later that evening and she answered immediately. The very sound of that husky voice sent frissons up and down his spine.

'It's Hugh . . . Hugh Driftwood.'

'No need to specify,' she said. 'You're the only Hugh I know.' She gave a breathless laugh. 'Have you recovered?'

'Ah . . . sort of. But I really—'

'Fun, huh?

It had definitely been that. 'Yes, but look, I wanted to—'

'And how about my other little idea. Still grab you?'

'That's what I wanted to talk to you about. I—'

'I've got it all worked out, you know. Right down to the last detail. I'm a great planner.'

'Listen, I honestly don't think—'

'Tell you what, why don't we meet up and I'll tell you all about it. Who knows, I might even give you a tiny appetiser . . .' She giggled. 'An *amuse-gueule*, if you'll excuse the French.'

It was too much for Hugh. Abandoning all good intentions, he surrendered to those base instincts yet again. 'When?' he asked.

'Sunday night?'

'Can't, I'm afraid,' said Hugh regretfully. 'I've got to attend this blasted Brass Monkeys ceremony. Driftwood International's sponsoring it and Vanessa's presenting the last award.' He consulted his diary. 'Then I'm going up north for a few days: the Midlands to open a tricycle museum, followed by the inauguration of the new Glasgow tram system. I'm back on Thursday, though. How about then? I've got a vote at ten but I could leave just after.'

'Sure,' said Ros breezily. 'You know the Poison Pen just behind the office? I'll meet you outside at ten thirty.'

Chapter 17

The Press, Radio And Television awards ceremony took place every year in May. In its early days in the 1950s it had been known by an acronym of its name, but the evolution of the English language had other ideas and the organisers eventually bowed to the inevitable and opted for a change. For its new title, they looked to the little statuette which was presented to all winners. Its genesis was shrouded in the mists of time. Originally gold-plated, nowadays it was made out of light aluminium topped with a thin veneer of brass. It was in the shape of a small, endearing baby chimpanzee. Thereafter, the awards became known as the Brass Monkeys.

The annual ceremony was held in the Royal London Theatre, a sprawling eyesore of a building just off the Strand which had been constructed in the 1960s in the grey concrete all too fashionable at the time. But the two auditoria inside the complex were surprisingly comfortable, with excellent acoustics, and had attracted some of the world's greatest acting talent to their stages over the years. The bigger of them, the Harold Wilson, boasted the largest stage in London and was an ideal venue for this type of show.

Hugh had been sent two tickets, and, on a whim he was sure he would regret, asked Will Cloud if he would like to accompany him. 'Black tie,' he instructed without much hope. Will had been living in the same pair of jeans ever since he'd arrived. But he was to be surprised. 'Sure, in my line of work you have to be prepared for every eventuality,' said Will, digging out a dinner suit which had clearly seen better days but was just about serviceable. 'Don't know what I'd do without the good old Oxfam shop,' he added with a grin.

As they arrived, it was evident that security for the event was unusually stringent. There were squad cars everywhere, and the outside of the theatre was bathed in floodlight, eerily illuminating the grey leviathans parked nearby which bore the BBC Outside Broadcast logo. 'Must be something up,' Hugh noted as they showed their passes at the door and submitted to an electronic search.

What had happened, in fact, was that Inspector Ffelcher of Scotland Yard, called in by Rowland Cranston, had investigated the anonymous E-mails and discovered the lengths to which the sender had gone to conceal his identity. That was deeply suspicious in itself, and the inspector decided that the threats had to be taken seriously. Given Vanessa's own prominent position, not to speak of her highly placed stepson, he was determined that anything that went wrong would not be down to him. So the huge security operation observed by Hugh had been swung into action.

Hugh and Will's invitation extended to the pre-ceremony cocktail reception, sponsored by Driftwood International, which was being held in a VIP suite at the side of the auditorium. The place was teeming with faces familiar from cinema and television. For someone who was out of the country so much, Will Cloud proved surprisingly adept at identifying them. Like most politicians, Hugh had little time for TV, except when he was on it, and was hopeless at playing the celebrity game. He listened indulgently to Will's running commentary. 'Look, there's Mattison Pick, the composer. Aren't they doing a bit from his latest show at the awards? And that's Mona da Ponte with him. She stars in it, I think. And who's the one over there? Is it not that girl who used to present the *Jolly Roger*? What's her name, Candida something. I had quite a fondness for her when I was young. She's not bad, even now.'

Vanessa was standing receiving guests under a massive sign bearing the Driftwood International logo. Elegantly attired in an azure ball gown that provided a vivid contrast to her red hair, she looked every inch the media mogul. As soon as she spotted them she came over, glass in hand. 'Hey, guys,' she said. 'Didn't anybody give you a drink?' She grabbed two champagne flutes from a passing waitress and thrust them into their hands.

'What about you?' asked Hugh, nodding at Vanessa's orange juice.

'I'm working tonight,' she replied with a grin. 'Gotta keep sober for my big speech.' She turned to Will. 'You must be Rosemary's cousin. Tell me, how's she getting on down under? Hugh never passes on any news.'

Hugh looked at him beseechingly and Will acceded to the unspoken request. 'Just fine,' he said, fixing Vanessa with his most engaging smile, and gearing up the accent again. 'She's a dear sweet girl, and she misses Hugh something rotten.'

'Now, who can I introduce you to?' asked Vanessa, noticing his eyes roaming. 'Have you met Mona da Ponte? She's the star of *Kennedy – the Musical*, which we're going to see an extract from during the show. Mona, come on over here and meet an old friend of mine . . .'

Like the practised hostess she was, Vanessa ushered them together. Mona, who had been standing sipping a fruit juice and chatting to Hilton Starr, put her glass down on the table and shook Will's hand. Vanessa was left facing Hilton and his companion. 'Hello, Hilly,' she said. Hugh looked over with interest to see if the rift he'd witnessed the other day had now been healed.

Evidently it had. Hilton looked pale and fragile, but not as tense as before. He nodded to Hugh, gave Vanessa a double-cheeked kiss in a friendly enough way and, as an afterthought, introduced them both to the tall blonde woman on his arm. She was wearing a long milkmaid-type dress, with chains of beads around her neck and a soupy, wistful expression on her face. 'This is Candida Blitz,' he said somewhat grudgingly. Hugh wondered why she was so familiar before realising that this was the *Jolly Roger* presenter Will had spotted earlier.

'Pleased to meet you,' he said to Candida. 'I used to be a great fan of yours years ago when I was a little boy.' As Candida looked sad, he reddened, wondering if he'd said the wrong thing. 'Of course, you were just starting out then,' he added in an attempt to hide his discomfiture. Then he asked, 'What are you up to nowadays?' which merely seemed to compound the error.

'I'm still doing the *Jolly Roger*,' said Candida disconsolately. 'For now.' Hugh was spared further embarrassment by an announcement over the Tannoy that the evening's entertainment was about to begin. 'Excuse me,' said Candida. 'Must go and collect Zoë.'

Hugh looked around for Vanessa but she had departed to go backstage, so he and Will made their own way into the auditorium. At the entrance, they bumped into Rowland Cranston. 'What's with all the security?' Hugh asked him.

Rowland appeared taken aback. 'Didn't Vanessa tell you? She's had a whole bunch of anonymous death threats about tonight. Probably just some nutter, but we're not running any risks. Half the bloody audience are plainclothes policemen.'

It was the first Hugh had heard of this, and as he followed Will to their seats, he felt distinctly troubled. 'You'd think Vanessa would have consulted me,' he said. 'I could have checked with the Home Office that they were taking it seriously.'

'Not much doubt on that score,' said Will grimly, glancing down an aisle which teemed with size eleven feet struggling to find enough room to put themselves.

As usual, Hugh too had to fold his long body up like a deckchair to fit into the cramped space. Fortunately, he was at the end of a row and was able to stretch out a little. In the next seat, Will made himself comfortable and, as the auditorium filled up, he continued his star-struck monologue like an over-excited child at a pantomime. 'Will you look over there!' he burbled. 'Are those not television cameras?'

Hugh followed his gaze. 'I think it's going out live on BBC1,' he said. At strategic points throughout the theatre, cameras had indeed been placed pointing towards the stage, where the massive scenery from the theatre's current production was only partly obscured by a sign bearing the awards logo. Still easily visible was the much vaunted final set of *Kennedy – the Musical*, featuring the full-size model of the motorcade from the climactic end scene. Downstage was a backcloth showing the Texas Book Depository and upstage a ten-foot model of the Brass Monkey statuette, of which thirty rather smaller editions were waiting behind the scenes to be presented.

Hugh's study of this was interrupted by the abrupt sound of a female voice to his right, talking as if to a child. 'Take your finger out of there this minute,' she said in a babyish voice. 'It's disgusting.' Turning round to find that the woman appeared to be staring straight in their direction, both Hugh and Will looked down guiltily at their hands. But then they realised that the words were being directed not at them, but at the undersized occupant of the seat next to Will. Their two new neighbours must have slipped in from the other end of the row. The woman burst into an infectious giggle, and Hugh recognised her as Hilton Starr's friend, Candida Blitz. 'You didn't think I meant you, did you?' she said. 'I was talking to Zoë here.'

Looking down, for a moment Hugh had the illusion that he was suffering from double vision. Seated next to her, as if in some psychedelic parody of the figure on stage, was a large chimpanzee dressed in a shimmering gold suit. It stared back at him with a deeply interested expression. 'The award organisers invited her along and gave her the costume as a bit of a publicity stunt,' Candida explained. 'She had a photocall in the lobby earlier. She loves imitating anything humans do, specially dressing up. Shake hands with the gentlemen, Zoë.'

Obediently, the animal offered its paw to Hugh and Will. Hugh shook it without much enthusiasm, surreptitiously wiping his hands with his handkerchief afterwards. But Will entered into the spirit of things, smiling animatedly at Candida and stroking Zoë behind the ear, an attention which she appeared to appreciate in no small measure. 'I've always been a huge fan,' he said, exaggerating the Irish lilt yet again, as Hugh had heard him do a million times as part of his chat-up technique. 'Sure, and I am even now. I still watch the *Jolly Roger* whenever I can,' he added, successfully avoiding the trap Hugh had fallen into earlier.

'Do you?' asked Candida with genuine delight. 'I'm ever so pleased. Our ratings always say we do have a lot of adult viewers.'

Further discussion was curtailed as the lights dimmed, and proceedings began in earnest with the arrival on stage of a BBC producer to give a pre-transmission speech. But he had hardly started when Hugh and Will became aware of something moving at their feet. Looking down, they discovered that the chimpanzee was scrabbling around below them and presently it was joined there by Candida.

'Contact lens,' she whispered. 'One's fallen out. But don't worry. Zoë's an expert at finding them.' Sure enough, within seconds Zoë indicated success by jumping up and down and emitting a low screech. She held the tiny piece of plastic delicately between two hairy fingers. 'Shhhhhh,' said all the people around about.

'Useful animal,' said Will.

Candida nodded. 'I can't see a thing without them.'

Oblivious to this little local difficulty, the BBC producer was in full flow. He began with a few tips to the audience on how to behave on air. He pointed out the cameras and asked people not to stare into them directly. Everyone stared into the cameras. He explained that, except for the final presentation to Hilton Starr for a lifetime's achievement in television, none of the winners knew of their awards in advance. 'If you're one of the lucky ones, try to overcome your astonishment at having won,' he said with painful irony. 'Embrace your loved one as rapidly as possible – only one loved one per person, please – and get up to the stage fast. Don't wait for the cameras – we'll catch up with you soon enough.' A red light would flash in front of them to indicate when their time was up and there were dire warnings of what would befall winners if their acceptance speeches overran the allotted two minutes.

It was just as he was about to finish his introduction that the producer was summoned to the side of the stage. There was a whispered consultation with someone out of sight and he returned a moment later looking distressed. 'Ladies and gentlemen, I'm sorry to have to announce that owing to the sudden indisposition of Mona da Ponte, we're going to have to drop the final scene from *Kennedy – the Musical* we had been planning to give you later this evening. I do apologise.'

A wave of disappointment rippled around the audience. *Kennedy*, by the highly successful American composer Mattison Pick, had been unanimously lauded by the critics who had particularly raved about the final assassination scene. The soaring melody of the song 'Ask Not What', sung by Jackie

Kennedy as she climbed blood-sodden from the motorcade, had been an international hit for Mona da Ponte, the actress playing the role, and tickets for the show itself were almost impossible to come by.

Once the hubbub of tutting had died down, the countdown for the start of transmission began. On two huge screens at each side of the Harold Wilson Auditorium, a view of the stage appeared and the orchestra struck up with 'There's No Business Like Show Business'. Finally an unseen presenter announced sonorously: 'From the Royal London Theatre in the heart of London's West End, the BBC is proud to present the annual Press, Radio And Television awards – the Brass Monkeys – and here is your host for the event, Freddie Murray.'

In a cramped room backstage, Inspector Ffelcher of Scotland Yard was supervising last-minute security arrangements with more than a little satisfaction. Normally confined to more routine police work, it was good to be doing something glamorous for a change and he was determined to cover every angle.

He reviewed the strategy one final time. As well as the plainclothes policemen and women planted in the audience, he had brought in a special squad of armed officers, who were due to fan out into the theatre just before Vanessa Driftwood made her presentation. There they would remain until she had left the stage. So even if a determined assassin had succeeded in penetrating the security shield, there was no way he could get anywhere near Vanessa during her speech.

Earlier in the day the entire theatre had been searched from balcony to orchestra pit. Since then, nobody had been permitted entry without a thorough frisking. Policemen were covering every door and window and even the trapdoors beneath the stage had been sealed to prevent anything unexpected from popping up during the show. Apart from the scrapping of the *Kennedy* extract, due, the inspector had been told in confidence, to Mona da Ponte having had 'one – or, knowing her, probably half a dozen – too many' at the pre-show party and now being confined to her dressing room, the ceremony was proceeding according to plan. There was, the inspector was certain, nothing that could possibly go wrong.

He allowed himself a brief respite. Not much to do now until Vanessa went on. Just enough time, perhaps, for another little chat with the attractive production assistant who was sitting at the side of the stage, organising the presenters. He'd been speaking to her earlier and was sure he'd made an impression.

Before opening the door, the inspector withdrew a small mirror from his pocket and carefully examined his hair. Ten years younger, he reflected contentedly. And almost unnoticeable. Even though he'd only had it for two days, his new wig already looked like it had been part of him since conception. Naturally, the lads at the Yard had ribbed him something rotten about it, but then they saw him every day. Anybody who'd never met him before – the production girl, to take one example – would never have suspected.

He looked out into the backstage area but saw with some disappointment that his quarry would be too preoccupied to talk. She was nervously lining up a gaggle of celebrities who were due on stage to announce the winners and present them with their trophies. As each stepped forward, she fed them with an envelope from the carefully ordered pile and handed them one of the statuettes. The awards themselves, she had explained during their earlier conversation, were identical for now; they would be taken away for engraving after the ceremony.

At the front of the queue, a Hollywood great was gasping at a last cigarette in flagrant contravention of London Fire Brigade regulations and the inspector's hapless friend was turning a blind eye. Inspector Ffelcher nodded to her and received in return a distracted grimace. This certainly beat arresting crack addicts down the Tottenham Court Road, he thought happily. Almost worth sending out one of these anonymous death threats himself next time . . .

Hugh sank into a mild stupor as the tedium of the awards ceremony took over. How was it that people found these affairs so fascinating, he wondered, when he could hardly keep awake.

The press awards were first, with interminable categories of reporting and feature writing. Then they moved on to radio: news, current affairs, drama, sport, light entertainment; would the list never end? As the winners each went up to the stage to receive their statuettes, Hugh noticed that their places were immediately reoccupied by special seat-fillers, presumably so that the audience would not look sparse when the cameras next panned in on that spot.

Finally, taking pride of place, came the television awards. Hugh stifled another yawn. Much the same again, but this time with clips from the programmes in question. Some way down were the awards for children's TV, and, as the nominations were read out, Hugh became uncomfortably aware from the screens high above that his image was being beamed out to the watching millions. But for once, he was not the person being targeted. Instead, the camera swooped to his right and a spotlight picked out Candida Blitz. Even from three seats away, he could feel her tense palpably as her name was called out in the category of best children's presenter. From the monitors he observed that she was trying to look nonchalant, but without much success.

There was a drum-roll as the presenter opened the envelope. 'And the winner is . . .' It was not to be Candida's day. 'The winner is . . . Georgie Plover for *The Skunk Show*.' No standby would be needed to fill Candida Blitz's seat tonight. Hugh could feel the disappointment radiating from beside him, her fixed smile on screen serving only to accentuate it, as Georgie Plover, a teenager with impetigo and a Mohican hairstyle, did a war dance in the aisle and dashed up to the stage.

The final awards were for best actor and actress on television. The woman's prize went to Faith Lilly, an ageing thespian who had belatedly won public affection for her portrayal of a psychopathic but loveable mass-murderer with a heart of gold in a soap opera about a women's prison. Her acceptance speech was long and effusive and the red light in front of her had to be flashed on and off dementedly to force her finally to quit the limelight. Then, the award for best actor was presented to a young heart-throb who had scored a hit as a robot in the latest space drama series.

As the items leading up to Vanessa's speech came to a close, Hugh was aware of increasing activity in the theatre. A number of men had slipped discreetly into the auditorium and were spreading out along the side aisles. One glance was enough to confirm Hugh's guess. Each had his hand warily placed inside the flap of his dinner jacket, and was eyeing his assigned segment of the audience with a practised eye, ready to act at the slightest sign of a would-be assassin.

The moment arrived. 'And now,' said the announcer, 'to present the special award for a lifetime's achievement in television, we welcome the chairman and chief executive of Driftwood International, herself a winner of no fewer than six Brass Monkey Awards. Ladies and gentlemen, Mrs Vanessa Driftwood.'

Vanessa entered stage left, and the policemen on the aisles tensed further. Most of the audience had become aware of their presence and were wondering what was up. Vanessa looked composed and confident, though, not like someone facing any kind of threat at all. Nobody could say his stepmother didn't have guts, thought Hugh with some pride. In her hands, she clutched the statuette which she was to present to Hilton Starr.

She began her speech slowly and quietly, thanking the ceremony's organisers for all their hard work. Then she talked for a while about the awards she had once won and the days in the not too distant past when she herself had come from America to become a successful television personality. 'You took me to your hearts,' she said, 'and for that I thank you from the bottom of mine.' There was loud applause and some cheering from the Driftwood employees in the audience. 'And that brings me finally to tonight's main award. When I first came to Britain to pursue my TV career, I worked with many people who have remained dear friends ever since. One of them had been an actor, a disc jockey, and had moved on to television, where he established for himself a very special place in the nation's affections.

'Ladies and gentlemen, you all know who I mean. The organisers of tonight's extravaganza have given me a whole list of nice things to say about this man. But I'm sure that I don't need to tell you what a great guy he is and I hope you won't mind if I depart from the script and say a few impromptu words of my own.'

Theatrically, Vanessa pushed her notes to one side and a hush of anticipation descended on the audience. Hugh wondered if news of Vanessa's impending announcement had got out, or, more likely, been leaked by Vanessa's own PR department.

'You may be aware,' she continued, 'that the co-sponsor of tonight's show, the British Broadcasting Corporation, is facing new competition from other providers of television services, including cable and satellite operators. With apologies to tonight's producer for taking advantage of his hospitality, I am pleased to announce here and now that Driftwood International will not be left behind in this race. On June 9th we will be launching a new satellite station, to be called Popviz, which will be beaming from the *Mistral* satellite direct into households throughout Europe. To receive it, all that's needed is one of our tiny new, and very inexpensive, satellite receivers.' Like a conjuror, she pulled one from her pocket and held it up to the camera. There was a gasp from the audience, not at the sight of the receiver, which was about six inches in diameter and resembled a Swiss cheese, but at Vanessa's sheer chutzpah in making such an announcement live on BBC television.

At the side of the stage, the assistant producer's complexion turned puce. He waved his hands about frantically and stabbed at the button which controlled the podium light. But Vanessa stuck her chin out and ignored him. 'From tomorrow,' she went on, 'these will be on the shelves of thousands of electrical retailers all over the country. And from June, Popviz will be providing an unparalleled line-up of news programmes, current affairs, light entertainment, comedy, and, of course, the latest movies.' She stopped to take a sip from a glass of water. 'Now, you may wonder why I'm using this occasion to tell you about these things,' she continued.

The producer certainly was. 'Get that fucking woman off the stage,' he screeched down his mike into the eardrum of his assistant. But short of bringing the curtain down on her, there was nothing either of them could do.

'I think you will understand the reason in a moment. For at the core of Popviz's commitment to high-quality entertainment will be a new innovative daily chat show called *Livewire*.' The light stopped flashing. The assistant producer had gone off in search of a valium tablet – or, failing that, a noose. Vanessa paused one last time in preparation for her final sprint. 'Such a programme will need as its presenter someone of stature, someone of experience, someone of humour, and someone of ability. But, of course, we couldn't have four presenters.' She allowed the ripple of laughter to die down. 'So we looked for one person with all these qualities and came up with the man to whom I am now about to present this statuette. I am absolutely delighted to announce that he will be joining Popviz as the star, and I use the word advisedly, of *Livewire*. Ladies and gentlemen, I know I don't need to tell you his name, just to say to you: Twinkle Twinkle . . .'

Rather sheepishly, those in the audience old enough to remember it joined in with the other half of the once famous catch-phrase. 'Hilton Starr,' they muttered self-consciously, not quite in unison. It fell rather flat but this did not deter the man himself from coming bounding on to the stage with an ecstatic grin on his face, opening and closing the palms of his hands in simulated twinkling. To polite applause he accepted the award from Vanessa with an effusive show of affection, kissing her on both cheeks, then stood back and, through a series of mimes, invited the audience to give her a round of applause in her own right. This they did graciously, until Vanessa finally retired stage right, to the transparent relief of the assistant producer who had returned to his post suitably sedated.

He was not the only one who was relieved. Backstage, Inspector Ffelcher watched Vanessa leave the podium and took a deep breath. In the distance, he could see Hilton Starr launching into his acceptance speech. He strolled over to the girl in charge of the awards. 'Thank God that's over,' he whispered.

'You can say that again,' she agreed. 'These things make me so nervous anyway, never mind the death threats on top.' She mopped her brow. 'My worst fear is always that I'll get all the envelopes mixed up and Lauren Bacall will end up with the award for most promising newcomer or something. I must have checked the order a hundred times.' She looked down and her face took on a puzzled expression. 'That's odd,' she said, glancing at her list, on which each name had now been meticulously ticked.

'What is?' asked the inspector.

The girl pointed to the back of the table where the statuettes had been arranged. 'There's one left over,' she said. Sure enough, a small Brass Monkey was sitting alone in the corner, looking rather forlorn. 'I could have sworn I counted them all. I had exactly the right number.'

'Perhaps someone didn't turn up?'

'No, they were all there.'

Inspector Ffelcher scratched his chin. 'That *is* peculiar,' he said. 'I wonder—' He stopped and suddenly his face froze and his body went rigid.

All at once, he knew. He knew with a terrible certainty what was about to happen. And he also knew, from somewhere deep within himself, that there was nothing he could do to prevent it. 'No!' he shouted, and started towards the stage where Hilton was in full flow. 'Stop!'

But it was too late.

'Well, that's that,' Hugh had whispered to Will a few moments earlier, as Hilton ploughed through endless thank-yous to people who had helped bring him to greatness. 'Just some crank after all. Gets a kick out of scaring people and wasting police time. What are you doing afterwards? Fancy a quick one in the bar?'

Will nodded. Hilton's speech was evidently about to reach its laborious climax. Hugh and Will gathered their things together and readied their smarting hands for a final burst of applause. On the stage, Hilton held the little brass statuette to his bosom and summoned a tear to his eye. 'In conclusion, ladies and gentlemen,' he emoted, 'I'd just like to say—'

They never did find out what it was he wanted to say. For at that moment an unseen timing device reached its appointed hour. And finally and decisively, it detonated the explosives hidden inside the little statuette clutched so tightly by Hilton Starr.

Compared to the theatrical pyrotechnics of most West End

shows, the ensuing blast was in fact remarkably restrained. Admittedly, the life-size model of the President's motorcade shook and rattled, and for a moment even threatened to roll off the stage and into the audience. But then it settled back harmlessly on its restraints. Likewise, the oversized Brass Monkey behind Hilton tottered a little but quickly regained its equilibrium.

The same, unfortunately, could not be said of Hilton Starr himself. Caught at the epicentre of the explosion, his equilibrium, corporeal and spiritual, had vanished for ever. Later, Candida Blitz would sadly explain to friends how Hilton had just 'gone off' and they would assume this was merely her own coy euphemism for describing death, born of years of presenting children's TV. In fact, she was stating no more than the literal truth. Quite simply, Hilton exploded like a firecracker. And then, without any further ado, his body disintegrated into its component parts as if it were no more than a piece of shoddily assembled DIY furniture.

As the theatre audience looked on goggle-eyed, bits of the diminutive quiz-show host flew off in every direction, splattering the final set of *Kennedy – the Musical* with genuine blood and guts and transforming it into a scene of carnage that was all too gruesomely real.

Meanwhile, in homes around the country, a wider audience of an estimated twenty million viewers sat mesmerised, stunned by the sheer spectacle of the occasion. Appreciatively they drank in every last detail. This was live television at its very best, a heady combination of action and pathos, genuine human interest and sudden violent death.

To all the participants in this spectacle, however – to Will and Hugh in the tenth row of the stalls, to Inspector Ffelcher standing open-mouthed in the wings, to the hundreds in the auditorium and the millions at home – one thing was crystal clear: Hilton Starr, quiz-show host extraordinaire, had finally made his very last comeback. From now on he would twinkle no longer, except perhaps in some far-off constellation on the other side of Kingdom Come.

Chapter 18

Zoë wore black for the funeral. Candida Blitz insisted the chimpanzee be allowed to attend and ordered her a custom-made suit for the occasion. 'Hilly was ever so fond of Zoë,' she sniffed dolefully. 'He would have wanted her there.'

Indeed, it would have been pretty odd if she hadn't been, because just about every other well-known face from the world of entertainment was present. Hilton Starr's funeral was a showbusiness spectacular, the media event of the season, and not to be seen at it would have been unthinkable. Hilton's career may have long since peaked and faded away in life, but in death he was a superstar. Nothing had become him so much as the manner of his going, that was the general consensus.

Zoë behaved herself impeccably throughout the service, standing at the front with Candida and holding on to her hand like a child, even letting out tiny sympathetic screeches when she saw the tears streaming down her face. 'I just can't see why anyone should want to do that to poor Hilly,' Candida sobbed. 'He never hurt anyone in his life.'

Inspector Ffelcher, who was standing at the back next to

Hugh Driftwood and Will Cloud, had a fairly good idea why Hilton had been killed, however. 'Clear as the nose on your face, sir,' he whispered to Hugh. He looked around to see if any of the press had spotted him hobnobbing with the Cabinet minister, but disappointingly the cameras were focused elsewhere. 'I'm afraid that bomb was meant for your stepmother, no doubt about it. If that scene from *Kennedy* hadn't been cancelled, Mrs Driftwood would have been on stage five minutes later than she was, and it would have been her holding that statuette when it went off instead of Mr Starr.'

Hugh felt the bile rise in his throat at the thought. 'But why?' he said. 'I mean I know Vanessa's made some enemies – who doesn't in business – but to do something like this . . .' His voice tailed off. It was too awful to contemplate.

'There are some very sick people out there,' said the inspector sententiously. They were buffeted by a sudden gust of wind and he grabbed at his head. 'And it's my job to find whoever's responsible,' he continued once his wig had been secured. 'I'll get him, I guarantee you of that. But in the meantime, it would be helpful if you'd impress on Mrs Driftwood the need to take extreme care. We've given her a twenty-four-hour armed guard, but I can see that she's a headstrong woman – begging your pardon, sir – and not used to doing what she's told.'

'I'll do my best,' said Hugh, without much hope. 'But even now she won't believe that someone's really out to harm her. She seems to think it's all some dreadful coincidence.'

'Well, at least she saw sense about not coming here,' said the inspector, checking the crowd suspiciously. 'Far too open a space. Murderer could well be in the crowd. They often like to go to their victim's funerals, you know,' he added with a ghoulish smile.

Hugh didn't know, but he also gazed around the assembled masses. They looked so respectable. It seemed hardly credible that there could be a killer among them, but then it seemed hardly credible that someone would put a lump of Semtex into a brass statuette in order to try and dispose of his stepmother.

'What about the bomb?' he asked the inspector. 'Have you any idea how it got in there?'

'We're working on that one, sir. It was a fairly sophisticated device. Quite carefully put together so it would only get the person holding the award and nobody else. We'll know a lot more when we get the ballistics report. They're still working on it. It was difficult to recover all the pieces, you see, because they were so firmly embedded in the corpse, or what was left of it, and—'

'Thank you . . . ah . . . Inspector,' said Hugh, now feeling distinctly nauseous.

'As you like, sir. But once we've got that report, we should be a lot clearer on how to proceed. And we'll also be looking further into the source of those anonymous E-mails. That might give us a lead or two.'

As the service broke up, Candida Blitz passed close to Hugh and Will, her long blonde hair swaying in the wind. She came over to speak to them, clutching her handkerchief. 'I wanted to thank you both,' she said tearfully, 'for your kindness on the night of the . . . of the . . . of poor Hilly's death. I don't know what I'd have done without you.' In the panic which had followed the explosion, they had helped get her and Zoë safely out of the theatre and had warded off the mass of reporters that had materialised with startling speed. She was in a highly distressed state, and Hugh had insisted she be allowed to get a good night's sleep before the inevitable police interviews. He had even sent her home in his official car, getting Will to go along to comfort her on the ride, while he stayed behind to find out exactly what had happened.

'Honestly,' said Will, stepping forward before Hugh could say anything. 'It was the least I . . . we could do. And if there's anything else, anything else at all . . .' He reached into his pocket, removed a slip of paper on which he had scribbled something in advance and handed it to her. 'I never got the chance to give you my number the other night,' he said. 'Please don't hesitate to get in touch.'

Candida took it with a mournful smile, and moved on miserably. 'Steady on, Will,' whispered Hugh. 'She's only just been bereaved, for God's sake.'

'I wouldn't like to have a mind like yours, indeed I would not,' said Will coldly. 'It was a perfectly genuine offer. No ulterior motive whatsoever. Sure, I feel for the poor girl.'

'I'm glad to hear it,' said Hugh, unconvinced. He knew Will too well.

Chapter 19

It had been a hard week and Alistair Sloach was feeling distinctly troubled. The Home Secretary's lot was not a happy one at the best of times, but recent days had seen three prison riots, a defeat at the European Court of Justice, a couple of deportations and, to top it all, this dreadful bombing at the Brass Monkey Awards. There had been questions in the House, and calls for him to take responsibility for the police's failure and resign.

All these were fairly routine, though, and the least of his worries. No, as he sat one evening later that week distractedly working through his interminable supply of red boxes, it was something quite different that was yet again preoccupying Alistair: namely the apparently unstoppable rise of the new Minister of Environment and Transport, the Rt Hon. Hugh Driftwood MP.

His last bid to sink Hugh having foundered with the unexpected eclipse of the Chancellor and his own thoroughly unwelcome transfer to the Home Office, Alistair realised that he had allowed himself to slip. As anticipated, his new job had proved a nightmare and it had taken him all his time to keep his head above water without worrying about Hugh. And anyway, now that he had moved departments, the original reason for wanting Hugh out of the way – namely the expansion of his own responsibilities – was no longer an issue.

However, to his intense horror, Alistair had found that another, vastly more important, motive had arisen for getting rid of Hugh Driftwood.

The Prime Minister was reeling from all these crises. As Alistair had known perfectly well when he had first chosen to champion Burgins for the leadership, the man was a walking disaster area – weak, panicky and quite incapable of even the most basic decision-making. His remaining time in the job could be numbered in weeks rather than months, so the day of Alistair's elevation was fast approaching.

Or was it? Certainly, Alistair knew he would still be the front-runner. None of the obvious candidates had any credibility compared to him. The new Chancellor, Percy Millbank, was a safe pair of hands – or as safe a pair of hands as you could expect from a doddery septuagenarian – but he was certainly no threat to anyone. Brought out of retirement to fill the gap, he had difficulty enough mounting the steps at Number 11 Downing Street, much less mounting a campaign for the succession.

But what about the less obvious candidates? Of late, disturbing rumours had begun reaching Alistair's ears. There was said to be a groundswell of opinion in the party in favour of moving back towards the centre ground and regaining the youthful vitality so tragically lost at the time of the Millennium disaster. And the name which was being touted around was one which left Alistair beside himself, not just with fury, but with incredulity. That they could even be considering that over-promoted simpleton for the leadership was sheer, unadulterated madness.

None the less, they were. A covert campaign was being orchestrated by someone, somewhere, to raise Hugh Driftwood's profile in the House and before the public, and with very considerable success. You couldn't turn on the blasted television or open a newspaper without seeing that inane face grinning out at you. Driftwood never actually said anything of note, but in the era of the soundbite that hardly mattered. The fact was that he was there and, given enough time, he just might snatch away Alistair's birthright from under his nose.

The very thought made the diminutive Home Secretary's blood sizzle in his veins. He should have sorted Driftwood out once and for all while he'd had the chance. But at that time Hugh had merely been a tiny obstacle in his path; it had not occurred to him for a single moment that Hugh might pose any threat to his real ambition. And now that the man was riding a wave of public popularity it was going to be more difficult to brush him aside.

Brush him aside was what he would do though. And the sooner the better. He had been too easy on him till now. From this moment on, he resolved, he would explore every avenue, leave no stone unturned, to discover Driftwood's Achilles' heel and exploit it come what may.

The following day was one of the Home Secretary's constituency days. Like all other members of the House of Commons, Alistair Sloach had been elected to represent a discrete area of the country, and regardless of how high one rose in office, every MP remained accountable first and foremost to those electors who had sent him or her to parliament in the first place.

As far as Cabinet ministers were concerned, this responsibility was accepted with varying degrees of enthusiasm. Many insisted on fulfilling their constituency obligations as conscientiously as if it were their only job, spending every possible weekend in their 'patches', as parliamentary jargon had it, in order properly to minister to their 'flocks'. Others, particularly those with big majorities, felt that the constant demands of state fully justified their delegating such minor affairs to local minions, and rarely showed their faces in their constituencies at all.

Alistair belonged to the latter school. He had been elected to the Commons by a drab inner-city area which bore constant witness to the failure of successive Home Secretaries of every party to reverse the country's decline into neglect and decay. Never very fond of his constituency in the first place, Alistair now found it a needless distraction from the business of exercising real power, which he could do quite comfortably from the headquarters of the Home Office in Queen Anne's Gate.

For that reason, despite its proximity to the Palace of Westminster, he very rarely visited the borough he represented, relying instead on his excellent constituency agent, Miss Wilks, to field the constant stream of requests, complaints, pleas, abuse, and sometimes carefully wrapped parcels of excrement which flowed into the local party headquarters. On his behalf, Miss Wilks would regularly conduct constituency 'surgeries', opportunities for people to take a question up with their MP in person. 'The minister's been held up at the Home Office,' she would explain, 'and asked me to listen to your problem and give him a full report of it so that he can take the appropriate action.'

Most constituents accepted this quite readily, basking in the reflected glory of having such an important parliamentary representative, and greatly impressed at their own prescience in choosing someone who had risen so high. And indeed their complaints were dealt with efficiently by the polite Miss Wilks, without ever even coming within ten miles of Alistair Sloach himself.

Occasionally, though, Alistair did feel the need to be seen in the constituency, mindful of his majority which, though still more than comfortable, had defied the national trend and dropped off slightly at the last election. The thing to do, he always felt, was to make a splash on the occasions when he was there. Press as much flesh as humanly possible and make sure the local papers were around to photograph him as if he were about the place day in, day out.

This visit to Caustwick had been scheduled some months ago, and for a while Alistair had been tempted to use the aftermath of the recent political crisis as a pretext for cancelling it. On second thoughts, though, given the reason for Matthew Potts's departure, he decided it would be a perfect opportunity to demonstrate his credentials as a faithful husband, both to his constituents and to whichever reporters could be blackmailed into following him around for the day. And to that end, he realised, his wife Margaret must somehow be persuaded to accompany him. He rarely saw her nowadays, as she spent all her time in their house in Berkshire while he lived permanently in the town flat in the Barbican, so he broached this delicate subject with her one evening by telephone.

'What on earth would I want to go there for?' she asked incredulously.

'It is my constituency, dear. Don't you remember when I was first selected you told them how much you loved that area? You said it had a delightfully unstuffy ambience about it.'

'Daddy told me to say that. I think it's a perfectly putrid place.'

'Of course it is, but we have to be seen there sometimes. My majority's slipping. You don't want to start redecorating Downing Street only to find that I get turfed out at the next election, do you?' That should get her, he thought.

He knew perfectly well that Margaret loathed him even more than she loathed the constituency. Her father, as she persistently reminded him, had been a former Prime Minister and twice the man he would ever be. And, she would invariably continue, if he didn't think she was perfectly aware he'd only married her for his own advancement, then he was even stupider than he looked. But Alistair also knew that, as long as there was a chance he might be instrumental in securing her return to Downing Street, she would never seek a divorce. Not that she was remotely fond of the Prime Ministerial residence, of course. In fact, quite the contrary: convinced her childhood had been totally destroyed by her first stay there during her father's administration, and having recently developed a penchant for the brutalist school of interior design, she was now intent on ripping the place to pieces by way of a revenge killing.

Eventually she agreed to go to the constituency. 'Oh, if I must, I'll come down for the day. But I refuse to go to any of those ghastly party meetings. And I want to catch the five fifteen back here.'

'Anything you say, dear. I'll be doing surgery in the evening, in any case. Just join me for lunch and for the opening of the new Karl Marx Mega Shopping Mall in the afternoon. If you catch the eleven thirty train, I'll send the car to pick you up.'

The day proved as depressing in reality as it had appeared in prospect. Alistair spent much of it mediating between his wife and Miss Wilks, who did not get on with one another. By the time they put Margaret into a taxi to catch her train home, open warfare had virtually broken out between them.

'Patronising cow,' muttered Miss Wilks, as the car drew away.

'Sorry?'

'I said, it's ... ah ... surprising how ... how quickly the day's gone by,' said Miss Wilks brightly. 'We see you so rarely, Minister, it's always such a treat.'

She's quite right, she is a patronising cow, thought Alistair to himself as they returned to the constituency office to begin the surgery. And it wasn't even as if her father had been any good as Prime Minister. Alistair's future reign would knock his into a cocked hat, of that he had no doubt.

That evening, there seemed to be an above-average quota of complete crackpots waiting to see him. The first person in line was typical. Superficially quite ordinary, she arrived with two infants in tow to whom Alistair felt it politic to chat and from whom he was forced to accept a generously proffered piece of Blackpool rock. He was still trying to disengage this from his fingers when she slapped a bundle of letters on the desk in front of him.

'What you going to do about them then?' she asked.

'About what?' Alistair replied, puzzled.

'About the Martians, of course.' She looked at him as if he were a backward child, and gestured towards the table. 'It's all in those letters. They've told me they need to use my toilet to launch a take-over of the Earth, and I've only got the one loo. I'm not like some of your toff friends with bathrooms "en sweet".' She pronounced the words with magnificent venom. 'Why can't they use one of yours, tell me that?'

He could not. In the end, the only way of appeasing her was to promise he'd get the PM to consult with the American President to see if a suitable compromise could not be brokered via the inter-planetary hotline to Mars.

'I'm sure the Prime Minister will be able to work something out with him,' he assured her. Knowing the current President, Alistair reflected, he would probably believe every word and launch a pre-emptive nuclear attack on this poor woman's bathroom facilities.

Constituent number two was normal enough. A council house problem. They got a lot of those at surgery and Alistair particularly enjoyed them, because in this area the council was controlled by the opposition and he could truthfully absolve himself from any responsibility. 'That's a local authority issue,

I'm afraid,' he would say, shaking his head sorrowfully. 'Of course, if you voters don't realise that that shower couldn't run a temperature, much less a country, then we at Westminster can't do much about it. Just make sure you don't let them back into government, that's my advice. Naturally, I'll take it up, but I don't hold out much hope.'

And then there was Reg Diggle.

He was number three in the queue, and in comparison to him the Martians' chosen representative on Earth began to look like the epitome of sanity. He came shuffling in, clutching a package close to his chest and began a long, rambling speech, which – like many of the constituents at surgery faced with the terrifying prospect of meeting their MP – he had obviously rehearsed endlessly beforehand. Despite this, it was almost impossible to decipher. Only gradually did an inkling of his story emerge from the string of disjointed mumbles, and Alistair Sloach began to pay more than a little attention.

'Now let me get this absolutely clear,' said the Home Secretary, adopting what he hoped was an encouraging smile. His inability to suffer fools, gladly or otherwise, was legendary in Whitehall, but he had gathered enough to suspect that, in the case of this particular fool, a little suffering might be amply repaid. Unfortunately, Alistair was also renowned for his verbosity and today was to be no exception: 'To recap,' he said, 'you are employed by Driftwood International and you have seen something of a . . . ah . . . scandalous nature which you wish to impart to me concerning my ministerial colleague. Am I correct in that surmise?'

Reg Diggle stared at the features so familiar from the nine o'clock news, which now bore a ferocious grimace, and tried to interpret this. He thought for a while, then his jaw went slack and he goggled back for a moment. 'Eh?' he said eventually, eyeing Miss Wilks with trepidation.

With difficulty, Alistair mustered himself and put the question more simply. But even though Reg seemed to understand this time, he continued to stare firmly at the package in his hands. 'I couldn't . . . that is . . . I wouldn't want to say anything in the presence of a lady,' he said.

His face more contorted by the second, Alistair turned to Miss Wilks. 'I think it might be best if you left us for a few moments, Elizabeth.'

With manifest reluctance, suggesting a prurience Alistair would never have suspected her of, Miss Wilks departed. Alistair shut the door firmly behind her and returned to Reg, his smile more fixed than ever. 'Now . . .' he said.

Finally, Reg managed to gather his wits and laboriously he related his tale.

'Disgusting it was,' he muttered. 'What they were doing together. Filth. No other word for it. I wouldn't even talk about it, and that's the truth, sir, except I was looking at the local paper, terrible rubbish, I don't usually read it, you know, it's just that it's good for finding out what's on the telly, and I saw as how you had a surgery tonight, and I thought, if there's anyone that could do something, quiet like, it would be you, because of you going on about morals in government, and quite right too, I've always felt. So maybe you could just talk to Mr Driftwood, sir, and, like, set him back on the straight and narrow. I mean, with you being his superior in the government and that. I wouldn't want to get him into any trouble or anything, and Mrs Driftwood mustn't hear about this.' He looked over at Alistair helplessly. 'I don't want to cause any fuss, you see.'

At long last, Alistair did see, and, having seen, the government's self-appointed chief moralist was agog to see more. 'Can you describe the nature of these – ah em – disgusting acts?' he asked, trying hard to keep the eagerness from his voice.

'Oh, I couldn't do that, sir,' said Reg. 'But if you'd just watch this video, it's all there.' He handed over the package that he had been holding so tightly. 'It will be all right, won't it, sir? I wouldn't want anyone in the press to get hold of it. The Driftwoods have always been very good to me.'

'Of course it will be all right,' said Alistair, suppressing his mounting excitement. 'I fully understand your concern, and I assure you that you have done exactly the right thing in coming to me. Now, what I suggest is that you leave this tape here and that you go home and forget about this unpleasant incident completely. I shall personally see to it that the Prime Minister has a sharp word with Hugh Driftwood, and that nothing of this sort ever happens again.'

With profuse thanks, Reg Diggle finally departed and Alistair Sloach called Miss Wilks back into the room. 'Elizabeth, my dear,' he said, 'something rather urgent has come up. Would you mind if I left the rest of tonight's surgery to you?'

Why should today be any different? thought Miss Wilks bitterly. But she mumbled, 'Of course, Home Secretary,' and took his place at the desk.

And a few moments later, Alistair Sloach left the building wreathed in smiles and clasping the videotape even more tightly than its previous owner.

Chapter 20

Stevie Cudlick was thoroughly fed up. For weeks now, he had been scrutinising Gilbert Falange's mail by morning and shadowing Hugh Driftwood by night without even a sniff of a scandal. Fortunately, Victor Quistling was doing a tour of his Far East operations and had not called him to account yet, but Stevie saw no prospect of having anything to report on Victor's return. The whole thing was a dead loss.

He resolved to have one last go at trailing Hugh Driftwood before throwing in the towel once and for all. Tonight, he knew, there was to be a three-line whip in the House, after which Hugh would be free for the rest of the evening. Please God, Stevie prayed, don't let him go straight home with those bloody red boxes again. Let the man have a bit of fun, just for once.

At last, his prayers were to be answered. At ten o'clock, Stevie arrived at the Houses of Parliament in his clapped-out Golf and circled Parliament Square repeatedly, not daring to stop in case the police arrested him as a suspected terrorist. At twenty past exactly, the MPs came spilling out of the Members' Entrance like so many remand prisoners on night release. A couple of ministerial Rovers slid smoothly out of the gates, dark glass at the windows, so you couldn't see who was in them. But Stevie knew the registration of Hugh's official car by heart, and was relieved to find that it was not among them. Perhaps he was driving himself tonight – always a promising sign.

Bingo! Out came the now familiar Volvo estate, with Hugh himself at the wheel, all alone. He turned left just before Westminster Bridge and Stevie crunched his gears and took off along the Embankment in hot pursuit. The Golf strained to keep up. He knew he ought to have had the bloody car serviced. It was wheezing like a strangulated hyena. Thank God for traffic lights. Each time it seemed as if Hugh's car was going to leave him far behind, its red brake-lights flashed and it stopped at yet another junction, allowing Stevie to lumber up behind.

But as the Volvo proceeded east towards Docklands, Stevie's heart began to sink again. It looked like Hugh was heading towards the offices of Driftwood International. Not a good sign. He must be going to meet his stepmother, which was no story at all.

Hang on, though. It was at least another mile to the Drift-wood building, but he was slowing down outside a pub. Someone was waiting for him on the pavement. Stevie swerved off and circled a roundabout to avoid approaching too closely. He peered into the darkness. Could it be? Yes! A woman, and a dark-haired, attractive woman at that. You have good taste, Hugh Driftwood, thought Stevie to himself.

Scenarios welled up in his fertile brain. First he dismissed the least enticing: could she be his fiancée? No. Stevie had checked that out and she was away in Australia. A cousin, an old friend, a political contact? Surely not. There could be no reason to meet at such an out-of-the-way spot. Then, the bright end of the spectrum: a prostitute? That would be joy

and rapture unrestrained. But unlikely. She looked a trifle too
sophisticated somehow.

The woman climbed into the car and they kissed. Briefly
and a bit self-consciously, but definitely with passion. So far
so good. The Volvo pulled away, and Stevie tugged heavily at
his steering wheel, slammed the car back into gear and took
off after them.

Blissfully unaware of his pursuer, Hugh tried to quieten his
pounding heart. He was sure it was drowning out the noise of
the engine.

'Where are we going?' he asked nervously. As soon as Ros
had got in, she'd taken command, instructing him to drive due
south across Caustwick Bridge.

'Wait and see,' she said. She gave him further directions
and they sped through the grey streets of south London.
Otherwise neither of them spoke and the tension in the air
became palpable. Hugh was already regretting his decision to
come out with her. It was utter madness. What if he'd been
seen picking her up? His face was not unknown to the public
now – anyone might have spotted him. But the die was cast,
and his libido was already drooling in anticipation of the treat
she had promised.

It was less than a quarter of an hour before they arrived at
their destination. Ros told him to slow down and take a left
turn and Hugh found to his surprise that he was driving into
the empty car park of the recently opened Karl Marx Shopping
Mall in Caustwick.

'Here we are,' said Ros.

'Yes, but what on earth for?' Hugh was totally bewildered.

'I'll show you.'

She had him steer the car into a space at the centre of the
deserted car park. It was unusually warm for the time of year, a
moonless spring night, almost pitch-black. Only the buildings

of the shopping centre were visible, looming up darkly in the middle distance like some concrete mountain range.

Ros opened the door and got out. She was wearing a tight white tee-shirt and a pair of blue Calvin Kleins. But not for very long. In an instant, to Hugh's intense excitement, she had slipped the shirt over her head, revealing, as he had already observed all too well, that she had nothing on underneath. Her firm breasts pointed at him tantalisingly, the nipple rings shimmering in the reflection of the car's feeble courtesy light.

'Come on,' she said. 'Nobody can see.' And, dancing erotically around the car, she took off the remainder of her clothing, piece by piece, until she stood totally and thrillingly naked in front of his driver's window.

Torn between his ingrained sense of caution and a tingling excitement that was almost unbearable, Hugh hesitated. But a look around confirmed she was right. There was no sign of life within a radius of at least half a mile; someone approaching would surely be spotted long before they could get anywhere near. Besides, why would anyone else come here at this time of night? Trembling, Hugh climbed out and stood fully clothed in front of her. He must have remained there, quite still, for fully thirty seconds. Then, tentatively, almost reluctantly, he too began to undress, taking off his suit, shirt and underwear and laying it all carefully out on the car seat.

And then they began.

An hour later, exhausted, they collapsed back in the car, the doors and windows wide open, their bodies clinging to the upholstery with the sweat of their exertions and the warmth of the evening.

Hugh drew a breath. 'That was . . . that was sensational. I've never known anything like it.'

Ros looked back at him coolly. 'Stick around and you'll find I can be even more inspired,' she said. 'When I'm in the mood.'

'Are you ever not?'

She gave that breathless laugh of hers. 'Not very often. You'd be amazed where I've fooled around over the years. And who with . . .'

After what he'd experienced, nothing would have surprised Hugh. 'Try me,' he said, with some curiosity.

'Well,' Ros began reflectively. 'The time aboard Airforce One was quite fun. But not public enough for my taste. I mean no real risk of being discovered, because we were all those miles up, and the secret service men knew better than to interrupt. I wanted to fit something in around the inauguration, but it got vetoed, unfortunately.'

'I'm glad to hear it,' said Hugh faintly.

'Then there was the racing driver. Had quite a cockpit, I can tell you. But I tend to get travel sick when I go around too many bends at a hundred miles an hour with my mouth full.'

'Certainly gives new meaning to having a high-speed blow-out,' said Hugh, fascinated. 'But haven't you ever been caught at it?'

'Not yet,' said Ros cheerfully. 'Had some close shaves, of course. But that just adds to the excitement.' She smiled and, lifting herself nimbly over the gearstick, moved over from the passenger's seat to sit astride him, the metal from her breast jewellery tickling the hairs on his chest. 'One more time?' she asked mischievously.

'I can't,' replied Hugh with regret. 'Battery's completely flat, I'm afraid.'

Ros kissed his forehead. 'That's all right,' she said. 'Save it for June 4th.'

Hugh inhaled sharply. 'The Popviz launch party? You can't still be serious about that!'

'Want a bet?'

'It's insane. I mean, I thought you were joking. I—'

'I meant every word. It'll be sensational. Just think, all

those people sitting around you and nobody will suspect a thing.'

'But . . .'

She placed a finger over his mouth. 'No buts. It's all arranged. I've planned it down to the last detail. There's nothing that can go wrong.'

Hugh knew that there was everything that could go wrong. His career, his reputation, his future. But even as these thoughts coursed through his mind he also knew, with a profound certainty, that he was going to go through with it. The thought filled him with the same exhilarating sense of danger he had experienced during the radio interview a few weeks before.

Ros giggled. 'What happened to the flat battery?' she asked.

'You just activated my automatic re-charge mechanism,' said Hugh shyly.

About three miles north, Stevie Cudlick could have done with one of those. His battered old Golf stood stranded at the side of the road where it had been dragged by some kindly passers-by.

The man from the breakdown service rubbed his forehead with an oily finger. 'You got a right heap of metal there,' he said. 'Difficult to tell which particular problem pushed it over the edge. So many to choose from. Have to tow it into a garage, I'm afraid. Hope you weren't on your way anywhere important.'

Stevie kicked his heels furiously against the kerb. He'd almost had him, he was sure of it. Every journalistic instinct he possessed told him he had come within an inch of landing his quarry once and for all. And he had blown it – this time.

But there would be other chances, he swore to himself. He would make bloody certain there were. From now on, Hugh Driftwood would not be able to break wind without Stevie being there to report on it. And next time he would make sure that nothing got in the way.

'No,' he said, smashing the car bonnet down savagely. 'Nowhere important.'

Chapter 21

That night Alistair Sloach arrived back at his flat in London's Barbican complex still in a state of high excitement, with the videotape carefully concealed under his jacket. To his dismay, he heard someone moving in the kitchen as he turned the key in the lock.

'Oh, it's you,' he said to Margaret, trying to hide his disappointment.

'Why, were you expecting someone else?' his wife asked. Hardly likely that he's having an affair, she thought. To her intense frustration, he hadn't displayed the slightest interest in sex since shortly after their marriage. Anyway, nobody other than her would put up with the jumped-up little prude.

'Of course I wasn't,' he replied irritably. 'I just thought you were going back to the country.'

'Points failure. There wasn't a single train out of Paddington. So I thought I'd stay over and pop into Harrods tomorrow morning.'

Damn, thought Alistair. He wanted desperately to watch that

tape. 'Look, are you going to bed now?' he said. 'It's just that I need to use the video – on my own.'

'A bit of Miss Whiplash and her naughty schoolboys?' she asked with some bitterness. 'I mean I know you're the guardian of the nation's morals, but you don't have to become its chief censor as well.'

'Nothing of the kind. It's . . . ah . . . a private report on the future of the prison service which I need to see before a meeting first thing tomorrow. And it's confidential.'

'Isn't it all, darling? Well, I was going to sit up and read for a while, but frankly the less time I spend in your company the better. So I'll leave you to it. Just try and keep off the bottle for once – if I *have* to spend the night in the same bed as you, I'd prefer you didn't smell like a distillery.' God, she thought as she made her way to the bedroom. Twenty years of being married to that self-righteous buzzard. She must have been out of her mind. And now all that was keeping her there was the prospect of moving back to a cramped flat above a council house in Downing Street. Was it really worth it?

In the living room, Alistair inserted Reg Diggle's cassette in the VCR, poured himself a drink, and settled back.

An hour later, his whisky and soda lying untouched beside him, he was still staring mesmerised at the TV set. The screen had gone blank, the tape long since having reached its conclusion and rewound. But Alistair sat on, oblivious to the hissing sound now coming from the speaker.

The scenes he had just witnessed were beyond belief. They were obscene, disgusting. They were . . . for once, words failed him. How could anyone commit such acts? And this was not just anyone, this was a government minister who, by virtue of his position, was part of Alistair's Moral Millennium Campaign. Not, the Home Secretary thought sourly, that the degenerate had ever given him any support in his crusade. Indeed, in his party conference speech, Hugh Driftwood had gone out of his way to set his face against it. Well, now he knew why. Evidently Hugh was quite an expert when it came to setting faces against . . . well, never mind that. It didn't bear thinking about.

But Alistair did think about it. He couldn't help it. What he had seen twisted around in his mind, churning up a welter of emotions ranging from outrage to hatred and fury and, although he would have died rather than admit it, even a tiny touch of envy. She was attractive, Hugh Driftwood's bit on the side, that much was indisputable.

The other thing that was indisputable was that this tape was potentially more explosive than anything that could fit inside a brass statuette. But the question was: how could Alistair turn it to his advantage? To the Home Secretary, just as to Reg Diggle before him, what to do with the recording posed a dilemma of the first order, and he analysed it with all the skills at his disposal.

The obvious thing, clearly, would be to destroy this appalling thing at once. Hugh Driftwood was a colleague and, whatever their differences, they were fighting for the same cause. If the tape ever got out, not only would it cause a total implosion of Hugh's career, but it would also be hideously embarrassing to the Moral Millennium government itself. Coming on top of the recent spate of revelations, it could easily sound its death knell.

Dispose of the tape immediately then, and perhaps, at some appropriate moment in the future, have a quiet word in Hugh's ear about what had happened, urging a modicum of discretion next time some woman went down on him during a live radio interview. Hugh's gratitude would be unbounded, and Alistair would be owed a useful debt. That was undoubtedly the right and proper course of action, and Alistair Sloach dismissed it without further delay.

If only the tape could be released to the media, he reflected malevolently, it would kill two birds with one stone in the most spectacular way. It would completely demolish Hugh Driftwood's reputation, so disposing of the one major threat to Alistair's succession, and it would produce yet another scandal for the existing PM which would hasten that glorious day when the removal vans trundled up Downing Street.

There was one major difficulty with that strategy, though, which Alistair identified immediately: it would be virtually impossible to make the tape public without implicating himself. He could hardly phone up the BBC and invite them to run it on next week's *Panorama*, enticing though the prospect was. He could send it anonymously to a journalist hostile to the government, but on closer inspection that tactic too was fraught with danger. All it needed was for Reg Diggle to pick up his paper to see what was on the telly that night, discover that his confidence had been betrayed, and then it might be the end of the career not only of Hugh Driftwood but of Alistair J. Sloach as well. No, whatever was done, there must be no trail which might lead some suspicious reporter back to the Home Secretary.

The tape itself, then, could not be used directly; there had to be some other way of exploiting its contents to discredit Hugh. Pensively, Alistair picked up the remote control, rewound the tape and viewed it one more time. The radio interview came to an end and Alistair listened idly to the discussion which followed on the screen. The sound quality was not the best, and he'd been so shocked he hadn't really paid much attention to it the first time around. Hugh, still reeling, was letting the girl do most of the talking.

Didn't he find it exhilarating, she asked, knowing that millions of people had been listening to them without the remotest inkling of what they were up to. It had been amazing, Hugh agreed, in a daze. She pressed him further. Had he ever been turned on like that in his life before? Never, he admitted, goggle-eyed. So, she said, looking at him slyly and sliding the tip of her tongue along her lower lip, how about a repeat performance some time?

A repeat performance? That was it! Alistair sat up straight. He might be powerless to bring them to book this time, but if they were seriously contemplating doing it again ... His hand trembling, he spun the tape back and strained to listen to Hugh's reply. Then he listened to it again. And again. Only when he was certain he had understood every detail of what they were planning did he finally switch off the machine and remove the tape with a triumphant cry. This time, he vowed, he would be prepared. A tip in the right quarters to make sure that a journalist, or even better a photographer, was strategically placed, and the whole episode could be captured for the enlightenment of the British nation in the next morning's papers.

He examined this new plan for any flaws and concluded there were none. Reg Diggle would no doubt read the story – the entire world would read this story – and would realise that his well-meaning efforts and those of the Home Secretary to warn Hugh of just such a catastrophe had been to no avail. Sadly, the culprit had offended once too often, and had been overtaken by the tragic fate which inevitably flowed from a life of evil and debauchery. The plan was foolproof.

Alistair moved purposefully over to his desk and selected a sheet of blank paper, holding it carefully at its corners to avoid leaving prints. One couldn't be too careful. Then he fed it into his old Smith Corona and began to compose:

To whom it may concern,

If you want to be in on the biggest political sex scandal since Profumo, read on.

On June 4th, Driftwood International celebrates the launch of its Popviz Satellite Channel at a dinner at the Grand Britannic Hotel. Be under the banqueting table without fail. Take a flash camera and be prepared to use it. For there you will be able to photograph a man who would be king engaged in an act of the grossest indecency imaginable. This is your chance for the scoop of a lifetime – don't miss it.

There, if that doesn't snare him, nothing will, thought Alistair. He wondered whether he ought to sign it with some sort of nom de plume and pondered for a while. Finally he remembered an alias used by one of his illustrious predecessors in the leaking business and hugged himself with delight. Then, still chuckling at his uncharacteristic flash of wit, he added his new signature at the bottom of the page and searched for his address book. Now who was that noxious chap at the *Flick* who had broken the story about Matthew Potts? Gilbert Falange, wasn't it? Christmas is coming early for you, Gilbert Falange, he thought gleefully.

He would post it somewhere near the House the next day. That way, if they ever tried to track it down via the postmark, the field of suspects would be as wide as Wembley arena.

Chapter 22

Vanessa Driftwood had a problem. Distressing though Hilton Starr's accidental murder had been, life had to go on, and more specifically Popviz had to go on. The launch party on June 4th was fast approaching, to be followed the next Friday by the first night's broadcasting and, with Hilton sadly departed, there was nobody to present *Livewire*, its flagship chat show.

She summoned Rowland Cranston and Dick Tockin, head of the Driftwood satellite operation. 'Well, neither of you wanted Hilly,' she said, 'and now you ain't got him. So who do you suggest?'

'A hard-hitter,' said Dick eagerly. 'To really put us on the map, get us talked about. How about that guy from *Newsnight* . . . or the *World at One* woman?'

'Nope,' said Vanessa with a firm shake of her head. 'Got to be someone soft-centred, at least for the first programme. Don't forget the Prime Minister. We promised him an easy ride, and he'll run a mile if he thinks we're reneging on that.'

'I suppose we could have a series of guest presenters,' said Rowland tentatively. 'Try out a few different styles and see how it goes. That way we can choose the right one to interview the PM without tying our hands.'

This idea met with general approval, but they still couldn't come up with any obvious candidates. Eventually, it was decided to mull it over and bring further suggestions to the next meeting. 'Now what about this launch party?' asked Vanessa. 'Is that all set?'

'Absolutely,' said Dick. 'The banqueting room at the Grand Britannic's been booked for months. Half the world's invited, over six hundred acceptances already.'

'Is the PM coming?'

'No. We asked him of course, but his office said he had a prior engagement. They're going to see if the Home Secretary can stand in for him.'

'Great,' said Vanessa. 'Now, I don't want any slip-ups. Who's responsible for organising it from your end?'

'My secretary, Alexis.'

Vanessa looked at him dubiously. 'Okay, but tell her to liaise with Ros Flato at my office. I want to clear every detail personally.'

Dick Tockin opened his mouth in protest, but apparently thought better of it. 'Okay,' he agreed glumly.

'Good,' said Vanessa, consulting her watch. 'You guys better scram. I got a meeting downstairs then I gotta see a policeman about a bomb.'

Inspector Ffelcher looked into the curiously hypnotic eyes of Ros Flato. 'Mrs Driftwood will be back in a moment,' she said. 'Do take a seat in her office.'

The inspector did as requested, wishing he had a secretary like that. The closest his own came to such an emerald green hue was in her complexion.

He took in his surroundings. Not so much an office, he thought, more like an exquisitely furnished airport terminal.

Vanessa Driftwood certainly didn't stint herself when it came to accommodation. He could have fitted twenty coppers in an area this size. He wandered over to the vast floor-to-ceiling windows and admired the view of the Thames snaking off to the right, with Canary Wharf towering in the distance.

Then he noticed a mirror hanging on the wall behind Vanessa's great oak desk and sidled over to it to check his wig. He still wasn't entirely comfortable with it and tended to worry about slippage. But no, he confirmed happily, it looked spot on. He stood for a moment, making minor adjustments, and his eye was caught by Vanessa's shelf of awards. Five little Brass Monkeys gazed malevolently out at him from among the memorabilia of her former showbusiness career. The inspector picked one up and examined it curiously. Apart from the inscription, *To Vanessa Zipsky, Best Newcomer to Television, 1976*, it was identical to all the others he'd seen on the table backstage at the New London Theatre. Its base was unsealed and inside it was quite hollow. A child's hand could have fitted in the hole without difficulty. It wouldn't have taken more than a few seconds to deposit a bomb in one.

'I'm pretty proud of those little guys,' said Vanessa, coming back into the room. 'Kinda cute, aren't they?'

'Kind of lethal,' said Inspector Ffelcher. 'You'd have to have a pretty sick mind to think of putting explosives into one of these things.'

'Tragic,' Vanessa agreed. 'Poor Hilly. He was one of my oldest friends. Anything I can do to help you find this maniac, you just need to ask.'

'Thank you, Mrs Driftwood,' said the inspector, withdrawing his notebook. 'I'll try not to take up too much of your time but I've got a few more points to check with you today.'

'Sure,' said Vanessa amiably. 'How's the investigation going anyhow?'

'It's slow,' the inspector admitted. 'We know a good deal

more about the bomb itself, but we're not much further forward on how it got into the statuette.' He didn't normally discuss investigations with members of the public but Vanessa hardly fitted into that category. 'We're pretty sure the boobytrapped award was added to the others just before the ceremony. Until then, they were all kept under guard along with the envelopes that held the winners' names, and nobody had access. But once they were laid out on the table backstage, anyone could have got at them.'

'One of the theatre crew?'

The inspector nodded. 'We've questioned all the backstage staff, of course. Without any success so far. But we'll keep at it. If any of them was involved, eventually they'll let something slip. Meantime, if I could just go through the events of the evening again with you, Mrs Driftwood. We often find people can remember useful details the second time around that didn't occur to them initially.'

'Fine,' said Vanessa, sitting back meditatively. 'I didn't arrive at the theatre till about six. Had to host the reception before the show.'

The inspector took a plan of the theatre from his case and carefully unfolded it on her desk. 'That took place here, didn't it?' He pointed to the reception suite off the main auditorium.

'Right,' said Vanessa. 'As the sponsor, Driftwood International had use of that room for client entertainment. Oh, and they also gave me access to the dressing area next door. That was where I freshened up first, then I went straight through this interconnecting door into the reception.'

'And who attended that?'

'I'll get my secretary to give you a copy of the full list if you want,' said Vanessa, making a note on a pad. 'But apart from our corporate guests, it was mostly the show's celebrity presenters and a few nominees. Plus, of course, some of the special performers; I guess it was there that Mona da Ponte had one too many and got soused.'

'Was she the actress who plays Jackie Kennedy?' said the inspector with interest.

'Yeah. She's got a reputation as a lush, apparently, but it's pretty unusual for her to get so tanked up that she couldn't go on. If she had, then the ceremony would have run to time and the bomb would have got me instead of Hilly like it was meant to.' She shrugged philosophically. 'Life's weird. I guess that award just had Hilton's name on it.'

'No,' said Inspector Ffelcher. 'The inscription isn't added until—' He broke off and smiled wanly. 'Oh, I see what you mean. Anyway, we believe that the most likely opportunity for the bomb to have been placed with the others was during your reception. Is there any way someone could have slipped out, say, and gone around to the side of the stage with the fake statuette?'

'Definitely,' said Vanessa, running a hand through her hair. 'There were a load of people there. Nobody would have noticed.'

'But you weren't aware of anyone leaving early?'

Vanessa cast her mind back. 'There was so much going on. People were coming in and out all the time. As the hostess, I was probably the only one who stayed put throughout. Rowland Cranston, my number two, was liaising with the Brass Monkey organisers, so he did all my running around for me.'

The inspector nodded. 'I've already talked to him. What about after you left the reception?'

'I went straight into the auditorium,' said Vanessa. 'They'd given me a seat on an aisle at the front so I could get backstage quickly at the end to do my shtick and present Hilton with his award.'

'There was no interval, then?'

'Nope. Because it went out live on TV they ran it straight

through. So I sat still till they called out the award to the best actress. That was my cue to go through this door' – she pointed on the plan – 'which took me to the side of the stage. Hilly was there too. Because his was a formal presentation that had been announced in advance, he came on from the wings, unlike the other winners. So while we were waiting, he and I talked a bit. We go – went – back a long way together, you know. He seemed very nervous. I guess it was some time since he'd been before a big audience. I tried to calm him down, then my name was announced, some girl stuck the statuette in my hands and I went on.'

'Ah,' said the inspector, writing furiously in his notebook while surreptitiously trying to scratch an itch where the wig was rubbing on the nape of his neck. 'Now please think carefully here. Did you notice anyone meddling with the Brass Monkeys, or anything else odd happening – anything at all – while you were in the wings?'

Vanessa considered. 'I don't think so,' she said at length. 'Of course, I don't really have much to compare it with. Sure, I'd been at the ceremony before when I won my own awards, but that was years ago. And then I was in the audience the whole time, never backstage.'

'What about the statuette? Did it feel perfectly normal to you?'

'I didn't spot it was any heavier for having a bomb inside, if that's what you mean,' said Vanessa, with a shudder. For the first time, she appeared distressed. She looked at the inspector with something approaching anguish. 'I've kind of put it out of my mind, but the thought that . . .' Her voice tailed off.

'Of course,' said the inspector sympathetically. 'Let's move on. Just a few final questions about possible motives, then we can wind up for today.'

'Sure thing,' said Vanessa, fighting visibly to regain her composure. 'Shoot.'

'Is there anyone who could have had a grudge against you?'

She gave her snorting laugh. 'I could count on the fingers of one hand the number of people who *don't* have a grudge against me, Inspector. This is a multinational company. It may be a cliché, but you don't get to sit in this seat without making a few enemies. Even as far afield as India, it seems.'

'India?'

'You should know better than me. That's where the anonymous E-mails came from, didn't they?'

'Ah,' said Inspector Ffelcher. 'I'm afraid that was a bit of a dead end – literally.' He consulted his notes. 'They came from India, right enough, but only because some fellow in Bombay was remailing them from there. Runs an anonymous service for Internet users. Or used to run, I should say. Not any more. When we got the Indian police to check it out, they discovered he'd been killed in a car accident the day before. Sad, really. His computers were programmed to delete all records immediately after they'd gone out, so he was the only person who might have given us a clue about the identity of the sender.'

'Can't you even establish which country they came from?' Vanessa asked incredulously.

'Unfortunately not.'

'Well, I guess you've got your work cut out for you,' Vanessa concluded. She checked the time. 'Now is there anything else you need to ask me? I've got a kinda busy morning.'

'I think that's it for now, Mrs Driftwood,' said the policeman, getting up. 'Thanks for your co-operation. We'll be keeping the armed guard around you for the meantime.'

Vanessa pulled a face. 'You really think that's necessary?'

'I certainly do. Whoever we're dealing with has killed and may try again.'

'Poor Hilly,' said Vanessa as the inspector prepared to leave. 'He never had much luck in life.'

'It's his girlfriend I feel most sorry for,' the inspector said conversationally. 'Miss Blitz.'

'The girl from children's TV?' asked Vanessa. 'Taking it hard, is she?'

'I'm afraid so. I had her in for an interview the other day and she was in a dreadful state. She and Starr were obviously very close, and she seems pretty lost without him. And as if that wasn't enough, it seems she's been sacked from her TV job. Apparently her ratings were down and when she didn't win the award, it was the final straw.'

'Is that a fact?' asked Vanessa. 'That's real bad luck. You'd think they'd at least have given her a reprieve under the circumstances.' She stared thoughtfully at her desk.

'Dog-eat-dog world, television,' said the inspector. 'I don't suppose I have to tell *you* that. Well, thanks once more for your time. I hope I won't have to trouble you again, Mrs Driftwood.'

Candida Blitz had indeed taken it badly. Apart from her visit to Inspector Ffelcher, she had not left the house since Hilton's murder and was spending all her time in the kitchen, living on nothing but Zoë's nuts and bananas and resorting to increasingly morose monologues with the chimpanzee about the nature of life.

Even Zoë was feeling the strain. Unable to maintain her usual expression of rapt concentration, she had taken to staring out of the window and scratching herself irritably whenever Candida launched into yet another diatribe.

This pattern was interrupted only by constant telephone calls and occasionally even knocks on the door from journalists. The media had latched on to Hilton's murder in a big way. Quite apart from his celebrity status, the manner of his going had shocked everyone, and the fact that twenty million viewers suffering from post-traumatic stress syndrome had taken out a class action against the BBC was news in itself.

Despite her dejected state, Candida had at first been unremittingly polite to any callers, but after a few days her patience wore thin. Eventually, faced with yet another persistent reporter from the *Flick*, she dredged her sparse reservoir of invective for something that might fit the bill. 'Bog off,' she shouted through the letterbox. 'Bog off or I'll set my monkey on you.' This bizarre threat had the desired effect, but more because of the patently genuine anguish in her voice than the fear of being mauled by an angry chimpanzee.

One resourceful individual had even tried to gain access to the house by pretending to be a plainclothes policeman. Candida let him into the living room and was about to show him up to Hilton's study where he seemed intent on looking for some papers, when, by a fortunate coincidence, Inspector Ffelcher himself telephoned. 'Oh,' said Candida. 'That's funny. I've got your detective here – what did you say your name was?' She looked up, just in time to see the man dashing down the front path and from then on she kept her door on the chain and demanded identification from everyone including the milkman.

One morning when she was at the depths of her despair the phone rang for the fifth time in as many minutes and she picked it up tearfully. 'Leave me alone,' she screamed. 'Please, please, leave me alone.'

'Certainly I will, if that's what you want,' said a vaguely familiar voice with a pleasantly lilting Irish accent. 'I just thought . . .'

'Who is that?' asked Candida.

'It's Will. Will Cloud. I doubt you'd remember me but—'

'Certainly I remember,' said Candida, full of remorse. 'You were ever so kind to me after the . . . after Hilton's accident. I'm terribly sorry, I didn't mean to shout before. I thought you were another of these beastly press people.'

'Now, I was wondering to myself how you were getting on.'

'I'm managing,' Candida gulped unconvincingly.

'Listen,' said Will. 'What are you doing today? I mean I wouldn't want to be forward or anything . . . but why don't you come out and have a wee bite of lunch with me.'

The thought of going anywhere filled Candida with panic. 'I couldn't,' she said. 'It's very kind of you but honestly, I . . . I've got so much to do. And anyway . . .' She looked around in search of any excuse and found one in the sleepy figure by the window. 'I can't leave Zoë alone. She got a dreadful shock when the bomb went off and she hasn't been the same since.'

'Well, bring the poor oul' soul along! I bet she could do with an outing too.'

'There aren't any restaurants that allow her in,' Candida objected.

'Sure, I bet you I can find one,' Will replied with certainty. 'Tell you what, if I can, will you come out with me? Go on!'

'Okay,' Candida finally agreed.

He rang back five minutes later to tell her he'd made a reservation at the Greasepot in Soho. 'Marcel, the owner, is a great fella and a good pal of mine,' he added. 'Said Zoë's table manners had to be better than fifty per cent of his normal clients.' That made Candida giggle and she gave in, arranging to meet him inside at one o'clock. Now that it was fixed, she was rather looking forward to seeing Will again.

She'd been to the Greasepot before. It was a relatively new restaurant, presided over by a French master chef who had studied under most of the top names, but had sought to open something a little out of the ordinary. His concept of a faux-plebeian lorry drivers' café had been a big hit with the chattering classes, ever eager for a new culinary novelty. They'd rolled up in their droves to enjoy exquisitely crafted chip butties made from imported Mongolian flatbreads and bacon and free-range eggs fried in unimpeachably virgin olive oil. The atmosphere was marred only occasionally by the arrival of a genuine lorry driver, who invariably disappeared in a faint on being handed an artfully chipped mug brimming with Lapsang Souchong or on being shown the menu – a brown paper bag on which the over-inflated prices had been painstakingly scrawled in pencil.

Candida and Zoë arrived at Old Compton Street just before one. There was no sign of Will, but Marcel greeted them like long-lost friends. 'Ah, Madame, et . . . Mademoiselle, welcome. Mr Cloud told me to expect you. Perhaps a little refreshment for madame and her . . . ah . . . delightful companion while you are waiting?' He showed them to a corner table and arranged a drink for Candida and a banana for Zoë.

As the chimp settled down contentedly at her feet, Candida glanced around. Anyone who was anyone seemed to be eating here today. In a discreet corner at the back, Candida recognised the ex-Chancellor, Matthew Potts, consorting smugly with some City types. She remembered reading somewhere that he had now been appointed chairman of a minor merchant bank. And at the table behind him she spotted Mattison Pick, the American composer of *Kennedy – the Musical*, finishing a pre-matinée snack with Mona da Ponte, his leading lady, who looked unusually sober. As well as being a Jackie Kennedy lookalike with a fine singing voice, she played the friendly cockney prostitute in a TV soap opera and was attracting much attention from the other diners.

Candida knew her slightly and nodded a greeting. To her surprise, Mona got up and came over. 'Candida, darling, I was so sorry about Hilton,' she simpered. 'Such a loss to the profession.' Candida murmured her thanks. 'I do hope they catch the . . . the *monster* who was responsible,' the actress continued. 'I know it's nothing compared to what you've been through, but I'm still recovering from whatever it was he gave me.'

'Gave you?' said Candida, puzzled.

'Didn't you hear, darling? Someone poisoned my drink at the awards. I was ill for days.'

This was the most novel excuse for a bit of over-indulgence that Candida had come across in ages. 'How dreadful,' she said doubtfully.

'What was worse, nobody believed me at first. I mean I know I enjoy the odd tipple, but, darling, *never*, *never*, before a performance. Fortunately I *insisted* they took a blood sample at the time and when they analysed it, I was quite right. I'd been slipped a Mickey Finn.'

'But why would anyone want to do that?' asked Candida.

'Heaven knows. I suppose it was another attempt to bump off Vanessa, and they put it in the wrong glass,' said Mona. 'There were so many drinks doing the rounds that night, it would have been easy to get them confused. Apparently Vanessa had orange juice, the same as me. God, what a mistake. I swear I'll never touch the bloody stuff again.'

They were interrupted by the arrival of Will Cloud. Candida recognised him immediately. Even though the circumstances of their first meeting had been traumatic for her, she had taken to the attractive Irishman with that tousled mop of dark hair and those impish blue eyes. He smiled a greeting to her and she introduced him to Mona da Ponte, who shook his hand appreciatively, even though she evidently did not remember that she had met him once before. Then he tickled Zoë under the chin. 'Wow!' he said to Candida once Mona had returned to her table. 'Don't you know a lot of famous people now!'

'Just in passing,' said Candida modestly. 'Mona and I sometimes bump into each other at the BBC canteen.' She gulped. 'Or at least, we used to.' Her thoughts returned morosely to the termination of her television career and she changed the subject. 'She told me something peculiar, though.' And as Marcel brought them the menus, Candida related what she'd just heard about the poisoned drink.

Will listened with interest. 'Now, isn't that an odd thing,' he said, stroking his chin pensively. 'I can't see why ... Oh, well, never mind.' He picked up his menu. 'Now what can I tempt you with?'

Candida studied the choice but none of the rugged-looking dishes appealed. 'I've been a bit off my food recently,' she said apologetically. 'I'll just have a glass of mineral water or something.'

'Nonsense,' said Will. He called Marcel over. 'Do you think you could come up with something a bit more delicate than black pudding for Miss Blitz, even if it is made from baby pigs suckled in Provence?' he asked.

'*Mais certainement*,' said the chef sympathetically, evidently jumping at the chance to do some real cooking for a change. '*Pas de problème*. For madame, how about a tiny soufflé to start with, and then maybe I could whip togezzer some of my special *Nonnettes de poulet François Mitterrand?* With a *soupçon* of *salade*, per'aps?' As Candida nodded her agreement, Marcel put a finger to his lips conspiratorially. 'But promise me you'll tell nobody! Otherwise they'll all be wanting it.'

'Now,' said Will after Marcel had bustled off. 'If you feel up to it, why don't you go over everything that's been happening. It'll do you good to get it off your chest.'

Gratefully, Candida began relating her troubles, right back to the moment when she had failed to win the award for best children's presenter. 'I know that seems like nothing compared to what happened after,' she said. 'But next to Hilly and Zoë, my job meant everything to me. The BBC didn't really fire me in the end. Once Hilton was murdered, I couldn't bear the thought that they might just keep me on for a few months out of sympathy. So the next day I rang up and quit.' She bit her lower lip. 'I suppose that was a bit silly. And now,' she hiccuped sadly, 'now I've got nothing – no Hilton, no job, nothing.' A tear rolled silently down her face and dripped into the soufflé which Marcel had just placed in front of her.

'There, there,' said Will soothingly, digging into his pocket and extracting a crumpled handkerchief. 'Would you look at that poor little face? Hush yourself, now.' He reached over and dabbed her cheek, then took her hand in his and squeezed it gently. 'Something will turn up, I promise you.'

Gazing into his eyes, Candida felt better already. She sniffed and looked around self-consciously to see if anyone else had noticed her distress. Fortunately the other diners were all too preoccupied with themselves. 'Now that you come to mention it, something did turn up this morning,' she said, brightening. 'Just after you phoned, I got a very odd call from my agent to say that Vanessa Driftwood wanted to see me. What in the world can that be about?'

'I've no idea,' said Will, intrigued. 'Maybe to talk to you about the murder?'

'That's exactly what I thought at first, but in that case, why not get in touch with me direct?'

They both agreed it was inexplicable. 'Oh, well,' said Candida. 'I've got a meeting with her this afternoon, so I'll find out then. It's funny, until you phoned, I'd hardly been out of the house. And now I've got two appointments in one day. Perhaps you bring me luck.'

Chapter 24

Stevie Cudlick looked down at the letter he was holding in a trembling hand and reread it for the umpteenth time. At last, he thought triumphantly. At last, after all these months of trawling through what had to be the most boring in-tray in the world, he had struck gold.

'*The biggest political sex scandal since Profumo*', the note said. That certainly sounded promising. But it was the last sentence which really caught Stevie's imagination. '*A man who would be king engaged in an act of the grossest indecency imaginable.*' The prospect made Stevie's heart miss a beat.

The grossest act of indecency might refer to anyone, since at least half of the Cabinet, not to mention the Shadow Cabinet, were probably engaged in any number of such acts at any one time. But '*a man who would be king*' – now that was much more specific. And as far as Stevie could work out, there were only two people who could fit that description. The most likely candidate, of course, was Alistair Sloach, the Home Secretary, but it could hardly be him that the writer was referring to. Whatever anyone said about Sloach, the one thing he was not was a pervert and looking at himself in the mirror in the morning was just about the grossest act of indecency he was ever likely to commit.

So that left only one alternative. One wonderful, mouth-watering, breathtaking, finger-tingling alternative. Hugh Driftwood! Could it really be? Could it really be that his prey was about to be delivered into his hands in so spectacular a manner? Stevie offered up a silent prayer. He had never believed in fairy godmothers up until now, but he was prepared to start today if only this tip-off had a scintilla of truth in it.

He glanced at the letter one more time to see if it held any clue to the identity of his mysterious benefactor. But there was very little to go on. All Gilbert Falange's anonymous correspondent had provided was a two-word nom de plume, typed at the bottom of the page. Hmm. It sounded familiar though. Wait a sec. Something was coming back to him. Wasn't that the name the mole in the Watergate scandal had used? It was. Stevie sniffed to himself disparagingly. Not very original, he thought, this new 'Deep Throat'.

There wasn't a second to waste. June 4th was only weeks away and Stevie's first priority must be to secure himself a ticket to the Driftwood satellite launch. But that was easier said than done. First, there was the traditional enmity between Victor Quistling's papers and the Driftwood Organisation. They were about as likely to send him an invitation to the party as the Montagus were to invite the Capulets round for a knees-up. Then, too, there was the security situation. Since the attempt on Vanessa's life at the Brass Monkey Awards, Stevie knew that the police presence around all Driftwood events had been tightened and getting into that hotel on the night of the party would be virtually impossible without a fully accredited invitation.

Fortunately, Stevie was not without his own contacts. He picked up the telephone and dialled the number of the *Pop*, where, within a few seconds, he was put through to an old chum.

'Hey, Pete. Stevie Cudlick at the *Flick*. How's it going over there?'

'Pretty rotten, mate, to tell you the truth. You not found a job for me yet?'

'You still looking?'

'You bet. What you got in mind?'

'Nothing right now, but I did get a tip-off that a spot might be coming up on the newsdesk in the next few weeks. Want me to keep you posted?'

'I'd be grateful.'

'I'll do that then. Talking of which, you know what they say about one good turn?'

'Aha,' said Pete resignedly. 'I thought there had to be a catch. What can I do for you?'

'This big shindig you lot are throwing at the Grand Britannic to launch your satellite station. I want in on it.'

'You're going to report on that for the *Flick*? You kidding? Victor Quistling'll skin you alive if you start giving free publicity to Vanessa.'

'Let me worry about that. D'you think you can wangle me an invitation?'

'I'll try my best. Give me half an hour and I'll call you back.'

At the very least, Stevie reflected as he replaced the receiver, he would get a good meal out of it. And maybe that would be all, for these sorts of tip-offs were notoriously unreliable. But Gilbert hadn't done too badly out of them, and Stevie had a hunch about this one. Anyway, he'd make sure he had his sturdy old Nikon with him, as instructed, and after that he'd trust to fate.

'Let's just see that it really works,' said the man suspiciously. 'Can't take any chances tonight.'

Stevie demonstrated the Nikon's bona fides to his satisfaction and proceeded into the reception area. He glanced around uneasily. His face was not unknown in the government, as he had assisted Gilbert Falange on exposing more than a few of its members in recent years, and he was nervous of being spotted by someone. As an extra precaution, he had made the ultimate sacrifice the night before. With the deepest regret he had taken a pair of scissors to his beloved ponytail, and now, suitably spruced up, he was almost unidentifiable. This had better be worth it, he thought to himself.

Once inside, he mingled as unobtrusively as possible with the other guests. Even he was impressed at the array of luminaries. He knew most of them by sight and some of them to speak to, and despite the absence of his hairy appendage, he was still concerned he might be recognised.

His fears were not unfounded. The former Industry Minister, Roger Breech, whom he had helped bring to his knees only months before, made a beeline for him. To Stevie's surprise, though, he started chatting quite amicably. 'Hello there, old chap, how are you?' he asked, sincerity oozing from his every syllable, even as his puzzled expression posed the quite different question, Where do I know you from?

'Oh, absolutely fine,' said Stevie with an ingratiating smile. 'I was so sorry to hear about your ... ah ... trouble. You've moved on now, I understand.'

'Yes, tragic really. I felt I had so much more to make ... I mean to offer ... in government.'

'It was the press that really did for you, wasn't it?' Stevie couldn't resist saying. 'Quite appalling really, what those vermin get up to.'

'Absolutely. Ruined my whole political career over a bit of innocuous share-dealing. Still, that's life, and, of course, now

that I'm no longer in government, I've managed to spend a bit more time with my family. Oh, and I've been able to spread my wings in other ways, too. Luckily enough, the company whose shares I had ... ah ... invested in, took me on to their board. They reckoned it was the least they could do, after all that free publicity. So things could have been worse.' He broke off, for he had spotted someone more interesting in the background. 'I say, isn't that Mona da Ponte over there? Did you see her in *Kennedy*? Fabulous! Do excuse me, old chap, must just go and say hello.'

He departed, still wearing a perplexed look. Stevie decided that discretion was the better part of valour, and, before he could be noticed by anyone with a better memory for faces, he repaired down the stairs to the banqueting room for an advance reconnaissance of tonight's field of operation.

'Under the banqueting table', the note had said. That was all very well, but which bloody table? His correspondent really might have been a bit more specific. There seemed to be hundreds of circular tables dotted throughout the room, and it would have needed an army of reporters to cover them all. However, a glance at the seating plan reassured him. It was evident that all the bigwigs in the audience would be seated not on the circular tables ranged around the waterfall but along the large U-shaped top table which skirted three sides of the hall. This was the most likely, and indeed the most capacious, venue for any shenanigans.

Stevie checked his own name. Table 39. Shit, he cursed inwardly. It was right in the middle. He would have to eat at his allotted place and, somehow, immediately after the meal – when the note had said the incident would occur – he would invent an excuse to slip away. Then all he needed was to find an entry route to the top table's nether regions and to roam around below, looking for something untoward.

Not for the first time in his journalistic career, it occurred to

Stevie what an absurd way this was of earning a living. But that thought didn't last long. If there was any truth in this tip-off at all, then his efforts would be amply repaid. And Stevie had done stranger things for his calling in the past.

The room began to fill up. Dinner had been announced and the guests were slowly filing through from the reception area. Stevie took his seat.

Hugh Driftwood was approaching the launch party with a sense of heightened sexual expectation. For the past week he had found it difficult to concentrate on work at all as he contemplated the adventure in store, with all its attendant risks. Several times he had determined anew to call the whole thing off, and had picked up the phone to tell Ros, only to replace it again without dialling.

And by the night of the banquet his excitement had reached fever pitch. As he made his way down to dinner, he could see Ros in the middle distance, discussing final details with the hotel management, and every so often, while he posed for photographs with Vanessa and chatted to the other guests, he caught tantalising glimpses of her stunning body swerving in and out of the crowds.

As befitted a government minister, not to mention a senior member of the Driftwood family, Hugh had been seated at the top table. But in the interests of sociability, he was some distance from Vanessa, who was in the middle beside the dais from which she was to make her speech. At the opposite end, he could see Will and Candida and he gave them a distracted wave. Then he sat down and looked around.

His partner for the evening, he discovered, was to be Faith Lilly, the ageing star of the prison soap opera who had taken so long to accept her award at the Brass Monkeys ceremony a few months before. No doubt she had been specially selected by Ros Flato as a suitably doddery neighbour, less likely to be

suspicious when events began taking their course under the table near her.

'Hello, I'm Hugh Driftwood,' said Hugh sociably, 'I *am* pleased to meet you.'

'Hello, dear,' replied Faith Lilly. She held out her hand vaguely. She had evidently never heard of him in her life.

'I'm the most enormous fan of your work,' said Hugh. He rarely had time to watch television and racked his brain for the name of the prison programme she starred in. It came to him just in time. 'I do love *Loose Screws*,' he said.

She batted two heavily mascaraed eyelashes back at him. 'I'm glad you like it, darling. We have such fun making it.'

'I was in the audience when you won your award for best actress last month.'

'Were you really? These award shows are such a bore, aren't they? But the fans seem to enjoy them, so one just has to grin and bear it.'

'Tell me,' said Hugh, 'are you going to be on Popviz as well?'

'Yes, I'm presenting the religious affairs show, *Faithlift*,' she said.

'Are you really? It must be so comforting to hold such deep religious beliefs,' he said.

'Not really,' she snapped back. 'I'm an atheist. Can't be doing with religion myself. But there's not a lot of work around at the moment. So needs must when the devil drives.'

At the other end of the top table, Will and Candida had been seated next to the Home Secretary, Alistair Sloach. For once, he was accompanied by his wife, the vitriolic Margaret, who had decided that this star-studded event was well worth the journey to London. But, dismayed at the prospect of an entire evening in the company of her husband, she had taken the precaution of slipping in beforehand and altering the place cards, so that

Alistair was three seats away from her next to Candida Blitz, while she was on the other side of the couple, in between Will Cloud and an attractive young Popviz weatherman.

Alistair, for his part, was no less alarmed at the thought of spending any time with his wife. As a consequence of this and his suppressed excitement at Hugh Driftwood's impending doom, he had already hit the whisky bottle earlier on in the evening. He arrived at the table the worse for drink, and immediately instructed a waiter to pour him a large glass of Chablis. Then he turned his back on his wife and laid into it.

Such was the picture of marital bliss which greeted Will and Candida when they filed down from the reception area to find their seats. Recalling his last brush with Alistair in the Strangers' Bar at the House of Commons, Will looked apprehensively to see if the Home Secretary would remember him. Fortunately, though, they were two seats apart, separated by Candida, and in any case Alistair was too far gone to notice anyone much.

Will and Candida took their places while Zoë settled at Candida's feet, her leash hanging loosely at the side of the chair. Every so often, Candida lifted the long white tablecloth which hung down to the ground to check on the chimp and feed her some of the favourite snacks she had brought along in her handbag.

'Sure, it must be fascinating being married to the Home Secretary,' said Will to Mrs Sloach, turning up his Irishness to try and break the ice.

As an opening gambit, it proved ill-judged. Not only did the ice remain resolutely unbroken, it shot down ten degrees and gained a few more layers. 'Must it?' snapped Mrs Sloach bitterly. 'Must it really?' And she swivelled around to concentrate on the weatherman on her other side.

Candida was having rather more success with Alistair. He'd begun by offering his condolences on Hilton's death. 'A tragic loss, my dear lady. The nation will be the poorer without him.' He moved closer and sent a blast of whisky-laden breath gusting in her direction. 'Television is terribly important, you know, and it's essential it provide the right moral message.' He launched into a monologue on his pet topic. 'You, of all people, must know just how much influence it can have on the young and impressionable. We have to act quickly to prevent the corruption of our youth. Why, only the other day, I saw a scene of the most disgusting filth on my television set. I—' He broke off, realising that the scene he had in mind was part, as it were, of a private screening. 'Well, let's not go into that. Now, tell me, I hear you're going to be interviewing my . . . ah . . . esteemed colleague, the Prime Minister, next week. What will you be talking to him about? Better keep off the subject of his wife's business interests, eh?' He chortled happily, for relations between him and his erstwhile protégé had turned rather sour of late.

'Oh, I shan't be asking him anything like that,' said Candida. And as the waiters began to serve dinner around them, she chattered on about the upcoming programme and told him how nervous she was.

For tonight's banquet, the combined forces of Vanessa Driftwood, Dick Tockin and the Grand Britannic Hotel had come up with a meal to be remembered. In a seven-course extravaganza, beginning with quails eggs in aspic and meandering dispeptically through a host of other delicacies to culminate in individual flambé desserts of rum-soaked crêpes formed into the shape of the Driftwood logo, no expense had been spared to provide the guests with a gastronomic experience of a lifetime. It was a meal guaranteed to stimulate their tastebuds for days to come – and to wreak havoc on their digestive systems for very much longer.

Left largely to his own devices as Candida prattled away to the Home Secretary and Mrs Sloach laconically attempted to seduce the weatherman, Will Cloud was able to savour every moment of this feast. Living off takeaways in Hugh's house for the past weeks had left him with a healthy appetite and he tucked in with gusto. It wasn't until they reached the dessert that Margaret Sloach tired of the blasts of hot air coming in from a southerly direction and returned her attention to Will. 'So what are you doing here?' she asked. 'Are you one of these television people?' She said it as if it were a new strain of bacteria.

'No,' said Will. 'I'm only here because of Candida. That's not my line of work at all.'

'Oh? So what is your "line of work" then?'

Will hesitated. 'Well, I'm just starting out,' he said, 'and I tend to keep it under my hat. Best to be a bit careful about these things, you know. But I'm sure you wouldn't be about to tell anyone my secrets, would you now?' Mrs Sloach raised an eyebrow and, taking this as an indication of discretion, Will continued. 'I'm an interpreter by profession but recently I've moved into the field of freelance private investigation.'

'What, like Hercule Poirot?' said Mrs Sloach, turning with sudden interest to face him full-on.

'Well, more like the other fella ... Simon Templar, I like to think,' said Will modestly. 'You know, the Saint. I get some paid work, of course, but a lot of the time I just help people out.' He waved a hand around airily. 'Championing the underprivileged, that sort of thing.'

'How marvellous,' mouthed Mrs Sloach. She had really perked up now. 'That's much more intriguing. I've never met a real-life private dick before. Now, I want you to tell me *all* about it.' She looked him up and down with new approval, her tongue flicking out to moisten her wafer-thin lips.

The meal could not be over soon enough for Hugh Driftwood. Faith Lilly had become more mellow as the evening progressed and had spent the dinner taking him on a Cook's tour of her life. She had begun on the quails eggs with her birth in 1932. By the time the crêpes flambées arrived, she had just reached the events at her fourth birthday party.

God spare me, thought Hugh. At least, though, he could switch off and concentrate on the feast of a different kind which was in store for him. Ros had told him that the best time for their adventure would be during the film show, and the cue came immediately after the coffee and petitsfours had been served, as the waiters were passing around with liqueurs and cigars. Vanessa moved to the dais and tapped the microphone. The loudspeakers boomed and an anticipatory hush descended on the room.

'My Lords, ladies and gentlemen,' she said. 'I promised no long speeches and I'm gonna keep my word on that. I will give you a little talk a bit later, but only so I can introduce you to the fabulous line-up of talent you'll be seeing on your television sets, courtesy of Popviz, from next Friday. First, though, I want to show you a short film we've specially prepared on all the work that went into getting this show on the road. I hope you find it as interesting and amusing as I have.' As she sat down, the lights were dimmed and the massive video screen flickered into life. Two thousand eyes shifted upwards.

At his more junior table, Stevie Cudlick had been placed between two Popviz technicians who had spent the evening competing for the most complete state of drunken paralysis. Under normal circumstances, Stevie would have happily joined in – and had no doubt he would have won handsdown – but on this occasion he had abandoned journalistic etiquette, and in the interests of keeping a clear head had stuck to mineral water. Without the added stimulus of alcohol, he had found the endless courses mind-numbingly boring.

As the lights went down, he recognised the ideal opportunity to steal away and begin his investigation. But just as he was about to do exactly that, he suddenly spotted a hotel official approaching him through the throngs, accompanied by a uniformed security man. Behind them both, just visible in the half-light and looking extremely irate, was Roger Breech. He had the look of a man recently cured of amnesia, and Stevie feared the worst.

'Excuse me, sir. I wonder if I might see your invitation?' the official whispered.

'I think I gave it to the man on the door,' Stevie said smoothly.

'I'm sorry, sir. I'm sure this is just a misunderstanding, but would you mind coming out to the lobby so that we can check it out?' His demeanour made it clear that this politeness was purely superficial.

'Sure thing,' said Stevie, easily.

He got up and followed them docilely through the labyrinth of tables towards the main entrance. It was only when he reached it that he decided to make a move. It was all or nothing now, he reckoned. Swiftly, taking advantage of the unaccustomed darkness, he took to his heels through the doors of the banqueting hall and swerved to the right.

For a second, the two men were left standing bewildered. Then, cursing, they followed him into the hallway and sped off in close pursuit. Stevie veered through a door marked private, and found that it led via a back passage into the hotel's delivery area. To his relief, as he tore through one corridor after another, the sound of his pursuers became increasingly distant. Finally he came to a halt in an unlit room, convinced that he had shaken them off.

He took stock of his situation. He appeared to be in a small store. In front of him was a slightly open door, through which he could hear the clinking and clattering of dishes. That must that I'm no longer in government, I've managed to spend a bit more time with my family. Oh, and I've been able to spread my wings in other ways, too. Luckily enough, the company whose shares I had . . . ah . . . invested in, took me on to their board. They reckoned it was the least they could do, after all that free publicity. So things could have been worse.' He broke off, for he had spotted someone more interesting in the background. 'I say, isn't that Mona da Ponte over there? Did you see her in *Kennedy*? Fabulous! Do excuse me, old chap, must just go and say hello.'

He departed, still wearing a perplexed look. Stevie decided that discretion was the better part of valour, and, before he could be noticed by anyone with a better memory for faces, he repaired down the stairs to the banqueting room for an advance reconnaissance of tonight's field of operation.

'Under the banqueting table', the note had said. That was all very well, but which bloody table? His correspondent really might have been a bit more specific. There seemed to be hundreds of circular tables dotted throughout the room, and it would have needed an army of reporters to cover them all. However, a glance at the seating plan reassured him. It was evident that all the bigwigs in the audience would be seated not on the circular tables ranged around the waterfall but along the large U-shaped top table which skirted three sides of the hall. This was the most likely, and indeed the most capacious, venue for any shenanigans.

Stevie checked his own name. Table 39. Shit, he cursed inwardly. It was right in the middle. He would have to eat at his allotted place and, somehow, immediately after the meal – when the note had said the incident would occur – he would invent an excuse to slip away. Then all he needed was to find an entry route to the top table's nether regions and to roam around below, looking for something untoward.

Not for the first time in his journalistic career, it occurred to

Stevie what an absurd way this was of earning a living. But that thought didn't last long. If there was any truth in this tip-off at all, then his efforts would be amply repaid. And Stevie had done stranger things for his calling in the past.

The room began to fill up. Dinner had been announced and the guests were slowly filing through from the reception area. Stevie took his seat.

Hugh Driftwood was approaching the launch party with a sense of heightened sexual expectation. For the past week he had found it difficult to concentrate on work at all as he contemplated the adventure in store, with all its attendant risks. Several times he had determined anew to call the whole thing off, and had picked up the phone to tell Ros, only to replace it again without dialling.

And by the night of the banquet his excitement had reached fever pitch. As he made his way down to dinner, he could see Ros in the middle distance, discussing final details with the hotel management, and every so often, while he posed for photographs with Vanessa and chatted to the other guests, he caught tantalising glimpses of her stunning body swerving in and out of the crowds.

As befitted a government minister, not to mention a senior member of the Driftwood family, Hugh had been seated at the top table. But in the interests of sociability, he was some distance from Vanessa, who was in the middle beside the dais from which she was to make her speech. At the opposite end, he could see Will and Candida and he gave them a distracted wave. Then he sat down and looked around.

His partner for the evening, he discovered, was to be Faith Lilly, the ageing star of the prison soap opera who had taken so long to accept her award at the Brass Monkeys ceremony a few months before. No doubt she had been specially selected by Ros Flato as a suitably doddery neighbour, less likely to be minutes. There's a whole lot of stuff about the work that went into bringing Popviz to the air followed by some trailers from the first night's programmes.'

'Fine. And did you manage to edit in the bit about Candida Blitz and *Livewire* like I told you?'

Dick nodded and Vanessa smiled with satisfaction. She was particularly pleased with her final choice of presenter for the chat show. Bringing in Candida had been an inspired piece of casting. Not only did it exploit the natural sympathy which the public were bound to feel for Hilton Starr's bereaved girlfriend, but, as a children's presenter, Candida was perfect to interview the Prime Minister on his return to television. Even he could hardly object to being quizzed by someone as patently bland and utterly guileless as the former *Jolly Roger* girl.

If Vanessa was pleased with the appointment, then Candida herself was over the moon, although she found the prospect of facing the PM on live television more than a little daunting. She confided these fears to Will Cloud when he collected her and Zoë from home to accompany them to the party.

'Thank goodness I won't have to ask him about politics,' she said. 'I wouldn't have a clue. But Vanessa was ever so nice. She promised I only needed to talk to him about some of the interesting places he'd been and people he'd met and suchlike. And they had to clear all my questions in advance with Downing Street,' she added. 'So the other night I sat down and typed out a whole lot of suggestions. Then yesterday the man at Popviz rang me to say that Mr Burgins was absolutely delighted with them and did I want to come over for tea at Downing Street on Thursday just to talk it all through in advance. Now, isn't that exciting?'

Will listened good-naturedly to her burbling. He was delighted to see Candida so animated, after all she'd been through. 'That's grand,' he said. 'And isn't it good of you to invite with increasing desperation in an attempt to find anything other than this celebration of kitsch which the Grand Britannic had to offer. But the Pearl Harbor Suite remained the only place in London that could cater in sufficient comfort to the upwards of a thousand guests expected, so that was where it had to be.

On Sunday, June 4th, the day of the party, preparations began early. By the time Vanessa Driftwood arrived at just after six p.m., fifty-two circular tables had been set up around the central waterfall and were already groaning under the weight of elaborate place settings for the banquet in store. The staff were just putting the finishing touches to the huge U-shaped top table, which stretched along three sides of the hall and would accommodate Vanessa, the Popviz management, and the most senior of the attending dignitaries.

Vanessa examined the arrangements with satisfaction. 'Well done,' she said to Dick Tockin, who had met her car at the door and was anxiously showing her around. 'Certainly seems you guys have covered everything. Looks a million dollars. Hey, and what's that up there?' She pointed to the ceiling above the waterfall, where a large black spherical object was spinning on its own axis, suspended on two thin wires.

'It's a replica of the *Mistral* satellite,' said Dick. 'I had the props department make it out of papier-mâché.'

'Nice touch!' said Vanessa with a low whistle.

'I thought you'd like it,' said Dick happily.

'Now, how about the movie show? Is that all set up?'

Wiping his brow, Dick indicated a wide screen on the wall above the top table. 'We had some technical problems earlier,' he said. 'But we managed to iron them out.'

'Good. So we banquet for a couple of hours, then I introduce this promotional video?'

'Correct. We thought you could do your main speech afterwards. But just after coffee's been served, you say a few words and we dim the lights and run the film. It only lasts twenty quite a few modern inconveniences. Electronically adjustable four-poster beds with easy-wash acrylic canopies were the order of the day, surrounded by a panoply of minibars, televisions, fax machines and video-conferencing facilities, all encased in mock antique mahogany cabinets with ornate gold-plated handles.

It was for the public rooms, though, that the new owners had reserved their greatest inspiration. Grand Victorian vestibules and hallways were consigned to oblivion and in their place came a 'themed' look. The hotel's new target market of wealthy overseas visitors and international pop stars would, it was calculated, want to be transported away from the fusty Englishness of Park Lane to something much more exotic. The Hawaiian islands were chosen as the ideal setting. Throughout the place, *lanai* terraces and paradise lounges were installed in which bored waitresses dressed as Hawaiian beauties ambiguously asked fat businessmen if they wanted a *lei*, and then, on being eagerly taken up on the offer, practically strangled them by forcing the floral garlands over their heads.

The apotheosis of all this was to be found in the Great Hall, a vast cavern of a room in the hotel's basement which had seen some of London's grandest balls in its distant past. With quite amazing crassness, or equally breathtaking triumphalism – nobody was quite sure which – the new Japanese owners had transformed the Great Hall into the Pearl Harbor Banqueting Suite, replete with artificial awnings, sky blue ceilings and marine walls, and every other South Sea accoutrement that a frenetic designer could cram in. Its centrepiece was a massive artificial waterfall, in which thousands of gallons of very real water descended from on high, gurgling and splashing convincingly over rock formations imported at vast expense from Maui and Kauai.

Surprising to say, the fact that the Popviz launch party was to take place in these nauseating surroundings was not entirely a matter of choice. Dick Tockin had toured every possible venue

The Grand Britannic in London's Park Lane was among the city's oldest hotels. Traditionally independent of the big chains, it had spent most of its existence being passed down through a family of the British landed classes. But inflation and death duties had put paid to that, and the place had finally been sold off in the late 1970s. Since then it had changed owners faster than a flu virus, coming under the control, in quick succession, of a dissolute French playboy, a Middle Eastern potentate and a retired New York gangster. Each had tried to milk it for maximum income with minimum investment and, as a result, it had sunk into a downward spiral of dilapidation and disrepair.

Finally the Grand Britannic had fallen into the dainty hands of a conglomerate of Japanese businessmen who were determined to turn its finances around once and for all. They had set about renovating it with an unlimited supply of cash and an equally unlimited absence of good taste. Out of each room went the sturdy fixtures and fittings which had remained unchanged for decades, and in came every modern convenience – and me along tonight!' he added, gazing at her affectionately. 'I do love this sort of occasion.' Since their lunch at the Greasepot they had been seeing a great deal of one another and he'd found himself growing fond of her wide-eyed naïveté in a way that he'd rarely allowed in his many previous liaisons.

Candida smiled back. 'It was the least I could do,' she said. 'Considering how you've cheered me up.'

'And you're sure, now, that they'll allow Zoë to come as well?' Will asked.

'I rang up and *insisted*,' said Candida, who'd gained a good deal in confidence since being appointed to the new position. 'I told them I was a very important member of the Popviz team and they'd jolly well have to let me take whoever I wanted. Talking of which, I thought you were going to be bringing Mr Driftwood with you?'

'Hugh? He's driving straight in from the constituency,' said Will. 'Just as well, really. He's been in a fearsome mood recently, which isn't like him at all, and this morning he seemed in a right ould state.'

'I expect it must be dreadful being in such an important job,' said Candida with feeling. 'All that pressure.'

Stevie Cudlick had succeeded in getting his invitation. Accredited as a freelancer, ostensibly writing an article for the colour supplement of one of Driftwood's US papers, he arrived at the hotel some time after Will and Candida and submitted himself to the security search with trepidation. A look around confirmed that the whole place was crawling with armed police.

'What's the camera for?' asked a guard, fingering his machine-gun threateningly.

'I was hoping to get some snaps of Mrs Driftwood during her speech. It's all been arranged in advance with her office,' Stevie lied.

'Let's just see that it really works,' said the man suspiciously. 'Can't take any chances tonight.'

Stevie demonstrated the Nikon's bona fides to his satisfaction and proceeded into the reception area. He glanced around uneasily. His face was not unknown in the government, as he had assisted Gilbert Falange on exposing more than a few of its members in recent years, and he was nervous of being spotted by someone. As an extra precaution, he had made the ultimate sacrifice the night before. With the deepest regret he had taken a pair of scissors to his beloved ponytail, and now, suitably spruced up, he was almost unidentifiable. This had better be worth it, he thought to himself.

Once inside, he mingled as unobtrusively as possible with the other guests. Even he was impressed at the array of luminaries. He knew most of them by sight and some of them to speak to, and despite the absence of his hairy appendage, he was still concerned he might be recognised.

His fears were not unfounded. The former Industry Minister, Roger Breech, whom he had helped bring to his knees only months before, made a beeline for him. To Stevie's surprise, though, he started chatting quite amicably. 'Hello there, old chap, how are you?' he asked, sincerity oozing from his every syllable, even as his puzzled expression posed the quite different question, Where do I know you from?

'Oh, absolutely fine,' said Stevie with an ingratiating smile. 'I was so sorry to hear about your ... ah ... trouble. You've moved on now, I understand.'

'Yes, tragic really. I felt I had so much more to make ... I mean to offer ... in government.'

'It was the press that really did for you, wasn't it?' Stevie couldn't resist saying. 'Quite appalling really, what those vermin get up to.'

'Absolutely. Ruined my whole political career over a bit of innocuous share-dealing. Still, that's life, and, of course, now suspicious when events began taking their course under the table near her.

'Hello, I'm Hugh Driftwood,' said Hugh sociably, 'I *am* pleased to meet you.'

'Hello, dear,' replied Faith Lilly. She held out her hand vaguely. She had evidently never heard of him in her life.

'I'm the most enormous fan of your work,' said Hugh. He rarely had time to watch television and racked his brain for the name of the prison programme she starred in. It came to him just in time. 'I do love *Loose Screws*,' he said.

She batted two heavily mascaraed eyelashes back at him. 'I'm glad you like it, darling. We have such fun making it.'

'I was in the audience when you won your award for best actress last month.'

'Were you really? These award shows are such a bore, aren't they? But the fans seem to enjoy them, so one just has to grin and bear it.'

'Tell me,' said Hugh, 'are you going to be on Popviz as well?'

'Yes, I'm presenting the religious affairs show, *Faithlift*,' she said.

'Are you really? It must be so comforting to hold such deep religious beliefs,' he said.

'Not really,' she snapped back. 'I'm an atheist. Can't be doing with religion myself. But there's not a lot of work around at the moment. So needs must when the devil drives.'

At the other end of the top table, Will and Candida had been seated next to the Home Secretary, Alistair Sloach. For once, he was accompanied by his wife, the vitriolic Margaret, who had decided that this star-studded event was well worth the journey to London. But, dismayed at the prospect of an entire evening in the company of her husband, she had taken the precaution of slipping in beforehand and altering the place cards, so that

Alistair was three seats away from her next to Candida Blitz, while she was on the other side of the couple, in between Will Cloud and an attractive young Popviz weatherman.

Alistair, for his part, was no less alarmed at the thought of spending any time with his wife. As a consequence of this and his suppressed excitement at Hugh Driftwood's impending doom, he had already hit the whisky bottle earlier on in the evening. He arrived at the table the worse for drink, and immediately instructed a waiter to pour him a large glass of Chablis. Then he turned his back on his wife and laid into it.

Such was the picture of marital bliss which greeted Will and Candida when they filed down from the reception area to find their seats. Recalling his last brush with Alistair in the Strangers' Bar at the House of Commons, Will looked apprehensively to see if the Home Secretary would remember him. Fortunately, though, they were two seats apart, separated by Candida, and in any case Alistair was too far gone to notice anyone much.

Will and Candida took their places while Zoë settled at Candida's feet, her leash hanging loosely at the side of the chair. Every so often, Candida lifted the long white tablecloth which hung down to the ground to check on the chimp and feed her some of the favourite snacks she had brought along in her handbag.

'Sure, it must be fascinating being married to the Home Secretary,' said Will to Mrs Sloach, turning up his Irishness to try and break the ice.

As an opening gambit, it proved ill-judged. Not only did the ice remain resolutely unbroken, it shot down ten degrees and gained a few more layers. 'Must it?' snapped Mrs Sloach bitterly. 'Must it really?' And she swivelled around to concentrate on the weatherman on her other side.

Candida was having rather more success with Alistair. He'd begun by offering his condolences on Hilton's death. 'A tragic loss, my dear lady. The nation will be the poorer without him.' He moved closer and sent a blast of whisky-laden breath gusting in her direction. 'Television is terribly important, you know, and it's essential it provide the right moral message.' He launched into a monologue on his pet topic. 'You, of all people, must know just how much influence it can have on the young and impressionable. We have to act quickly to prevent the corruption of our youth. Why, only the other day, I saw a scene of the most disgusting filth on my television set. I—' He broke off, realising that the scene he had in mind was part, as it were, of a private screening. 'Well, let's not go into that. Now, tell me, I hear you're going to be interviewing my . . . ah . . . esteemed colleague, the Prime Minister, next week. What will you be talking to him about? Better keep off the subject of his wife's business interests, eh?' He chortled happily, for relations between him and his erstwhile protégé had turned rather sour of late.

'Oh, I shan't be asking him anything like that,' said Candida. And as the waiters began to serve dinner around them, she chattered on about the upcoming programme and told him how nervous she was.

For tonight's banquet, the combined forces of Vanessa Driftwood, Dick Tockin and the Grand Britannic Hotel had come up with a meal to be remembered. In a seven-course extravaganza, beginning with quails eggs in aspic and meandering dispeptically through a host of other delicacies to culminate in individual flambé desserts of rum-soaked crêpes formed into the shape of the Driftwood logo, no expense had been spared to provide the guests with a gastronomic experience of a lifetime. It was a meal guaranteed to stimulate their tastebuds for days to come – and to wreak havoc on their digestive systems for very much longer.

Left largely to his own devices as Candida prattled away to the Home Secretary and Mrs Sloach laconically attempted to seduce the weatherman, Will Cloud was able to savour every moment of this feast. Living off takeaways in Hugh's house for the past weeks had left him with a healthy appetite and he tucked in with gusto. It wasn't until they reached the dessert that Margaret Sloach tired of the blasts of hot air coming in from a southerly direction and returned her attention to Will. 'So what are you doing here?' she asked. 'Are you one of these television people?' She said it as if it were a new strain of bacteria.

'No,' said Will. 'I'm only here because of Candida. That's not my line of work at all.'

'Oh? So what is your "line of work" then?'

Will hesitated. 'Well, I'm just starting out,' he said, 'and I tend to keep it under my hat. Best to be a bit careful about these things, you know. But I'm sure you wouldn't be about to tell anyone my secrets, would you now?' Mrs Sloach raised an eyebrow and, taking this as an indication of discretion, Will continued. 'I'm an interpreter by profession but recently I've moved into the field of freelance private investigation.'

'What, like Hercule Poirot?' said Mrs Sloach, turning with sudden interest to face him full-on.

'Well, more like the other fella ... Simon Templar, I like to think,' said Will modestly. 'You know, the Saint. I get some paid work, of course, but a lot of the time I just help people out.' He waved a hand around airily. 'Championing the underprivileged, that sort of thing.'

'How marvellous,' mouthed Mrs Sloach. She had really perked up now. 'That's much more intriguing. I've never met a real-life private dick before. Now, I want you to tell me *all* about it.' She looked him up and down with new approval, her tongue flicking out to moisten her wafer-thin lips.

The meal could not be over soon enough for Hugh Driftwood. Faith Lilly had become more mellow as the evening progressed the table dwarfed anything he had ever experienced before. An expression of complete ecstasy overtook his face.

When it was all over, Hugh felt his flies being closed and he leaned back in his chair with a surge of relief. It had been blissful. It had been worth every last risk. Apprehensively, he looked around at his fellow dinner guests. But they were still staring up at the screen, oblivious to the scene that had just unfolded beneath them.

There, Ros squatted for a moment, equally delighted with this new addition to her portfolio of sexual escapades. And then, with just as much caution as before, she stole back to her place. Her absence had not been noticed, and neither was her return. Smoothly she slipped out from under the tablecloth and retook her seat. She stole a glance across at Hugh. Despite the gloom, she fancied she could see him smiling happily back at her.

And that should have been the end of the affair. It should have been, yet it wasn't – at least not as far as Zoë was concerned. For the chimpanzee had observed Ros's antics under the table with some fascination. She had stayed at a safe distance behind throughout the incident and had mentally noted her every move. And although puzzled by the exact motivation behind these strange activities, she was a long-standing student of human nature and keen to learn more. In her experience, many things that human beings got up to were more enjoyable than they appeared at first sight. Maybe this was one of them, she reflected, and it would be as well to find out.

Zoë was not a very patient creature. The concept of delayed gratification was something entirely alien to her. If she was going to try out this new trick she wanted to do it now. The first thing, she realised, was to select a target. Accordingly, after returning to her place to make sure Candida had not noticed her absence, she looked around tentatively among the mass of legs that surrounded her. The ones directly adjacent to Candida were short and easily accessible, and, more to the point, conveniently located. Lazy as well as impatient, Zoë did not believe in travelling any further than she needed to on a mission. She moved over, crouched down just as Ros had, and went to work.

The excellent wines, on top of numerous pre-prandial whiskies, had combined in Alistair Sloach's bloodstream to produce a comfortable stupor and the Home Secretary had taken advantage of the film show to drift off to sleep. His thoughts were far away. He was picturing the not-too-distant day in the future when he would take over the helm of the nation. Hugh would be safely ousted from public life, his acts of licentiousness having long since been exposed to a shocked populace. Alistair would reign supreme, and decency and efficiency, and, most importantly, morality, would be the order of the day. From this happy picture his dreams meandered on tangentially, as dreams tend to do, and he wondered what it was like to be the subject of that perverted act which he had seen performed on Driftwood. Disgusting as it was, he fancied there might be a certain eroticism associated with it. A kind of warm, sensual feeling, which he could almost imagine. Not unpleasant at all . . .

Zoë had set about her task with the dedication she devoted to all her apings of human endeavours. And she was rewarded with some immediate results. This was one curious banana, she mused to herself. At first apparently soft and ripe, now increasingly hard and unyielding. She continued to lick on it speculatively.

Such was the vista which greeted Stevie Cudlick as he finally made his way painstakingly along the underside of the top table. It was quite dark there and it took some time for his eyes to adjust. He had advanced about twenty yards, crouched on hands and knees, when he turned a corner and came on what appeared to be a hairy chimpanzee attached to the lower portions of a short gentleman. He blinked. Surely his eyes were deceiving him. Prolonged alcohol deprivation could have some weird effects.

But no. There was the animal, apparently performing fellatio on one of Vanessa's guests, who, unless Stevie was completely out of his mind, was sitting quite still, a willing collaborator. But who on earth was it? One person it certainly was not was Hugh Driftwood, he realised. The legs were not long enough. But this was no time for disappointment. Whatever the man's identity, it was still a mind-boggling story. Stevie cast his memory back to the table arrangements. He had mentally mapped most of the government ministers present and knew roughly where they would be sitting. Jesus Christ. It couldn't be, could it? The Macclesfield Machiavelli – Mr Moral Millennium – himself? It bloody well could!

Not in his wildest imaginings could Stevie have pictured such a mouth-watering scenario. As he withdrew his camera from his pocket, his hand was trembling with excitement. The film was ready, the flash was primed. He began clicking furiously before this mirage could dissolve before him.

Zoë's study of oral sex had been punctilious but not quite as exact as it might have been. She had mastered the tactics with a certain dexterity, but the strategic objectives were way beyond her ken. When the first flash went off, she had just opened her jaws wide. Now she lost her bearings completely. If Alistair Sloach had ever wondered how a monkey-wrench had got its name, then he was about to find out. For, suddenly startled, she snapped them shut again with a decisive crunch, her yellowing but still sturdy teeth enclosing the Home Secretary's appendage in a vicelike grip.

To say that the reaction above table level was cataclysmic would be putting it mildly. The film had just reached an end, and the lights were coming back up. As the buzz of conversation resumed, the last thing anyone expected was the sound which issued forth from the august person of Alistair Sloach, who was discovering what resulted when you combined a monkey with his organ-grinder. Alistair's primordial scream echoed through the hall like the howl of an injured hyena, causing at least three waitresses to faint and countless waiters to drop their trays. In the cacophony of crashing brandy glasses, the minister rose from his table like a man possessed, his hands clutched to his groin, where a once proud organ now hung down like a piece of mangled macaroni, forlornly *al dente*, and hurtled screaming along the aisles between the tables towards the exit.

And that was not all. In hot pursuit, carrying a camera which he clicked and flashed frenetically, came Stevie Cudlick. On hearing the shriek, he had decided that he might as well blow his cover and get in for the kill. To add to the pictures he had taken under the table, he managed at least ten good snaps of the Home Secretary fleeing for the door.

Taken completely unawares and startled by the sudden noise, the armed police manning the entrance-way drew their machine-guns towards their breasts. What they saw filled them with the fear of God. Charging towards them, apparently unstoppable, was what looked like two human elephants, at least one of them with a distinctly lacerated trunk. In panic, one of the officers raised his gun and prepared to shoot.

'No!' shouted the policeman next to him, realising what a terrible mistake was about to be made. He reached out desperately but it was too late. A terrifying crackle rang out in the hall. The whole room went suddenly and eerily silent, as all eyes stared at the two running men. But then there was a gasp of relief. Hesitating only momentarily, the two figures had continued to dash towards the door, rushing through the exit and disappearing from view. Mercifully, the last-minute intervention of his colleague had succeeded in upsetting the marksman's aim. His arm had jerked upwards and the hail of bullets had been loosed off relatively harmlessly into the air.

Not quite harmlessly enough, though. Certainly they did not hit anyone, although the sound of them added to the general pandemonium which now broke out everywhere. None the less, the bullets had not been totally unsuccessful in finding a target. With a satisfied splutter, they had embedded themselves firmly in the enormous replica of the *Mistral* satellite which Dick Tockin had suspended in the centre of the room. For a second, the huge sphere shook and strained precariously on its moorings. Then, almost as if in slow motion, it threw off its shackles and launched itself triumphantly into space, where no doubt it felt it belonged.

It was to be a brief orbit. Unlike the real thing, the satellite had strong gravitational forces to contend with, and so was unable to maintain its trajectory for more than an instant. With an almighty splash it landed at the base of the waterfall below, sending out a great monsoon and drenching everyone in the immediate vicinity.

As they watched these events unfold, the remainder of the audience pulled back smugly, delighted that nobody had been hurt by the shots, and glad at least to have been spared the effects of the downpour. Their relief was also to be short-lived, though. Settling itself contentedly into its new housing, the papier-mâché of the satellite rapidly expanded to form a most effective plug, completely preventing the cascades of water from reaching the drains underneath. And deprived of its means of escape, the waterfall rapidly began seeking other outlets, gushing forth in every direction.

Within moments, the whole of the Pearl Harbor Banqueting Suite had been submerged in swirling torrents several feet deep. The room's basement location meant that the water was contained effectively within it, and as its level began to rise inexorably, an armada of tables and chairs took to the waves, along with mini-flotillas of napkins and table mats and shoals of cigars and after-dinner mints. These were closely followed by most of the guests, or at least those unable to escape fast enough through the emergency exits.

Fortunately, some of the water also found an escape route through the floorboards and into the hotel's foundations, and, after a few moments of terror, the fears of those still trapped were allayed when the tide settled at a depth of no more than four feet. Resorting to upturned tables as temporary life-rafts, they crowded together and awaited the arrival of a plumber capable of switching off the waterfall's pumping mechanism.

In the centre of this deluge was Vanessa Driftwood who, with typical resourcefulness and fully living up to her surname, upended the dais she had been speaking from and launched herself into the mêlée. She converted the toastmaster's gavel to an oar and propelled herself easily around the room on this makeshift gondola, comforting semi-submerged dignitaries and directing rescue operations in her usual authoritative manner.

Sweeping down the white-water rapids to table 32, she chanced on an ashen-faced Dick Tockin, sinking fast on an abandoned wine-trolley. 'Ahoy there,' she said cheerfully. 'Bit choppy out tonight, eh?'

'Oh, Christ,' moaned Dick, looking like he was about to be violently sea-sick. 'Vanessa, I'm so sorry. God knows what happened. If I ever get out of this place alive, I'll bloody well skin everyone who had anything to do with it.'

But, to his astonishment, instead of the expected tongue-lashing, all he received from Vanessa was a playful slosh round the head with her gavel. 'You'll do nothing of the kind,' she said, grinning from ear to ear. She shook water off her red hair like a pond-sodden poodle. 'First thing you do when you get out of here is ring up that goddamned factory in Hong Kong. I want another million of those satellite receivers here by next week.' And she let out her hoot of a laugh. 'After the publicity we get from this, we're sure as hell gonna need them.'

*   *   *

Oblivious to the mayhem he had left in his wake, Stevie Cudlick sat in the rear seat of a black cab bound for the offices of the *Flick*. He had just managed to flee the clutches of the security men by the skin of his teeth. When he'd followed Alistair to the exit they had been on the verge of capturing him, but the howls of the injured Home Secretary had claimed their more urgent attentions, and as they were directing the poor man towards the first-aid room and calling for an ambulance, Stevie had made good his escape.

Now, his brain performing a little internal waltz, he settled back in the taxi. True, he hadn't managed to get the goods on Hugh Driftwood as he was supposed to. But what did he care about that? The scalp of the Home Secretary was just as good – no, better. And after his name appeared in tomorrow's *Flick* above this story, he would no longer need Victor Quistling's approbation. In fact, he would no longer need anyone's approbation. He would be able to walk into the offices of any paper in Britain and take his pick of the plum jobs on the strength of this little scoop.

Eat your guts out, Woodward and Bernstein, Stevie chortled to himself. His Deep Throat had been more aptly named than theirs had ever been. For a brief instant he wondered if he would ever know the identity of the person – his fairy godmother, his angel from heaven – who had presented him with this story of a lifetime. But he quickly dismissed such speculation as futile. Whoever it was, he just silently thanked him from the bottom of his soaring heart.

Chapter 26

The injuries to the Home Secretary's penis proved relatively minor. A visit at high speed to the casualty department of Westminster Hospital, accompanied by over a dozen screaming police cars, revealed the damage as no more than a few minor cuts and contusions, and the specialist rushed in by helicopter from his Surrey home confirmed that the unfortunate organ would heal up in no time.

The same could not be said of Alistair Sloach's amour-propre, however, or indeed his reputation. When he returned suitably swathed in bandages to his flat at the Barbican, his wife Margaret was awaiting him with impatience. After establishing at the hotel that the attack was not life-threatening, she had decided to come straight home rather than accompany him to the hospital. 'I haven't looked at that bloody thing for twenty years and I don't intend to start now,' she declared to anyone who would listen.

She was standing by the kitchen door as he let himself in. 'How's the willy?' she asked. 'Still hanging in there? Not that it really matters, for all the use you make of it. I heard exactly what happened, you know. It was all round the hall.'

'What was all round the hall?'

'Just out of interest, just when exactly did you develop your penchant for seducing chimpanzees in public places? I mean, one wouldn't want to pry, but it might help with my memoirs.'

Alistair stared at her aghast. 'It must be clear, even to you, that it was a totally unprovoked attack,' he said desperately. 'The animal has obviously been trained by seditious forces in an attempt to destabilise the government.'

'Well, it's certainly managed to do that,' said his wife. 'I've just listened to the news on the radio. You're a complete laughing stock. And the press haven't stopped phoning up.'

Alistair turned white. 'It's preposterous,' he said frantically. 'I'll sue them, I'll . . .'

Just then the telephone rang again.

'For God's sake, you get it. Say I'm still recovering from tonight's terrorist attack.'

'By a chimpanzee? You cannot be serious.'

But it turned out not to be the press at all. It was Mildred from Number 10 Downing Street. She was one of the Garden Girls, the team of civil servants which serves as the Premier's personal secretariat. 'I have the Prime Minister to speak to the Home Secretary,' she announced.

Edward Burgins began by enquiring solicitously after his colleague's injury. 'Most unfortunate incident,' he said, tutting furiously and trying to keep any hint of levity from his voice.

'I suspect insurgents,' said Alistair. 'It was a blatant attempt to smear me by the enemies of my Moral Millennium Campaign.'

'Absolutely,' said the PM nervously. 'And I assure you that we'll hold an immediate public enquiry into it.'

'Public?'

'Private,' the PM hurriedly conceded. 'You're absolutely right – matters of such delicacy need to be discussed behind closed doors. But be assured, my dear chap, that we'll get to the bottom . . . ah . . . the nub . . . of it all. However . . . ahem . . . I have to say that the press are going to have a field day over this. Quite unjustifiably, of course, but there it is. And for the survival of the government, I wonder if it mightn't be best if you took a somewhat lower profile in the near future. I'm certain that the enquiry, when it does report, will clear you of any . . . ah . . . collusion in this unfortunate incident, but I do think that with the current standing of the government so bad, it might be best to . . .'

'Are you suggesting that I resign over this appalling attack? In the name of heaven . . . do I need to remind you that I was its victim?'

'Well, not resign exactly. But we have to be seen to be taking rapid action. How about a spell as Governor of the Falklands?'

'Certainly not!'

'Bermuda, then?' asked the PM. 'Lots of sunshine and recreation.'

'Will you listen? There's no question—'

'I've got it!' Burgins interrupted in the tone of a man who has just had a brainwave. 'Gibraltar! Now that should be right up your street.'

'What on earth do you mean?'

The PM coughed. 'The Spanish are a *most* broad-minded people,' he said. 'And those Barbary apes . . .' He lowered his voice discreetly. 'Most approachable, don't you know. Why, last time I was there, one came right up to me and—'

'How dare you!' Alistair practically screamed.

'Then,' the PM rounded off soothingly, 'after the fuss has blown over, you can come back to your old role.'

'For the last time,' said Alistair through clenched teeth. 'I have no intention of resigning over this. Quite the opposite. I have no doubt that there will be huge public sympathy for this unconscionable plot against me. So if you want me out, then you'll have to sack me and face the consequences.' And with that, he slammed down the phone.

The following morning's papers did not, however, bear out his confidence in the British sense of justice. Waking up the next day after a troubled night's sleep, Alistair reluctantly picked up the selection of the papers which had arrived on his doormat. The Driftwood presses were the most understanding, at least accepting that he was an unwitting victim. 'MINISTER IN SAVAGE ATTACK' was the headline in the *Pop*.

In the *Flick*, however, the story was much worse. In a world exclusive, headlined 'HE'S OFF HIS CHIMP!', Stevie Cudlick claimed that the crazed minister had somehow orchestrated the whole venture himself in an attempt at some bizarre sex act. What was more, he had the photographs to prove it. Pictures taken underneath the table, seconds before Alistair had realised what was happening, extended over pages one to five of the *Flick*, with a special full-length souvenir pull-out on the centre spread. They showed the Home Secretary's easily identifiable lower regions enjoying a gentle oral massage from the chimpanzee without any suggestion that he was not a willing collaborator. The caption read: 'The Home Secretary and friend enjoy a quiet moment together before they are unmasked.'

Alistair buried his head in his hands. It was the end, and he knew it. No amount of righteous protestation would be proof against those photographs. And all taken by someone who had been under the table at Alistair's own instigation. But not for a second did it occur to him that there was some kind of poetic justice in what had happened – that the petard with which he had been hoisted was well and truly of his own making. It had to be a plot. A plot by the forces of evil, or by the opposition, to discredit him and to put paid to his attempts to improve Britain's moral standards.

Or maybe not. All at once a thought crossed his mind. Maybe it was not his opponents at all. Perhaps it was even more insidious than that. Sloach's first rule of politics: when someone does the dirty on you, look first to the enemy within. Hugh Driftwood! What if Hugh Driftwood was behind all this? Alistair cast his memory back to the traumatic events of the previous evening. Candida Blitz had brought that chimpanzee with her. And she had been accompanied by that man whose face had seemed vaguely familiar. Where had he seen him before? Hadn't he spent most of the evening talking to Margaret?

His wife was in the kitchen. 'Him?' she said curtly in response to Alistair's question. 'Yes, I remember him. At first I thought he was a complete wimp, then I found out he was a private detective or something. His name's Will Cloud and he's a pal of your great friend, Hugh Driftwood.'

Of course! Alistair remembered now. Of course! The man who had been with Driftwood in the Strangers' Bar that day, smoking some suspicious substance. He could have kicked himself for not recognising him.

'I've got his address and phone number written down somewhere,' Margaret continued, 'if it's not illegible from the soaking. I'm going to invite him to speak to my Women's Guild annual luncheon. They'll eat him up.'

But Alistair was no longer listening. He had his answer. It was all falling into place now. Who was it who had most to gain from discrediting him? Driftwood. With Alistair gone, Driftwood was the heir-apparent. Who was with that monkey? The shady-looking Irishman who was Driftwood's friend. He was undoubtedly an animal trainer who had spent months teaching it to attack him in that humiliating way. Alistair saw it all so clearly. Hugh Driftwood was behind everything. For a moment, he considered the idea that the whole episode was a set-up from the beginning, including that blasted man who said he worked for Driftwood International and who came to his surgery with the video. But that could not be. Driftwood would never have deliberately exposed himself in that way, both literally and metaphorically.

The video! That was it! He still had it carefully locked away in his desk drawer. That tape was dynamite and Alistair no longer cared whether or not he was implicated in its release. He *would* resign. But if he was finished, then he would bloody well take that bastard Driftwood with him. He would show the world that it was Hugh Driftwood, not he, who was the disgusting pervert at the heart of the British government.

His messianic zeal revived, Alistair rushed into his study, unlocked the desk drawer and took out the videotape. His hand was trembling as he slid it in the machine. It was as disgusting as ever. Just wait and see what the *Flick* makes of this, he thought to himself malevolently. Better still, wait and see what they all make of it. He would call a press conference. He would invite everyone. He would announce his resignation and he would show the tape to the world. He reached for the phone.

'What on earth is that on the video machine?' His wife had entered the room unnoticed. 'Does that turn you on too? I've discovered a whole new side to your personality in the last day. Shame you didn't mention it years ago. We might have had some fun before it was too late.'

'It's Driftwood,' said Alistair, his voice rising with anger. 'It's that degenerate performing the most disgusting acts.' The words tumbling out, he related the story of the videotape and how it had come into his possession. Then he told her about his decision to resign, and to take Hugh with him.

When he had finished, Margaret sat down, her legs weak. 'You mean it's all over,' she said flatly, as if it had only just come home to her.

'Yes,' said Alistair. 'It's all over.'

She started to cry, and he was touched. They had not got

on with each other for a long time, and he was gratified that now, in his moment of greatest adversity, she felt for him.

But it soon became clear they were tears of anger, not sympathy. 'All these years,' she suddenly shrieked. 'All these years I've put up with you, and what for? Don't you think I would have liked to have some fun like that.' She pointed to the television. 'When we first got married, I even felt attracted to you. But no. You were Alistair Sloach. You were Mr Morality. You . . . you . . . you . . . And now look what's happened, you self-righteous little shit. Now . . . now I'll never get to redo Downing Street in concrete cladding.'

She stood there ranting and raving, distraught with self-pity and seething with anger at the same time, then rushed into the bedroom and slammed the door behind her.

Chapter 27

After the momentous events at the Grand Britannic, Will, Candida and Zoë headed back to the house in Hampstead she had once shared with Hilton Starr, soaked to the skin and totally exhausted. Once the waterfall had been switched off and the floods had begun to abate, they had finally been rescued by apologetic hotel officials and offered a room upstairs in which to dry off. But Candida had been more anxious to get Zoë, who was still trembling and in a complete state of shock, back to her own home.

'I'm sure she would never have done anything like that by herself,' said Candida tearfully. 'It's so unlike her. She's never harmed anyone in her life. That nasty man must have forced her into it.'

They tumbled out of the taxi and Candida fiddled in her purse for her latchkey. She threw the door open and together they looked unbelievingly at the scene of devastation which faced them. It was almost as bad as the one they had just left behind.

'Jesus!' said Will. 'Looks like you've been burgled, I'm afraid.'

'Oh, no,' cried Candida hysterically. 'As if I haven't had enough trouble already.'

Nothing had been left untouched. Sofas and chairs had been tipped over, ornaments had been broken and scattered on the floor. Countless star-shaped frames containing Hilton's photograph collection and featuring the deceased quiz-show host hobnobbing with the rich and famous had been ripped from the wall and smashed, apparently in an act of wanton destruction. Even the fitted carpets had been pulled up.

But not, it transpired despite initial appearances, by burglars. A preliminary search by Candida revealed that nothing of any value – indeed nothing at all – seemed to be missing.

Will did his best to comfort her and eventually Candida did begin to calm down a little. Finally she went off to put Zoë to bed and Will telephoned the police. By the time Candida came back downstairs, Inspector Ffelcher and his men had arrived. He examined the debris with grim satisfaction. 'I don't know what they were looking for,' he said, 'but it doesn't look as if they found it.'

'Do you think it's connected with Hilton's murder?' asked Candida.

The inspector rubbed his chin. 'Could be. But I don't know how.'

'Have you not made any progress at all in your enquiries?' asked Will with a hint of impatience.

'We've made a good deal of progress,' said the inspector, throwing him a nasty glance. 'But I can't discuss it with *you*. It's possible this incident might just give us our final lead. Have you any idea what they might have been after?' he asked Candida.

'None. I haven't touched any of Hilly's things since he died. I wouldn't know what . . .' A thought occurred to her. 'Unless . . .'

'Yes?'

'Hilton had a safe, in the bedroom. I'd completely forgotten.

I wasn't meant to know about it, but I saw him take some money out of it once.'

They repaired to the master bedroom. It too had been ransacked, but the safe was concealed behind a wardrobe and appeared untouched. Candida did not know the combination.

'I'll send some more lads over to pick it up,' said the inspector. 'I've got a feeling we're going to find something interesting in there. And meanwhile I'm going to arrange around-the-clock security for you too, Miss Blitz. You might be in some considerable danger.'

It was nearly four a.m. when the inspector and his officers left. Candida and Will, exhausted but still tense, sat in the remains of the living room. Will reached into his coat pocket.

'Look,' he said. 'I know you won't approve, but I have to have myself a joint or I'll sure as hell explode.'

'I don't think drugs are the answer to anything,' said Candida primly. But then she relented. 'You *have* been wonderful though, so I won't stop you – just this once.'

Despite herself, she watched with fascination as he lit up, drew a long gasp and lounged back in his chair. 'It must be very relaxing,' she said slightly enviously. 'I knew lots of people who used to do it when I was at the BBC. Perhaps I should have a try? I do feel ever so wound up.'

'No, that wouldn't be a good idea at all,' said Will firmly. 'I'd feel very guilty about introducing you to grass, considering your views. And, you might have a bad reaction if it's your first time.'

'I expect you're right,' agreed Candida with regret. 'Besides, I couldn't stand having to inhale the smoke.'

'You don't need to, of course,' said Will unthinkingly. 'Some people prefer to eat the stuff.' He giggled a little, as the drug began having an effect. 'Americans even cook it in brownies sometimes.' And taking another gasp, he closed his eyes contentedly and so did not notice the wide-eyed expression of interest which filled Candida's face at these words.

Chapter 28

Rarely had a meeting at the House of Commons been so well attended. Not surprisingly after his recent tribulations, the Home Secretary's announcement of a news conference had excited widespread interest and the Grand Committee Room at the House of Commons was so heavily packed with journalists and photographers that many of them ended up standing outside in the draughty reaches of Westminster Hall. There was widespread speculation that Alistair was going to announce his resignation, and all the national and international media were there to hear it.

To the angry protests of Gilbert Falange, Victor Quistling had insisted that Stevie be allowed to follow his story through, even though Gilbert was still the *Flick*'s chief parliamentary correspondent for now. Accordingly, Stevie slipped into the meeting just as it was about to start. He was unsure if he would be welcome after yesterday's publication, but he needn't have worried. Shorn of his ponytail, he was noticed by only a few of his rivals from other papers, who congratulated him grudgingly on his scoop.

He looked around the room. He had been to hundreds of press conferences of this type before, although never in such interesting circumstances. At the head of the room was a table from which presumably Alistair Sloach would speak. Stevie noticed that a video projector and screen had been set up there. That was odd; he'd assumed Alistair was simply going to protest his innocence and resign, but clearly there was to be more to it.

The Home Secretary arrived in the room accompanied by a posse of security men. He was limping slightly and a titter went round as he took his place behind the table. 'Ladies and gentlemen, thank you for coming,' he began.

'More than you'll be able to do for a while,' someone called out.

Alistair ignored him. 'I'll get straight to the point,' he said. 'You will all know of the appalling attack on my . . . ah . . . person, and I hope you will be pleased to hear that my physicians expect me to make a full recovery from the injuries I sustained. Clearly, this unprovoked assault has caused great anguish both to me and my family, but that was as nothing compared to the even greater distress which has resulted from the scurrilous articles and disgusting photographs which appeared in this morning's press.'

A few eyes turned on Stevie, who, hardened hack though he was, had the grace to blush.

'I have come to the conclusion that there is only one way for me to proceed,' the Home Secretary continued. 'I intend to clear my name at all costs, and this will involve me in extensive legal action, which would not be compatible with my role in government, much less with my position as Home Secretary. I have, therefore, with the deepest regret, today handed my resignation to the Prime Minister, as you will see from the copy of my letter which you will shortly receive. You will also receive a copy of the Prime Minister's reply to me, in which he is good enough to suggest that my contribution to the government has been ... ah ... not insubstantial, and in which he expresses the hope that once I have pursued my legal action to a successful conclusion I shall be able to return to high office with my reputation intact. This, I confirm, is exactly what I intend to do.'

A young assistant began circulating with a sheaf of photocopied papers and Alistair paused for a drink of water before resuming.

'I do have some other points I wish to make,' he said, 'and a brief video which I want to show you. But before that, I would like to pay a special tribute to my wife, who is still recovering from the shock of last night's attack and unfortunately cannot be here with us. Margaret, you have stood by me through thick and thin, and at this sad moment, I want to thank you for everything. I know that nothing can dim the love we share together.

'The work I have tried to do in government is, I hope, known to you all. If, in my small way, I have contributed to the good of the nation by leaving behind me a cleaner, more moral society, in which perverts and junkies no longer wallow in a cesspool of their own making, then I will have achieved something very close to my heart. But I have to tell you that there is still a long way to go. Even at the very core of government there is immorality and perversion.'

Someone shouted, 'You should know!' and one of the security men stood up ready to eject him. But Alistair waved him away, his eyes blazing. He was in his stride now, and did not want to be distracted.

'There is immorality at the very heart of government, and I call on you all here to witness it. Please start the videotape.' The last remark was addressed to the minion who sat close by with a remote control. The screen above the Home Secretary's head lit up and within seconds it was filled with a picture of

Hugh Driftwood. Alistair sat down, his face contorted in a demoniacal grin, to watch the reaction.

But he was to be sadly disappointed. A look, not of shock, but of boredom came over the faces of all the pressmen and women in attendance as the film started up. There were wolf whistles. There were jeers. Startled, Alistair looked up at the screen. On it, undoubtedly, was the unmistakable image of Hugh Driftwood. But instead of leaning back against the desk in his stepmother's office receiving a blow-job at the mouth of her beautiful assistant, the picture in fact showed him making his famous speech at last year's party conference.

'Morality, yes,' he was saying hesitantly, as he looked down at his text with a somewhat goggle-eyed expression. 'Of course we must aim for the highest standards, and I am fully in accord with my colleague Alistair Sloach on the subject. However, we must also remember that other great virtue, tolerance. We must have charity and understanding for people who may choose lifestyles different from our own, but which are no less valid for all that. In a tolerant society, no one person should have the right to dictate which way is right or which is wrong. Down that road lies fascism. If one section of the community chooses to march to the beat of a different drum, so be it, provided that they do not do so at the expense of their fellow man.' His voice rose to a crescendo. 'Let us revel in our differences, let us rejoice in our diversity, and let us condemn no person who lives according to his own interpretation of moral standards, if he does so with respect for others.'

'Old hat,' one of the journalists heckled. 'Give us something exciting.'

'Yeah, come on, Sloachy,' shouted another. 'Bring back the performing monkey.'

'How about a League for Penile Re-form,' said a third. 'Bet you could do with one of those.'

But the Macclesfield Machiavelli was oblivious to all the

Chapter 29

Inspector Ffelcher rubbed the corner of his toupee and looked at his right-hand man, Sergeant Dorf. 'Take a gander at this!' he observed, staring down at the contents of Hilton Starr's safe. The lads had retrieved it from the house in Hampstead and had spent most of the day working on getting it open without damaging anything inside.

Together, the inspector and the sergeant withdrew a number of items from the safe's recesses. First of all came a box containing money. A lot of money. 'Flippin' heck,' said Sergeant Dorf. 'Must be twenty thousand pounds in here. What would he be doing with that?'

The inspector shook his head and reached for the next object. It was a little leather-bound book. Eagerly, he opened it up and began examining the tiny, practically illegible notes. 'Been doing some serious accounting, our dearly departed has,' he said, adding up the columns of figures in it. At length, he put it on his desk and sat down heavily. Then suddenly a light of inspiration came into his eyes and he let out a yelp.

'What is it?' asked the sergeant.

'Just remembered something Vanessa Driftwood said to me the other day,' replied the inspector. He pondered further. 'Bugger me,' he said at length. 'I reckon we've struck gold here, my lad. I want you to get the ballistics people up right away. Tell them to bring everything they've been able to piece together from that statuette. Not the bomb. Just the statuette. I think we may be on to something big here.'

Then he sat back and considered the implications of what he had just discovered. 'Bugger me,' he repeated.

Apparently this invitation held little appeal for Sergeant Dorf, however, since he hurried off post-haste to carry out his superior's instructions while the inspector continued to scratch himself speculatively.

Chapter 30

The Home Secretary's resignation, and his committal to the Margaret Thatcher Rest Home for Retired Politicians in Dulwich, created yet another public relations disaster for the government. Murmurings in the media suggested that the scandal that had engulfed Alistair Sloach – which they themselves had done so much to precipitate – would be the final fatal blow to a weak Prime Minister, whatever the size of his majority. And all signs confirmed that the widespread public sympathy the new leftwing government had enjoyed after taking office in the wake of the millennium disaster had now completely vanished.

There was one person, however, who did not believe those findings for a moment. And that was the Prime Minister, Edward Burgins himself. Sitting in his study at Downing Street on the day after Alistair's resignation, he reflected insouciantly that he had seen it all before – and he had not the slightest doubt that this momentary unpopularity would soon pass and he would once again bask in the glow of public affection.

An amiable man, famous for his wide avuncular smile, he had

never been given much to introspection. Admittedly, during this recent period of crisis there had been times when he had suffered occasional fits of melancholy, dreaming longingly of retiring to the country to tend his geraniums and collection of Stalinist memorabilia.

But after all, he'd been on the very point of doing that once before, he reasoned, and look what had happened then. Six months ago, just as his mind had been turning to retirement after more than twenty years on the backbenches, Alistair Sloach had persuaded him that he was the only person capable of carrying the torch of the left forward into the new millennium. And how right he'd been! Burgins thought with pride of what he had achieved in such a short time. Not just the renationalisations, but also the introduction of the new maximum wage, the return to the good old ninety per cent tax rate, the compulsory establishment of workers' co-operatives throughout the City, and the unilateral disarmament of both nuclear and conventional weapons.

Who'd have thought he'd ever get to do all that? Until the millennium disaster, he'd assumed that his career was long over. He'd served his time in a previous government all those decades before, but in that administration he'd always been boxed in by the pigmies of the woolly centre. Just as he was getting his teeth into one government job they would shunt him on to another, preventing him from implementing anything that really helped the working man. Buggins Turn, the press had called it, making fun of their favourite nickname for him. Eventually the then Prime Minister had simply sidelined him into a sinecure as Deputy Prime Minister and left him there to rot.

If only that bastard was still alive now, thought Burgins triumphantly. He'd see how a proper socialist government was run. And the deceased Premier was not the only one. The same went for his own late father, the noble Lord Burgins. He remembered how much vindictive pleasure the old man had taken at all the slights they'd inflicted on him. 'See,' he'd cackled. 'I told you you should have stuck to your own class. They're making a fool out of you, all those jumped-up grammar-school boys.'

Well, they'd all be laughing on the other side of their graves now, Burgins reflected to himself. And this was just the beginning. There was much, much more he intended to achieve before his time in office was out. When he was done, there wouldn't be a single means of production left that had not proudly taken up its rightful place in the public sector.

So he just thanked God he *hadn't* yielded to that temptation to retire. He must have been prevented by some sixth sense, he liked to think. Perhaps it was the hand of fate which had known that the day would come when, like Churchill, he would be triumphantly recalled to take the reins at a time of national catastrophe.

Unlike Churchill, though, he was resolved that there was one thing he would not do, and that was outstay his welcome. He would not remain in office one moment longer than was absolutely necessary to achieve his objectives – nine or ten years, he reckoned, or perhaps just a little bit more. And at that point he would make a gracious and dignified exit and retire undefeated.

In the meantime, he was certain that his country and his party still needed him and he fully intended to stick around. Not for a second did he believe all these polls which suggested his unpopularity was lower than that of any leader since Caligula. What people really needed, he felt, was to see him as he was. A decent man trying to do the best possible job in difficult circumstances. The trouble was that the populace were very rarely presented with the true picture. They saw scandal, they saw crises, they saw their politicians being belittled on television by sharp-suited right-wing interviewers with machine-gun tongues, who were only interested in scoring points, not in establishing the truth at all.

Well, this Popviz interview would soon put an end to that. Ever since those disgusting questions on *Panorama* about his wife's entirely legitimate private company, the PM's distrust of television had been total. But this time things were going to be different. Driftwood International had proved itself a staunch friend of the government and the interviewer Candida Blitz was a most charming young woman. A little simple, perhaps, and she had seemed a trifle nervy when she had come to tea at Downing Street the other day, but then that was to be expected in the presence of such an important man as himself.

Most crucially, on the issue of questions, Candida had proved utterly sound. She had submitted the list in advance and there was not one which would give him a single moment's difficulty. They had even discussed some of the amusing stories he would be able to relate about his youth, and especially that one about a visit to the House of Commons when he was a boy scout. He'd tried to sit down on the green leather bench which was reserved for the Prime Minister, but an irate policeman had chased him off. Wouldn't that make them all laugh!

The Popviz interview, the PM decided, was going to be just the ticket to help him recover from this terrible chimpanzee business.

With that, the PM's mind turned back to Alistair. Despite the undoubted debt of gratitude he owed Sloach for helping him – in a really rather minor way, Burgins felt in retrospect – to attain the premiership, he had always been convinced there was something odd about the chap. All that fanatical morality might go down well with the electorate but it had never seemed healthy in an educated man in this day and age. And now he turned out to be a dedicated chimpanzee fetishist! It just went to show.

Now Hugh Driftwood, there was a good fellow, straightforward and reliable. None of those perverse foibles in him. The Prime Minister had no doubt he would make a fine Home Secretary, and perhaps one day when – in the distant future – he decided to retire, Hugh might even become his chosen successor. But he wouldn't need to worry about that for a very long time, of course.

All in all, Edward Burgins concluded with rising enthusiasm, the worst was now behind him. This interview would mark the start of a new era, the beginning of a comeback which would take him all the way through to the next election. Then, he would be swept back to a resounding victory on a wave of popular support.

The Prime Minister was nothing if not an optimist.

Chapter 31

Candida Blitz was also beginning to focus on the interview with Edward Burgins, and with no small degree of trepidation. For some weeks she had been rehearsing at the spanking new Popviz studios in the Isle of Dogs under the watchful eye of its director of current affairs, Phil Zimper.

Since the huge extra publicity generated both by the murder of Hilton Starr and the waterlogged chimpanzee incident at the Grand Britannic Hotel, the new station had acquired a reputation for danger and unpredictability, and the satellite dishes had indeed been disappearing off shelves in record quantities just as Vanessa had predicted. As the launch approached, supplies were completely exhausted, and the dishes were thought to be changing hands on the black market for up to ten times their recommended price. In all, somewhere in excess of five million were in circulation by the so-called PopDay on Friday, June 9th.

That first evening of official transmissions was due to be an eventful one, not only for Candida, but also for Vanessa Driftwood and her team. Vanessa arrived at the studio early in the morning, much to the dismay of her staff, to supervise the final preparations in person. The line-up for the night was relentlessly impressive. Although its highlight was the interview with the Prime Minister on the new channel's flagship current affairs programme, *Livewire*, there were a host of other attractions to tickle the fancy of less politicised couch potatoes. *Livewire* was to be followed by a specially commissioned television play by Hollywood director Kurt Bocklemaster on the traumas of a relationship between two airline stewardesses. Much advance publicity had been devoted to this, including numerous interviews with the director in which he maintained that the scenes of intimate lesbian love-making were essential for the integrity of a deeply moving story. Carefully selected extracts had even been shown on the terrestrial channels, stimulating a refreshing interest in the dramatic arts – and coincidentally in Popviz too – in many working men's clubs throughout the country. The play would be followed by another Popviz innovation, the first in a series of pro-am boxing matches. Finally, to round off the evening, there was to be a documentary profile of the popular American composer of musicals, Mattison Pick, and his erstwhile writing partner, Sam Kaskin, in the new weekly culture slot, *Your Arts Desire*.

Even though most of these programmes had been recorded months in advance, much remained to be done on the day itself. It was a central plank of the new station's philosophy that all its news and current affairs output would be up-to-the-minute, and so the whole of *Livewire*, including Candida's interview with the PM, was, as its name implied, due to be transmitted live. On top of that, programme links had to be planned, announcers co-ordinated, and the switchboards manned both for the expected influx of complaints from viewers about the explicit sex scenes and the not unrelated flood of new subscribers. A busy day was in store for everyone.

Candida had asked Will if he would be there during the

broadcast to give her moral support, and he had willingly agreed. He arrived at the bustling studio at about seven p.m. After checking in at the gleaming reception area, he was shown through a series of identical corridors to Candida's dressing room and arrived there feeling like he'd just negotiated the maze on an especially nasty video game.

When he'd left her at the house that morning, Candida had been as on edge as he'd ever known her during their brief relationship, and Will was not looking forward to seeing her again now. However, he was in for a pleasant surprise – at least initially. As he entered, she greeted him full of cheer. 'Hello, Willy Billy,' she said in a playful voice. She peered at him myopically, then groped for her glasses. 'Hardly recognised you without my contacts in.' She had rarely let him see her in spectacles, which wasn't surprising as they were thick as bottle ends and altered her appearance completely, giving her an even more endearing air of vulnerability. He moved over to her and kissed her on the forehead. 'You're going to be grand,' he said, 'I know it.'

'Of course I am,' she said brightly. 'No problem. *Kein Problem. Pas de problème*. I don't know why I was so nervous before.'

Will looked at her with some curiosity. 'Today's rehearsals went well then?'

'Couldn't have been better. Listen, as Phil said, I'm so used to interviewing roller-skating parrots and talking donkeys on the *Jolly Roger* that someone as straightforward as a Prime Minister should be a piece of cake.' She giggled.

'And you've got all your other questions sorted out now, have you?' She had been rehearsing in front of the mirror at home for days.

'Certainly,' said Candida airily. 'And I cleared them with the PM personally, so that should all be hunky-dory.' She threw back her long blonde hair in a confident sweep as she inserted her lenses.

'Have you got them memorised?' Will asked dubiously.

'Don't fuss so, Willy. Don't you know anything about broadcasting? I'll have an autocue, of course. I'll do some ad-libbing when I need to, and Phil will be able to feed me any extra instructions from the control box through my earpiece. Easy as pie.'

Will tried to square this picture of super-cool with the gibbering wreck he had left at home earlier. A suspicion was beginning to dawn on him, one which he only hoped was unfounded. Just in case, though, he thought he'd better confront it at once.

'You wouldn't by any chance have been been eating brownies recently, would you?' he asked tentatively.

'Brownies?' Innocence beamed from her every pore.

'Yes, brownies. Hash brownies, to be precise.'

'Now, why would I want to do anything like that, sweetie-pie?'

Laid-back though he was, even Will was not proof to the fears which now surged within him. 'How much did you put in them?' he asked in measured tones.

'I don't know what you're talking about!'

He tried to remember what quantity he'd deposited in the secret hiding place in Candida's kitchen the day before. He'd been spending so many of his nights there that it seemed like a good idea at the time.

'I don't like brownies anyway,' Candida twittered. 'Nasty sickly chocolatey things.' Then suddenly, she burst into song. 'But if I'd known you were coming, I'd have baked a cake, baked a cake, baked a cake,' she warbled.

'You baked it in a cake?' asked Will weakly.

'Yes, and a very nice cake it was too. Sponge, with lots of hundreds and thousands on top.'

'Jesus, how much did you put in the bloody thing?'

'You didn't say how much to put in,' replied Candida in

a baby voice. 'So I just used whatever it was you left under the tea-cosy and then I ate it all up. Yum yum. And you're quite right, it does relax you.' She did a little dance around the dressing room to demonstrate.

'Oh, fuck,' said Will and sat down heavily.

Candida wiggled an admonitory digit at him. 'Language, Willy Billy!' she said. But then the sound of the word seemed to take on an appeal for her, and she began repeating it ad nauseam. 'Fuck, fuck, fuck,' she burbled. 'Fuck, fuck, fuck, fuck.'

Will's heart had filled with apprehension. And though he was not much given to self-recrimination, he had a fair dose of that too. This was all his fault. He should never have introduced the stuff into her house in the first place. Now what was he going to do?

But it was too late for him to do anything much, for at that moment there was a tap on the door and a young man with a toilet-brush hairstyle poked his head around it. 'Candida, darling,' he said in a phoney mid-Atlantic accent. 'You better get your ass upstairs. The PM's about to arrive and they want to begin voice-level tests.'

'Thanks, Joey-oey,' said Candida sweetly. 'I'll be on my way in a momentito.' Joe, too, looked at her oddly. 'Joey, this is my friend Will.'

'Hey there, Will, great to meet you,' said Joe in an indifferent monotone. He continued to study Candida speculatively.

'Do you think you could maybe get Will into the control room for the broadcast? I'm sure he'll find it very interesting.'

'I'm certain he will,' said Joe, with feeling. 'Sure. I'll smuggle him in. Now you'd better get a move on.'

'Wish me luck!' said Candida.

'Good luck,' said Will, giving her a kiss and a hug.

'You're gonna be great,' said Joe. 'I just know it.' As Candida rushed off happily, he turned to Will and drew his index finger across his throat. 'She's dead,' he said with absolute certainty.

Up in the control room, Will discovered that the scene was one of controlled chaos. Joe ushered him in and sat him down in the corner. 'Stay there and keep your mouth shut, and nobody'll notice you,' he advised.

Will looked around. He had not realised it took so many people to stage one of these programmes. There seemed to be enough personnel and equipment here for a small lunar landing. Regiments of technicians were sitting in front of computers and television monitors, and the whole business was being co-ordinated by an Albert Einstein lookalike who sat in the middle with a cigarette hanging from his lips. This, Will guessed, must be the director, Phil Zimper, he had heard so much about. On the man's left was a young woman whose sole job appeared to be to furnish him with a constant supply of pre-lit Marlboros.

An anticipatory murmur went around as the familiar figure of Edward Burgins, the Prime Minister, arrived on the studio floor accompanied by Candida. Will wondered if anyone else had noticed the slightly unfocused expression in her eyes. Well, he reflected philosophically, the die was cast now. As a student of human nature, he had no doubt the next hour would be fraught with interest. The proof of this particular pudding was very definitely going to come well after the eating.

Candida took her seat with great confidence and tried to cross her legs, but it didn't quite work. Her right one seemed to have gone slightly out of control, and eventually she lifted it with both hands and placed it very carefully over her left. All this was watched with some consternation by the Prime Minister.

'Are you quite all right, Miss Blitz?' he asked solicitously.

'I'm just dandy, thank you, PM, and how are you? The main

thing about these interviews is not to be nervous. Just you sit back and relax.' To illustrate the point, she lolled back comfortably in her chair, almost falling backwards. 'Whoopsadaisy!' she giggled.

In the control room there was a growing realisation that all was not right. 'Oh, my God, she's high as a kite,' said Phil Zimper. But there was no time to stop her now, since, after a few voice-level tests and a brief exchange between the technical people, someone began counting down from ten and it was evident that the broadcast would shortly be under way. Just as they were about to start, the door to the control room opened once again and Will saw a red-headed figure slide in. The director, alerted to the new arrival by a blast of cold air, turned around angrily but bit back his curse when he recognised Vanessa Driftwood.

At the start, it all went better than Will had feared. Candida was after all a seasoned broadcaster, and as soon as the red light on the camera told her that she was on air she rose impressively to the occasion. She was, perhaps, slightly over-bright, but not to an extent that anybody but a close acquaintance would have noticed. With the help of the autocue, she sailed through the introduction and the preliminary questions with a self-assurance not previously associated with her. They had a brief and solemn chat about Hilton Starr and his tragic passing, and both agreed that terrorism ought not to be allowed. After that, in short order, they covered the Prime Minister's happy home life, his fondness for geraniums and his famous collection of Stalinist memorabilia. Then he told an amusing tale involving the First Lady's dog and a Gurkha's regimental hat from the last time he'd stayed at the White House.

Every so often Phil muttered a few words of encouragement to Candida through his microphone, but even this was hardly necessary. She was breezing away with aplomb, and it didn't seem as though anything could put her off her stride.

Unfortunately this was not to last. It was when they reached the Prime Minister's early years that things started to go awry. A photograph of him as a spotty child on a school trip to the Houses of Parliament filled the screen, and he told the story about the policemen and the Prime Minister's bench in the House of Commons. Candida laughed uproariously, burbling away with an enthusiasm far out of proportion to the mediocre anecdote.

Then she shifted him on to his military career. He had won a medal in the Korean War and this was one of the points his advisers were anxious to have publicised in an attempt to counter his reputation for gutlessness. Burgins chuntered on for a while about comradeship in the armed forces. His time there, he said, had been challenging and character-forming. All eyes were on the PM except for Will's; mesmerised, he had been watching Candida ever since the beginning of the programme. Suddenly he noticed her becoming distracted. A look of consternation overtook her face and she began to feel around her knees frantically. Will knew at once what the problem was, having seen it once before on the night of the awards ceremony. One of her contact lenses had fallen out, and this time Zoë was not around to help her locate it. Fortunately, the live camera was still focused on the PM. Candida peered myopically ahead of her, trying to see her next question on the autocue, but Phil Zimper was speaking in a low voice to one of the cameramen and seemed oblivious to her difficulty.

Finally, as the PM ground to a halt on the topic of the army, he looked expectantly across for the next prompt. Candida appeared centre screen. She had stopped feeling around between her legs just in time, and pulled herself together to read with apparent confidence from the autocue. 'Of course,' she said with a bright smile of admiration, 'it was as a result of your activities in the army that you got the famous VD from that queen, wasn't it?'

The Prime Minister looked shell-shocked, his Adam's apple bobbing up and down like a buoy on a stormy sea. 'I don't think that incident's anyone's business but mine,' he began to mumble.

In the control room, Phil burst frenetically into life. 'VC, VC!' he screamed into his microphone. 'He got the famous *VC* from *the* Queen, you stupid bitch. The bloody Victoria Cross.'

A hundred decibels travelled rapidly through the wire into Candida's skull, and she rose several inches into the air. She interrupted the Prime Minister before he could make any more accidental revelations about his medical and sexual history to a fascinated nation. 'Sorry, of course I meant to say that you were awarded the . . . the VC . . . by the Queen for . . . for acts of bravery. That must have been a proud moment for you?'

Relief flooded over the Prime Minister. 'I don't think these things are a question of pride,' he said rather shakily. 'I saw what had to be done and I did it. I do consider myself a man of action.' He struck a Churchillian pose and began somewhat uncertainly to relate the circumstances of his military feat.

The director continued to curse, clearly quite unaware of the reason for Candida's slip-up. Will coughed theatrically, and despite receiving a withering look, decided to make a contribution. 'I think,' he whispered, 'that Candida has dropped a contact lens. She can't see a thing without them.'

'Shit,' said Phil.

'Shit,' said all his assistants in unison.

Behind them, however, a stifled laugh rang out. 'Buggins just admitted on prime time television that some faggot gave him the clap,' Vanessa chortled, 'and just because she misread the line? What an asshole!'

'Shhhh!' Phil did not care who he offended now. His single aim in life was to rescue his show from catastrophe. 'Candida, my darling,' he said, with a voice of infinite patience. 'Sorry for shouting at you there. Now, love, are we right in thinking you've lost a lens, hmmm? If so, just blink once.' Candida blinked. 'Fuck,' he screamed violently, banging his head on the table.

Candida's face went even whiter and Phil hastened to reassure her. 'Not a problem. No problem at all. Nothing to worry about,' he said soothingly. The blood vessels on his forehead were pumping like pigs' bladders. 'Now, here's what we'll do. Don't try and look for your lens now. We can find it later. In the meantime, I'm going to give you lots of easy prompts through the earpiece and you can ad-lib a little from those. Don't, don't, for God's sake, try to do any more of your own reading. Okay?'

Candida blinked her agreement, but she didn't look convinced. As the PM continued prattling on about the importance of leadership, Will watched her trying to regain her composure. It was a lost cause. The combination of adrenaline and drugs seemed to have severed any connection between her brain and the rest of her body and all trace of intelligent life had disappeared from her features. She was now totally reliant on the crucial drip-feed of questions being transmitted into her ear.

'Right,' said Phil as calmly as he could, 'just five more minutes to go, then we can all go home and slash our wrists. Now, when he finishes on the army, we're going to ask him very nicely about his vision for the country's future.'

'No, we're not!' A strident voice suddenly rang out like a rifle shot from the back of the control room. Startled, everyone turned around. 'That's not what we're going to ask at all,' said Vanessa, like a woman possessed. She sounded as if she had just been subject to some great revelation.

'Sorry?' asked Phil, taken aback. He looked down at his notes. 'I thought—'

But moving rapidly up to the front, Vanessa cut him off.

'I'm taking over here now,' she said with authority. 'Gimme that goddamned mike.' Without further ado she pushed the shell-shocked director off his chair and plumped herself firmly down in his place. 'Now listen, Candida,' she said urgently. 'This is Vanessa Driftwood talking. There's been a change to the published programme. Okay?'

Candida blinked.

'Here's what I want you to do. You're gonna pull yourself together and repeat everything I tell you. Are you with me?'

Candida blinked again.

'Great! Now, the next question's gonna be about this sorry excuse for a government. I want you to ask the Prime Minister how he explains all the corruption and vice in his Cabinet when they keep on blabbering on about moral millenniums. Got that?'

Candida blinked a third time, and as Burgins wound down on the subject of leadership, she repeated what Vanessa had said, word for word.

The PM stared at her like a frightened rabbit. 'Sorry?' he asked weakly.

Guided by Vanessa, Candida put the question again.

'Well, eh . . .' said the Prime Minister, clearly flummoxed by this unexpected departure from the script. Hesitatingly, he launched into an impromptu reply. Yes, he conceded, this had indeed been a sticky period. He had been as shocked as anyone when, shortly after his appointment, his trusted private secretary had been discovered with her legs wide apart and the three envoys from an Asian embassy somewhere in between. This, he added, was not what he had in mind at all when he had called for a greater opening out to the East. And, too, the resignation of the Chancellor of the Exchequer had been an embarrassment he could have done without. But it had not been Matthew Potts but his girlfriend who had committed the peccadillo, and weren't we all slaves to our loved ones, if

Candida knew what he meant? As for poor old Alistair, well he really couldn't comment on that because the case was sub judice, but at least no one could now claim that his government had no animal lovers in it.

All these, he indicated with an expansive gesture, were just minor setbacks – part of the rough and tumble of politics. Once the dust had settled, he had no doubt that the average man and woman in the street – he looked ingratiatingly at the camera – would realise that his was an honourable government of good intent, and that no other party could assure the long-term stability and prosperity of the nation.

Somehow it all fell rather flat. To the audience in the studio, and to the millions of viewers watching in every corner of the British Isles, this neat précis of his administration's brief but dreadful history served not to reassure but to highlight just how bankrupt it had become. And as the PM spluttered to a close, his mouth gaping open like an oyster, Vanessa moved in for the kill. Sitting forward in her chair, she spoke slowly and deliberately into the microphone. The tension in the control booth was palpable as everyone watched Candida listening vacantly to the words. Her eyes were glazed over, yet some auto-record mechanism in her brain seemed to take it all in, for presently she turned to face Burgins.

'One final question, Prime Minister,' she said sweetly, tilting her head to one side as if about to ask him about his marble collection. 'What would you say to the charge that you are' – her internal recorder moved perceptibly into playback mode – 'a corrupt, incompetent, slimy, lazy, lying, cheating, good-for-nothing son of a bitch' – she smiled encouragingly – 'who couldn't organise an orgy in a whorehouse, much less run a country?' She stopped, then evidently recalled there was one further bit. 'And don't you think it's time you gave us all a goddamn break and got the hell out before the whole country rises up and *drives* you out?'

To say that this question hit the Premier like a bolt out of the blue would be something of an understatement. For at least fifteen seconds he just sat there and goggled. His eyes popped and his jaw, never known for its steadfastness in the first place, gently settled itself somewhere close to his lap. At length, though, he clearly felt that a reply was called for. His mouth opened. Nothing came out. It opened again. 'I . . . I beg your pardon?' he gulped.

If this was intended as a lightning riposte, it undoubtedly lacked bite. But Candida merely took it at face value, supposing that her question had not been fully understood. Obligingly she provided a short résumé. 'Don't-you-think-you're-just-a-good-for-nothing-son-of-a-bitch?' she repeated all in one breath. 'And-isn't-it-time-you-gave-us-all-a-break-and-got-out-before-the-country-rises-up-and-*drives*-you-out?'

By now, though, the Prime Minister had had more than enough. With as much dignity as he could muster – which wasn't much – he rose unsteadily to his feet. 'I have never been so insulted in my entire career,' he stuttered. 'I don't think there's any point in continuing this interview. Don't imagine I shall ever appear on this station again. My office will be making an official complaint first thing in the morning.' And with that, he picked up his papers and was gone, a puddle of perspiration on his chair the only sign that he'd ever been there in the first place.

'Oh, my God,' said Candida, the true awfulness of what she had said just beginning to seep through to her befuddled brain.

'Oh, my God,' said Phil Zimper.

'Oh, my God,' said all his assistants.

'Cut!' said Vanessa Driftwood smugly. 'Cue the credits.'

Uproar and confusion broke out everywhere, but Will's sympathies were elsewhere. Poor Candida, he thought. She would be devastated. He rushed downstairs to discover how right he was. Head in hands, she was still sitting on the studio floor where the Prime Minister had left her. The effects of the drug were gradually wearing off and she looked as pale as whitewash.

'I'm completely finished,' she said, inconsolably. 'I'll never work again.' Will took her in his arms. But much as he would have liked to, he couldn't really disagree.

It was two a.m. It had been a long and eventful day for Vanessa. Stooping with fatigue, but still with a glint of triumph in her eye, she gathered her strength and prepared to depart from the studio. Her car was waiting for her but she imagined there might be an onslaught of reporters to be dealt with first.

She was not wrong. Outside, the area was mobbed. The world's media had gathered with lightning speed. The vilification of a Prime Minister was a very big story indeed.

'Mrs Driftwood!' they shouted. 'Could you look over here please?' Cameras clicked and flashbulbs flashed. 'Number 10 have issued a strongly worded complaint to the broadcasting authority. What do you have to say to that?'

'Naturally we're very sorry about what's happened,' said Vanessa, trying hard to get to her car. 'Upsetting the Prime Minister was the very last thing we wanted to do. Tomorrow we'll be issuing a full apology.'

'What about Candida Blitz,' someone called. 'Are you going to fire her?'

'No comment,' said Vanessa, pushing her way through the throngs. But suddenly she was blocked by someone who was not from the media at all. She stopped in her tracks.

'Vanessa Driftwood?' asked the man in front of her with a sinister calmness.

'Yes?' Vanessa scowled and looked up. 'Oh, it's you, Inspector Ffelcher. What are *you* doing here?'

'I regret to say, Madam, that I am here to place you under arrest.'

'Come now, Inspector,' said Vanessa, startled. 'This is a free country. It may not be very nice to insult the Premier, but it's not exactly a crime.'

'It's nothing to do with that, Madam, I'm afraid.'

There was a sudden hush among all the members of the media as Vanessa looked at him questioningly. 'What the hell do you mean?'

'Mrs Vanessa Driftwood,' said the inspector sonorously, 'I am hereby charging you with the murder of Hilton Starr. I have to warn you that you are not obliged to say anything but that anything you do say will be taken down in writing and . . .'

And then he read her rights.

Chapter 32

The Prime Minister awoke with a start the following morning in the flat above Number 10 Downing Street. He had just had the most dreadful dream that some woman had verbally abused him on television in front of millions of viewers. Extraordinary what tricks the mind plays when one's under stress, he thought to himself.

But gradually, as he gained full consciousness, or at least came as near to full consciousness as he would ever be capable of, the Prime Minister began to realise that it had not been a dream after all. He really had appeared on that live chat show, and, having been promised a cosy non-political interview, had been subjected to the most disgusting display of vituperation he had ever come across in his life. It was unimaginable. It was the most staggering piece of political treachery in history. But what in God's name was he going to do about it?

He looked around for his wife, who was magnificent in a crisis and much brighter than he was. She would no doubt have been able to shed some light on the question. But then he remembered she was away in the States, negotiating some deal or other for The Millicent Burgins Government Contract Advisory Service. He would telephone her a bit later to see if she had heard about this awful interview, but in the meantime he must work things out on his own.

He thought carefully about the events of the previous day and, at length, his perennially sunny outlook on life came back to the fore and he began to feel less depressed. Of course, there would always be those opposed to him who would use this episode as a weapon. But, after all, the British were famous for their sense of fair play. They would realise that this kind of treatment simply wasn't cricket. It was cheating to lure him into a studio like that and then insult him so scandalously.

On further reflection, the Prime Minister was convinced that the real people of the country, the ordinary men and women in the street, would see how shoddily their Premier had been treated and would rally around him. Reassured by this line of reasoning, and exuding a quiet confidence, he was prepared to face the day. He pressed the bell above his headboard to tell his staff that he was ready for his early cup of tea, and sat up in bed. He felt much better already. There was a gentle tap on the door.

'Come in,' said the PM assertively. But it was not his tea. It was George, his principal private secretary.

'Bit early for you, George,' said the Prime Minister. 'Nothing up, I hope?'

'Well, there is something, Prime Minister. Ah ...' He seemed lost for words.

'Well, come on, man, spit it out. Foreign affairs crisis, eh? Run on the pound overnight in the Far East?' Edward Burgins was prepared for anything the vicissitudes of government might throw at him.

'No, none of those things,' said George nervously. 'Eh, perhaps it would be better if I showed you, Prime Minister. If you would care to step over here.' Mystified, the Prime

Minister pulled on a dressing-gown and allowed himself to be led over to the side of the room. George drew back the thick curtains and threw open the windows.

The sight that greeted them was stunning beyond description. Indeed, Edward Burgins had to pinch himself to make sure it was not some kind of mirage. As far as the eye could see, starting in Horseguards Parade and fanning out through St James's Park, the Mall and beyond, there spread forth a sea of faces. Thousands upon thousands of waving and chanting figures, of all shapes and sizes, were assembled before him.

'Goodness gracious,' said the Prime Minister. 'There must be ten thousand people out there.'

'We believe it's nearer a hundred thousand, at last count,' said George dolefully. 'They've been travelling in from all over the country overnight. The stations and airports have come to a standstill. The arterial roads into London are clogged with cars.'

The Prime Minister was overwhelmed. A spontaneous show of support! This he really had not expected. Tears welled in his eyes. The previous day had shocked him, but he had not realised how much it had affected his fellow countrymen too. They had felt so strongly that they had come from far and wide to demonstrate their support for him. It was most moving.

'They appear to be chanting something,' he said. 'I'm afraid I can't quite make it out. Can you?'

'Yes, Prime Minister.'

'What is it?'

George's voice faltered. He wished more than anything that he could be somewhere else at this moment. 'I think, Prime Minister,' he said tremulously, 'it's "Get out, you good-for-nothing son of a bitch."'

He was quite right. From every corner of the British Isles, the people had obeyed Candida's call to arms and risen up in their tens of thousands: stockbrokers from the City had forsaken their dealing desks and made common cause with miners from Derbyshire; middle-aged matrons from the Home Counties, wearing their best twin-sets and pearls, were embracing the homeless from the Embankment and helping them carry their cardboard boxes; little old ladies from Aberdeen had gathered their knitting to their breasts and, militantly waving their needles in the air, had teamed up with oil-rig workers who had helicoptered in from the North Sea; in hospitals all over the land, patients had discharged themselves and had hobbled and crawled on bended knee to be here; schools had declared an unofficial holiday so that their pupils would not miss this historical occasion; factory workers from the Midlands, fishermen from Cornwall, farmers from the Borders, sex workers from Soho, pensioners from Sussex. No element of the British people was unrepresented – every race, religion, ethnic group, interest group, hue of opinion and colour of skin.

And, a nation united – and at last at ease with itself – they had all made their way to the seat of government. To a man, woman and child they had assembled in front of 10 Downing Street overnight and, arms linked in a spirit of genuine camaraderie, they were chanting the words like some mystical incantation: '*Get out,*' they screamed in unison. '*Get out, you good-for-nothing son of a bitch.*'

The Prime Minister stared out dismally into the heaving crowds. Even he, with his eternal optimism, could recognise the end when he saw it. And he had no doubt that the end, in the shape of one hundred thousand of Britain's best and brightest, was standing outside the doors of Number 10 Downing Street at that very moment.

Chapter 33

Just after nine that same morning, Hugh Driftwood stood miserably on the doorstep of Candida's house in Hampstead. 'Vanessa's been arrested,' he said as soon as she answered the door. The distress radiated from his unshaven face. His eyes were red and he looked like he might dissolve into tears at any moment. 'I've been at Paddington Green police station all night. I didn't want to go home and I couldn't think where else to go.'

'How dreadful!' said Candida, looking no less upset herself and evidently suffering from an almighty hangover after her drug-induced trip at the Popviz studio the evening before. 'You were quite right to come here.' She showed him into the living room where Will was sitting playing with Zoë the chimpanzee. 'Hugh has some more bad news,' said Candida sadly. 'We've certainly had our fill today.' It was barely fourteen hours since her disastrous interview with the Premier and she had been near-suicidal for most of that time. Will had stayed up with her all night, trying to raise her spirits, but nothing he could say could console her. 'I'm finished,' she kept on snapping at him with an uncharacteristic harshness. 'Completely finished. And all because of you and your dope.'

Then Hugh had rung them up and asked if he could come over, and now there was this further catastrophe to add to the air of depression. 'What have they charged her with?' Will asked with some curiosity.

'I just can't believe it,' Hugh said, sitting down heavily. 'They're accusing her of murdering Hilton Starr. They say that she wrote those anonymous letters herself, that it was all a plot, that she planned for the bomb to explode after she gave it to Hilton at the awards all along.'

'But that's absurd. How could she have?' asked Candida, her own problems momentarily forgotten. 'I mean, she wasn't to know that the timing of the show would change and that the bomb would go off when it did.' But suddenly something clicked in her mind. 'Oh,' she said. 'Mona da Ponte and the orange juice . . .'

'Exactly,' said Hugh. He buried his head in his hands. 'It turns out that Mona da Ponte wasn't drunk at all. She was deliberately got at. Someone poisoned her juice so that she wouldn't be able to go on. And they're saying it was Vanessa who did it by switching glasses with her. That way she brought forward the show's running order and made it seem as if she was the real target.'

'But how could she have put a bomb into the statuette?' Candida was thinking it through. 'The whole idea's impossible.'

'I wish it was,' replied Hugh with a glazed expression. He got up and paced around the room. 'But unfortunately it's not. It seems it was *her* own statuette that had the bomb in it. One of the ones she was awarded years ago when she was in TV. You see, someone had substituted it for the real award. They've managed to piece it back together from all the bits. It even had her name on it, and none of the new statuettes had been engraved yet. So they checked out Vanessa's office at Driftwood House, and found that one of hers is missing.'

'Oh, my God,' said Candida. 'For heaven's sake, why should she want to kill Hilly?' The full implications of the terrible accusation were just beginning to sink in. 'What possible motive could she have had?'

'That's what makes it even worse.' Hugh's whole body was sagging from the sleepless night and the weight of his misery. 'The police are saying that Hilton was blackmailing Vanessa – had been for ages. That was why she had to let him have the job on *Livewire*. They don't know what he was blackmailing her about, but apparently they've found evidence that she's been depositing money in his bank account and giving him cash every week for ages now. It was all in Hilton's safe.' He gestured helplessly towards the bedroom. 'The one they removed from upstairs.'

'You mean it was Vanessa who sent those burglars here?' asked Candida, deeply shocked.

'So they're claiming. She needed to get the incriminating evidence back.' Finally, he abandoned the unequal struggle and broke down. 'I just don't know what to think,' he sobbed.

Candida moved over immediately to comfort him. She put an arm around his shoulder. 'I don't believe it for a moment,' she said stoutly. 'I knew Hilly better than anyone else, and he wasn't a blackmailer. It's simply not true. The police must have made it all up because they can't find the real murderers.'

But opposition to this view came from a surprising quarter. Will Cloud, who had been sitting staring pensively into the middle distance, had hardly spoken during the exchange, but now he stirred. 'Let's not be too hasty here,' he said evenly. 'We wouldn't want our judgement to be clouded by our own personal feelings.'

'You mean you suspected her all along?' asked Hugh with incredulity.

'Well now, it was always a possibility, so it was. And what does Vanessa have to say for herself?'

'I haven't been able talk to her properly yet,' said Hugh. 'They won't let her out of . . . out of custody until they've fixed bail. But apparently she claims she doesn't know anything about it, that she never paid any money to Hilton Starr, and that she offered him the job on the satellite station out of the goodness of her heart. She says someone must have framed her.'

'That must be right then!' said Candida decisively. 'I'm sure Vanessa would never lie.'

Hugh nodded his agreement but Will looked at them both with pursed lips. 'How does she explain the statuette being the one with her name on it?' he asked.

'She can't. She can't explain it at all,' Hugh replied. 'She says she didn't even know the bloody thing was missing from her office. According to her, someone must have taken it when she wasn't looking. But that's virtually impossible – hardly anyone's allowed in except Vanessa's own staff. And the rest of the time it's always kept locked. They have round-the-clock security in that place. You can hardly nick your finger, much less a statuette, without being spotted.' He rubbed his eyes. 'Some Prime Minister I would make,' he said, smiling dolefully through the tears. 'Can't even keep from blubbing.'

'I think you'll make a great Prime Minister,' said Candida fiercely.

'That's just it,' said Hugh. 'I hate to think about myself at a time like this, but it looks like I'm sunk as well. Burgins is finished after last night' – he cast a rather reproachful glance at Candida – 'and there's bound to be a leadership contest. But I can hardly put myself forward when my step-mother's just been arrested for murder. The whole situation's completely hopeless.' He appeared as if he might collapse again and Candida offered to get him something to steady his nerves.

'I'm really sorry,' said Will as she went off to raid Hilton's drinks cabinet. 'I don't know what to say.'

'There's nothing you can say,' Hugh replied with a sad shake of the head.

They sat in silence until Candida returned with a brandy and some news. 'I just turned on the radio in the kitchen,' she told them. 'The Prime Minister's resigned. For health reasons.'

This did nothing to bolster Hugh's spirits. 'It's all over then,' he muttered. 'If he'd held on a bit, then maybe I could have . . . I don't know what I could have done. But now the nominations will have to be in by tomorrow night, so I've no chance. Well, I suppose it was fun while it lasted.'

'Stop talking like that,' said Candida. 'You mustn't give up hope. Must he, Will?' She turned to the Irishman expectantly.

But Will wasn't even listening. Instead he was sitting tickling Zoë's ear with a faraway expression in his eyes. 'What was that?' he asked.

'I said we mustn't let Hugh give up hope,' Candida repeated, not without some irritation.

'Ah . . . no, I suppose not,' Will replied absently. 'Not unless you feel like it, that is.' Then suddenly he got to his feet. 'Look,' he said. 'I'm sure you don't want me hanging around here. Now you two are getting on so well, why don't you carry on chatting and I'll just nip back to the house in Islington for a while. I've got something I need to do on my own, you see. You don't mind, do you, Candida?' She looked at him angrily but the question had been a purely rhetorical one. He was already on his way out into the hallway. Without any further explanation, he collected up his jacket, shouted, 'Bye then,' and departed through the front door without a backward glance.

'Well!' said Candida, staring in fury at the door. 'Doesn't that just show him in his true colours! Of course,' she added, 'you know why he needs to be alone.' Hugh raised a weary eyebrow and she did an exaggerated mime of a drug addict injecting himself. 'Dope. That's his answer to everything. Look at the trouble he's got me into with all that.' She slammed her cup down on the coffee table, startling Zoë, who was dozing underneath. 'You're just a useless pothead,' she shouted after him, although he must have been halfway down the road by that time. 'And I wish . . . I wish I'd never set eyes on you.'

It was Hugh's turn to comfort Candida. He wiped her cheeks gently with his handkerchief and give her a sip of the brandy. 'Well, at least you and I can stick together,' he said. 'We're both in the same boat now – neither of us has got any future . . .'

Chapter 34

In guessing at the reason for Will Cloud's abrupt departure, Candida had not been entirely wrong. He was indeed longing for a smoke. But that was by no means the only motive for his Garboesque quest for solitude. The truth was that he desperately needed to think. Used to solving problems for a living, he was sure he had his most challenging puzzle to date if only he could crack it.

Not having a car and unable to find a taxi, he decided to walk back down to Islington. It was a pleasant June day, the weather warm but overcast, and it was muggy as only London could be at that time of year. He set off jauntily down Hampstead High Street towards Camden Town and presently took a quick look around to check that the coast was clear before reaching into his pocket. Not that he was that bothered about being spotted, but he could do without the hassle right now. He extracted one of the pre-rolled joints he always kept in his jacket and lit it up, luxuriantly breathing in the smoke and waiting for the mildly narcotic effects to spread through his bloodstream. They did not disappoint, and, swinging his arms loosely by his side, he sauntered along and allowed the world to float serenely past him.

He simply didn't understand this whole affair at all, he mused as he walked. And yet he was sure he ought to. There was one piece of the riddle missing, but he couldn't for the life of him work out what it was, or where to begin looking. Methodically, he ticked off all the elements in his mind: Vanessa and the brass statuettes, Mona da Ponte and the orange juices, Candida and the burglars who had found nothing they wanted to steal, the Kennedy motorcade bizarrely strewn with pieces of Hilton Starr. But none of it made any sense to him. There had to be a key somewhere – and he just needed to find it.

As Hampstead gave way to Belsize Park, and it in turn to Camden Town, he lit up a second joint, reflecting that in this part of the world he would be more likely to stand out if he wasn't smoking dope than if he was. He passed a doorway where a group of drunks were sleeping rough. 'Spare some change, mate?' asked one. Absently Will dug into his pocket.

'Thanks!' said the man groggily, peering up at him, bottle in hand. He looked ill, his skin drawn, his cheeks empty; but his eyes were bright with a strangely translucent quality. He vaguely reminded Will of someone, but for the moment he couldn't think who.

Walking on through Camden High Street, he took a left, and with another puff let the events of the past few months wash over him once again. One image after another swam dreamily into his mind. All at once, a startling picture came to him in garish close-up. It was of another face, sallow and unhealthy, which had also stared maniacally out at him, its eyes like those of a Hallowe'en pumpkin hollowed out and lit from within.

And it was at that precise moment that Will knew – he knew with absolute certainty – what had really happened on the night of the Brass Monkey Awards ceremony. Finally, walking through the streets of Camden Town stoned out of his mind, he had found that elusive key and suddenly it was all a million times clearer to him than it could ever have been when he was stone cold sober.

In a daze, he found a seat at a bus stop and sank on to it. What he needed to do now, he knew, was think through the consequences of this startling revelation. Gradually, he emptied his head of everything else and allowed the other elements of the bizarre kaleidoscope to click decisively into place in his brain.

It was fully half an hour before he stood up again. The effects of the drugs were just beginning to pass their peak and a glint of reality was stealing back into his befuddled consciousness. But that didn't matter any longer. With a lopsided grin, Will set off on the last stage of his journey, a sense of optimism coursing through his veins to replace the waning narcotic.

There was one thing, however, which still troubled him about his discovery, he reflected as he finally reached the outskirts of Islington. And that was evidence – or the absence of it. It was all very well having a theory, and a bloody good theory at that. But it would do him no good if he had nothing to back it up. And, given the circumstances, such proof was going to be pretty difficult to come by.

Shaking his head ruefully, he turned into Hugh's street and let himself into the house with his latchkey. Since he had virtually moved in with Candida, it was a while since he had been there and even Hugh had not slept in the house the night before. The mail had piled up on the mat and Will sifted through it distractedly. As usual, it was almost all for his friend, consisting of the typical postal monsoon of invitations, petitions, requests for help and demands for money that filled the in-trays of even the most minor MP. At the bottom, however, there was a thick package which was addressed to Will himself. He stared at it in some perplexity. He had given Hugh's address to very few people and he couldn't think who it could be from.

After ripping it open, he was no less confused. Inside, all he could find was a carefully wrapped video-cassette. Why would anyone want to send him one of those? he wondered. Nor did there seem to be any identification with it. No, wait. There was a letter, scrawled on lavender notepaper, which he'd almost missed.

With mounting curiosity, he read it through.

Dear Will Cloud,
    I so enjoyed our little chat at the banquet.
    I think you will find the enclosed of interest. Please pass it on to your friend, Hugh Driftwood, or do whatever else you think appropriate with it.
    I couldn't let the bastard ruin another career as well.
    I do hope we'll run into each other again soon.
    Yours sincerely,
    Margaret Sloach

Well, well. Now, what on earth could all that be about? Mystified, he took the cassette through to the lounge, slipped it into the VCR, and settled down to watch it.

Chapter 35

It wasn't until the following morning that the telephone calls started coming.

Candida had stayed in bed, sobbing gently to herself. There was nothing really to get up for, she thought miserably. Both her career and her new friendship with Will Cloud, in which she'd set such store, were over, dead and buried. There would be nothing to get out of bed for ever again.

Will had not arrived back until late the night before and had made no attempt to explain his odd behaviour of earlier in the day. She'd greeted him frostily, but he'd virtually ignored her anyway. He'd just gone upstairs and spent most of the evening searching through Hilton's papers, even though the police had already removed most of them.

After that they'd had an almighty argument. 'You just don't care,' she'd shouted. 'I see what you're really like now. Here we all are in the middle of the most terrible catastrophe ever and you're not the slightest bit interested. Well, I'm glad I've found out now, before it's too late.'

Will had sat through all this stoically, almost not listening, as if his mind were on more important things. Then, with a shrug, he'd gone to sleep in the spare room and left early in the morning without another word.

The first of the calls was from her agent, Milton Grimble. He hadn't been in touch since the débâcle, which had hardly surprised her. After what had happened, she doubted if she would ever hear from him again.

'Well?' he said brightly. 'Where's it to be? New York or Los Angeles? I would go for LA myself. Of course, you'll get more offers from New York, but then the weather in California is so much better. Or I guess you could stay in London, if you can stand all the media attention.'

'What in heaven are you talking about?' asked Candida, completely baffled.

'For Christ's sake, darling!' he exclaimed. 'Haven't you seen today's papers?'

'No, they're still on the mat.'

'Then get your pretty little bum downstairs and call me back when you've read them.'

She staggered into the hall and collected the morning's newspapers from the doormat. The *Flick* was the first to come to hand and to her astonishment she stared down at a huge image of herself on the front page, below one of the outgoing Prime Minister, Edward Burgins. 'BUGGINS TURNED OUT!' screamed the headline. And above the picture of Candida it said: 'AND IT WAS HER WOT DID IT!' Underneath there was a long article. 'Is acid-tongued Candida Blitz the most feared interviewer in television history?' it began, and went on to suggest that she had changed the face of political journalism for ever with her rapier-like tell-it-as-it-is style.

'Everyone knew that it was time for Buggins to go', said an editorial, 'but nobody could say it to his face. This woman was the one who did it and that took guts. The *Flick* takes its hat off to plucky Candida Blitz.' There was much more of the same in the *Pop* and even in the respectable broadsheets. The *Financial Times*'s headline – 'RESIGNATION OF "GOOD-FOR-NOTHING SON OF A BITCH" SENDS STERLING SOARING' – gave her almost all the credit for the ecstatic response of the world's currency markets to Edward Burgins's removal.

Candida could hardly believe it. She rang her agent back. 'I see what you mean,' she said delightedly. 'Have you had much other reaction?'

'Are you bloody kidding?' he gurgled. 'The fax machine is close to exploding. I'm going to have to draft in extra switchboard staff. BBC, ITV, NBC, ABC, you name it, they all want you. *Time* magazine and *Newsweek* would both like to profile you on next week's cover. Also, the White House have just phoned. The President's about to launch a new initiative to get closer to what people really think about him. Would you be interested in doing a one-off special, a no-holds-barred interview for public television? You just need to name the figure.'

Candida's knees buckled underneath her. 'I . . . I don't know what to say.'

'Just say yes,' advised her agent.

After that the phone didn't stop ringing all day, with people calling up to congratulate her and ask for interviews. Even Will didn't manage to get through until the afternoon.

'Jesus,' he said. 'Your phone's been engaged for an age!' Such was Candida's elation that she decided to forgive him for his earlier behaviour. But although he was delighted to hear her good news, that was not what he had called about. 'Can you get down to Docklands later this afternoon?' he asked.

'Well, it looks like I've got some job interviews lined up now, but . . . is it important?'

'Indeed it is!'

'Okay,' said Candida. 'Where?'

'Vanessa's office. Four o'clock. And be sure to bring Zoë. I want *everyone* at this meeting.'

'We'll be there,' Candida promised. 'What's it all about, though?' she asked curiously.

But Will had already rung off.

Chapter 36

Will Cloud surveyed the room thoughtfully. It was a full house. All the people he had invited had appeared at the appointed time, and even Vanessa's enormous office seemed crowded. Hugh and Candida were there, of course, accompanied by Zoë as requested. So too was Vanessa. She had been released from custody that morning on bail of two million pounds and was sitting at her desk, chain-smoking and looking uncharacteristically drained.

Ros Flato was there, wearing a short tight dress that enclosed her long legs like clingfilm, and oozing just as much sensuality as on the day when Will had first met her on the plane from Morocco.

Even Reg Diggle was there. To Ros's surprise, Will had phoned her up and, after getting her to check out certain facts about Vanessa and the Driftwood Organisation, had asked her to invite Reg to the gathering. She had done so rather reluctantly. 'All will be explained,' said Will, mysteriously. It was something he had always wanted to be able to say, ever since reading countless detective books in the course of his misspent Dublin youth.

Only Edward Burgins and Alistair Sloach were absent. Alistair's wife, the brittle Margaret, had come, though, and was sitting perched on the edge of Vanessa's coffee table. Will had requested her presence as a special favour to himself, and she'd accepted on the condition that her husband wasn't invited. In fact, there was little chance of that as Alistair had been confined to a padded cell for his own safety and was likely to remain so restrained for some considerable time to come.

Finally, Inspector Ffelcher was there, standing moodily beside the huge window and looking extremely bald. He had finally buckled under the jibes of his colleagues and with deep regret had jettisoned his hairpiece. He'd only agreed to attend this event after Hugh Driftwood, at Will's insistence, had exerted political pressure via the Metropolitan Police Commissioner and he appeared distinctly disgruntled at having been so impelled.

'Good, we all seem to be present and correct,' said Will. 'So let's get started.' He paced up and down the room for a moment in best Hercule Poirot fashion, gathering his thoughts. Then, somewhat melodramatically, he began to recite a familiar rhyme. 'Twinkle, twinkle, Hilton Starr,' he said, his gentle Irish inflexion taking the edges off the words. 'How I wonder what you are!' He paused for effect. 'It appears to me that this whole case ultimately revolves around the personality of Hilton Starr,' he continued.

'Now, I never actually met Hilton Starr until the night of his death. But I've heard so much about him from Candida that I really feel I knew him well. And the thing that strikes me most about the man is how bitter he must have been.' He held up his hand to forestall Candida's defence of her erstwhile lover. 'But it wasn't, it seems to me, a bitterness born of hardship or adversity. Sure, that was just the way he was. For Hilton, if anything ever went wrong in his life – even if it was something relatively minor – he always had to allocate blame, and rarely to himself.

'Of course, maybe I'm doing the poor fella an injustice, because he did have one thing to be resentful about.' Will turned and faced Vanessa. 'Hilton had helped Vanessa Driftwood, or Vanessa Zipsky as she was then, in many ways. He had given her a spot on his show when she first arrived from the States. He had helped to make her a star in her own right. And then he fell in love with her. And what did she do in return?' Vanessa stared at Will defiantly. 'She threw him over to marry Charles Driftwood. Hilton was beside himself with anger. And, as usual, he looked around for someone to blame, and Vanessa seemed the obvious candidate.

'Then, after she left his show, the ratings started to drop off. Hilton blamed Vanessa for that too. His career was falling to bits. Again, it had to be Vanessa's fault. So, becoming more and more embittered, he took to the gin bottle good and proper and his health began to go downhill. And even though he eventually found some brief happiness with Candida here, it didn't do anything to alleviate the deep sense of injustice in his heart.'

Captivated by his own lyricism, Will paused for breath and gazed out of the huge window on to the buildings of Canary Wharf. 'I only saw Hilton Starr in person that one time, on the very day he died, but he appeared to me to be very thin, almost emaciated compared to how I remember him from television in the seventies. He hadn't just grown older, he'd also shrunk. Didn't you ever notice?' he asked Candida, who shook her head sadly. 'I suppose people who were with him every day might not have seen the change. And he was always very secretive, of course.

'But last night I searched through some of Hilton's personal papers and then today I went to see a certain doctor in Harley Street. He was prepared to talk to me, because, after all, his patient is now no longer. And I discovered something that nobody else seems to have been aware of. Hilton was very ill, you see. All that gin over the years had taken its toll. Seems his liver had shrivelled up like a walnut – advanced cirrhosis, and by the time they found out, it was totally incurable. The doctor had told him that he had no more than a year to live.'

A little cry issued forth from Candida Blitz, and Hugh went over and put his arm around her. Will glanced over at him gratefully but he himself did not break stride as he continued to pace around the office.

'I don't know whether Hilton had a sense of irony,' he continued. 'I doubt it, but it must have been ironical all the same: he would have got the news of his illness at just about the same time that Vanessa rang him up to offer him the spot on Popviz. She really did do it out of kindness, and I suppose a certain amount of guilt, but I doubt if Hilton appreciated it one little bit. I'm speculating, but my guess is that this was the final straw. Vanessa had ruined everything for him and now he was dying as well. He wanted his revenge on her and he was determined to have it before he went. So that was when –' Will stopped dramatically in the middle of room – 'that was when he hatched his plot. He decided to frame Vanessa for his own murder.'

By now, Will's audience were spellbound, all except Inspector Ffelcher, who yawned ostentatiously and continued to stare out of the window with a sedulously bored expression. Will ignored him.

'Hilton really ought to have been a writer, you know,' he continued. 'He had a most bizarre imagination. He wasn't blackmailing Vanessa at all, of course. There was nothing for him to blackmail her about. It was all part of this extraordinary fiction which he managed to fabricate in his mind, and made the police believe even after his death.' A snorting noise emanated from the direction of Inspector Ffelcher, but Will pushed on.

'Hilton began by writing all those threatening letters and sent them off in various ways to Vanessa's office. Then, after that, he laid his plans for the awards ceremony itself. He arranged for the manufacture of the bomb, a tiny device specially made to fit into the brass monkey statuette. He even poisoned Mona da Ponte's drink on the night of the awards so that she would fall sick, and the show's timing would be altered. That was also designed to cast suspicion on Vanessa when it was finally discovered. Then, he accepted the award in front of twenty million viewers and . . . kaboom!' Will threw his hands up in the air with a flourish. 'He blew himself to smithereens. That must really have satisfied the showman in him. In death, he was finally famous again. Twinkle, twinkle, Hilton Starr.'

As Will's little speech drew to a close, there was a collective gasp from the assembled gathering. Vanessa shook her head admiringly. 'That's the smartest bit of detective work I ever heard,' she said. 'Absolutely unbelievable.'

Only Inspector Ffelcher was left unmoved. 'Unbelievable's the word,' he said with disdain. 'And I, for one, don't believe it. It's a very nice *theory*, of course. But that's *all* it is. And if you analyse it in any detail, you'll find it doesn't hold water for a second. For a start, what about the burglary at the house in Hampstead? That happened long after Hilton was dead. Or did he,' he asked with heavy sarcasm, 'manage to piece himself back together and come back from the grave to break into his own house?'

Will smiled over at him serenely. 'You're almost right there,' he said. 'I was coming on to that. You see, for his plot to succeed, Hilton had to make sure that the finger of suspicion would eventually be pointed at Vanessa. So he decided to leave around a few little clues.' Will counted them off on his fingers. 'First, he made anonymous payments into his own bank account – not difficult if you've stored up some cash for just that purpose. Then he painstakingly constructed a notebook detailing just how much she was supposed to have paid to meet his blackmail demands – all completely fictitious, of course. Naturally, he had to be certain all this evidence would turn up in the event that the police didn't have the intelligence to unearth it by themselves.' Here, Will allowed himself a sidelong glance at the inspector, who glared back at him defiantly. 'So, before his suicide, he arranged that a few weeks later there would be a little visit to his house, just to mess things up a bit and draw attention to the safe's existence. Not difficult to fix, really, if you know the right people.' He wheeled round to face Inspector Ffelcher full on. 'Do you really think that any self-respecting burglar would have missed that safe?' he demanded. 'Of course not,' he answered himself. 'Not unless he'd been instructed in advance to leave it alone. Hilton didn't want the contents stolen, just exposed. And naturally, the break-in would be put down to Vanessa too.'

At long last the inspector spoke. 'Very clever,' he said. 'Very clever indeed. You think you've got all the answers, don't you! But I'll tell you something.' His lips turned up in an angry sneer. 'All I'm hearing from you is *I guess this* and *I suspect that*, and I'm wondering to myself: is this just something that's been cobbled together to save a Very Important Person from getting her *ass*' – he pronounced it in a fair imitation of Vanessa's New York drawl – 'her *ass* hauled off to the poky? Because that's what I *suspect* it is. You see,' he continued dismissively, 'when it comes right down to it, you don't have a shred of evidence for this . . . this unbelievably far-fetched hypothesis. And if you think it's going to stop me pursuing the prosecution of Mrs Vanessa Driftwood here then you've got another think coming. I fully intend to carry on right up to the moment when she's found guilty in a court of law, which is exactly what will happen, have no doubt on that score.'

'Ah,' Will replied. 'Now, on the evidence front, I have to admit, you have a point, indeed you do. And I thought the same way for a while. It seemed to me there would never be any way of proving Vanessa's innocence, however sure we were of what really happened. But then,' he added triumphantly, 'I'd reckoned without the hand of fate.' He paused again for effect. He was really beginning to enjoy himself now. He stuck his hands in his pockets and sauntered around the room. 'You see, on the day when Vanessa was introduced at the Brass Monkeys ceremony, they said she had once won six awards in her own right. But if you look at that bookcase over there' – he pointed to the spot – 'now there are only five.'

'Precisely,' said Inspector Ffelcher, his own tone no less triumphant than Will's. 'That was exactly what put me on to her in the first place. She used the other for the bomb. When we pieced back together the one that killed poor Hilton Starr, her name was engraved all over it. Pretty conclusive that, don't you think?' He was now making no attempt to keep the smugness from his voice.

Will continued as if the inspector had not spoken. 'Obviously, one of the awards had been removed,' he said. 'And that's just the point I want to come on to. Now at this juncture' – and here he made a quick switch from Hercule Poirot to Perry Mason – 'at this juncture, I would ask you to consider, if you will, the humble videotape recorder. Useful little gadget, don't you think?' They all looked back at him blankly. 'Well, I know Vanessa thinks so, because she's treated herself to a fair number of the things.' He pointed up to the corner of the office. 'You can't see it, but somewhere up there is a hidden camera, and it leads to a room where everything that goes on in this building is monitored and recorded.'

'How the hell did you know that?' asked Vanessa, glaring at Reg Diggle, who looked down nervously.

'I'm coming to that too,' said Will. 'And I wouldn't be too critical of poor old Reg here, because he may just have saved your bacon. You see, a tape recording was made of everything that happened in this room on the day that Hilton came in to sign his contract, and by an odd series of coincidences' – he threw a sidelong glance over at Margaret Sloach – 'that tape has come into my possession. And what I now propose to do is play it to you.'

'No!' shouted Hugh and Ros simultaneously. 'I don't think that's a very good idea,' Hugh added weakly.

Will held up his hand. 'Trust me,' he said. 'I'm a detective.' Ignoring their further protests, he crossed to the video machine situated beside Vanessa's desk and pressed a button. On her large television screen there appeared a slightly disconcerting picture of the very room they were currently in. The image of Vanessa could be clearly seen, sitting at her desk exactly as she was now, with the unmistakable figure of Hilton Starr in front of her. They were evidently in the middle of a furious argument.

'You *cannot* be serious!' Vanessa was shouting. 'I'm doing you a favour, for Chrissake. Have you any idea how much flak I'm getting here for giving you the goddamned job?' Then there was a brief gap, during which Hilton could be heard mumbling something indecipherable and Vanessa said: 'Just forget it. I'm going to lunch, and if that contract's not sitting signed on my desk when I get back, then the whole goddamned deal's off. Got that?' And with that she stalked out of the camera's vision. 'You ready, Hugh honey?' she could be heard to say. 'I'm just gonna powder my nose then we're outta here.'

'Now watch this carefully,' said Will. His words were quite superfluous. Nothing could have dragged his audience's eyes from that screen. On it, Hilton could be observed waiting until he was quite certain Vanessa had gone. Then, stealthily, and ensuring he could not be seen through the semi-open door, he picked up his briefcase and slipped behind the desk where he stood facing the shelf of awards. Finally, with a quick flick of his wrist, he scooped up one of the Brass Monkey statuettes and deposited it in his case. It was the work of no more than a few seconds, and he was back in the guest chair at the other side of the room by the time Ros Flato came in to usher him out of the office.

There was a stunned silence as Will stepped back to the video player and switched it off. 'I think that's pretty conclusive, don't you, Inspector?' he asked innocently.

With a face like thunder, Inspector Ffelcher looked down at his size eleven boots. At long last, some of his bumptiousness had left him and he seemed deflated. 'I suppose so,' he muttered. But there was some defiance in him yet. 'We'll want to examine that tape very carefully,' he said threateningly. 'Make sure it's genuine and that there's been no hanky-panky with it. It's not unknown to fake these things.'

'I'm sure hanky-panky's the last thing you'll find on this tape,' said Will, staring blandly at Hugh and Ros Flato as he ejected it from the machine. 'But your experts may discover one odd thing about it: for some reason, the last half an hour or so's been completely erased. I can't think how that could have happened. But it shouldn't matter for your purposes, should it now?'

The inspector stood up angrily. Sensing that some sort of apology was expected of him, he cleared his throat and addressed himself to Vanessa, still looking straight down at his feet. 'Ah, clearly a serious miscarriage of justice has been averted here, Mrs Driftwood,' he said from between clenched teeth. 'You'll understand that I was just doing my duty. But of course I'll arrange for all charges against you to be dropped at once.' And with that he snatched the video-cassette from Will Cloud's hand and stalked out of the office.

The atmosphere he left behind him was exultant. The entire gathering burst into spontaneous applause, and, sensing the air of elation, Zoë jumped up and down excitedly on her chair.

'All *right*,' shouted Vanessa, punching her hand into the air with a whoop of joy. Candida threw her arms around Will and gave him a great hug. Even Mrs Sloach allowed herself a lemony smile.

'What a genius!' Candida exclaimed. 'I always knew you wouldn't let us down.'

'Elementary, my dear Candida,' said Will.

'Isn't he wonderful, Vanessa?' Candida continued happily.

'Yeah,' said Vanessa with feeling. 'He sure is.' But grateful though she evidently was, it was clear that her mind was already shifting on to more important matters. All the old vitality had come back to her face as she turned purposefully to her stepson. 'Hugh,' she said with urgency. 'What time do the nominations for the leadership close?'

'Oh, my God,' said Hugh, clutching his brow. 'I'd completely forgotten.' He checked his watch in dismay. 'In half an hour's time. There's no way I can make it now.'

But a look of implacable determination had set like concrete on Vanessa's face. 'You wanna take a bet on that?' she asked, reaching for the phone.

Chapter 37

The BBC make-up girl dabbed at his forehead. 'I think that should just about do it for now, Mr Driftwood,' she said, standing back and studying his face critically.

Hugh wiped his sweaty palms on a handkerchief. 'Have we got time for one more run-through?' he asked the producer.

The man next to the camera consulted the clock. ''Fraid not, sir,' he said. 'We go out in less than ten minutes.'

'Oh, Lord,' said Hugh anxiously. 'I think I'll just read through the last paragraph again. It sounded a bit weak the first time around.' He leafed through the script on his desk as an assistant adjusted the autocue to the correct position. Then, brushing his hair out of his eyes, he stared into the camera with as much calm authority as he could muster.

'In conclusion,' he read, 'I would like you to know how conscious I am of the great responsibility which you have entrusted in me. I will endeavour to serve every single one of you to the very best of my abilities. But in accepting this high office, let me also ask something of you, the British people.' He paused, took off his glasses and clasped his hands in front of him.

'The tasks before us and the challenges we face are immense,' he continued. 'They far exceed the capabilities of any single man. But if we tackle them as a country united, if each and every one of us pulls together in the interests of all, then—' He broke off. 'You don't think this sounds a bit too pompous?' he asked the cameraman nervously.

The man shrugged his shoulders. 'Don't ask me, guv,' he said. 'I just take the pictures.'

'It hits exactly the right note,' the producer cut in hastily.

Only slightly reassured, Hugh resumed. 'If each and every one of us pulls together, in the interests of all, then, I promise you, we will be able to march forward into this new millennium with our backs held straight and our heads held high.' He stopped. 'How was that?'

'Absolutely fabulous, love. I mean, Prime Minister,' said the producer. Instinctively, Hugh glanced over his shoulder to see who he was addressing. Then he smiled. It was going to take some getting used to, this new title, he reflected to himself wryly.

'Two minutes,' said the assistant. Even though he was seated, Hugh suddenly felt weak at the knees. He clutched at the edges of the desk for support. It was an exquisitely carved piece of furniture, made out of solid mahogany and almost as broad as it was long. Hugh thought with awe of his illustrious predecessors who had sat there before him and he tried to take strength from their memory.

Finally, as the assistant counted down, the red light on top of the camera lit up and the director gave him his cue. His heart racing ten to the dozen, Hugh began his broadcast. 'I am speaking to you tonight from the study at Number 10 Downing Street,' he said. 'This afternoon I was granted an audience with Her Majesty the Queen and she graciously requested that I form a government. I accepted with great pride, but also with humility . . .'

*   *   *

Below him, in the recesses beneath the desk and hidden from camera shot by its stout mahogany frontispiece, a crouched figure stirred uncomfortably. It had been a long and boring wait, and Ros Flato was anxious to get on with the job at hand.

Lest Hugh should spoil her little surprise by discovering her presence too soon, she had smuggled herself into Downing Street some hours before and had been concealed in her hiding place ever since. But she needn't have worried. Above her head, Hugh had other things on his mind – for now. Oblivious to her presence, he continued his speech. 'I would like you all to know,' he said simply but solemnly, 'what a very great honour this is for me.'

Deciding that this was as good a cue as any, Ros finally made her move. Silently and stealthily, she shifted over to face the Prime Ministerial trouser legs.

Not half as much of an honour as it is for me, she reflected contentedly as she reached forward.